Advance Praise for *How to Escape from a Leper Colony*

"In this Widest of Sargasso Seas Tiphanie Yanique gives us the pan-Caribbean, from the old lepers' colony on Chacachacare, off the coast of Trinidad, to St. John, Accra, and London. It's an astonishing debut collection—as brutal, sexual, magical, and seductively disturbing as if Jean Rhys had written it today."—Robert Antoni

"*How To Escape from a Leper Colony* is fiction of the first rank. Tiphanie Yanique explores the ferociously complex terrain of her native Caribbean to show what it means to live in a world where accidents of culture, country, history, race, and place figure so bewilderingly in, as the author puts it, 'the divine risks of love.' Every single one of these extraordinary stories delivers a necessary revelation. So few of us can hope to see with any clarity, much less make sense of, this world, but Yanique—and we should be profoundly grateful for this—sees and understands a very great deal indeed."—Ben Fountain

"With turns to the wild, clever, and magical that seem at once fantastic and inevitable, Tiphanie Yanique has crafted a beautiful collection of short and not-so-short fiction. This is an exciting new voice."—Percival Everett

"This splendid debut collection reveals a storyteller of multiple gifts and ample heart. Yanique's writing is very fine, her characters are authentic and memorable, and her vision is deeply humane."—Sigrid Nunez

"Tiphanie Yanique has written powerful stories, in luminous prose, that reveal a Caribbean beyond tourist brochures, stories that tell of human triumphs and failures. A wonderful read."—Elizabeth Nunez, author of *Anna In-Between*

"These are fiercely original, poetic, and bold stories from a writer who is a force to be reckoned with. I loved every minute of this book and was in awe of nearly every paragraph."—Cristina Henriquez, author of *The World in Half*

"In these powerful, poetic stories set in landscapes real and imagined, Tiphanie Yanique explores beautifully race, family, and the complicated movements of the heart."—Chitra Banerjee Divakaruni, author of *Sister of My Heart* and *The Palace of Illusions*

"Tiphanie Yanique has a gift for writing about physical displacement and the longing for connection that ensues. The unique stories in *How to Escape from a Leper Colony* meditate on confused expressions of love and spirituality in fresh and surprising ways."—Emily Raboteau

"Tiphanie Yanique is a writer to watch. Although *How to Escape from a Leper Colony* is her debut, she writes with the wisdom and confidence of an old soul. The title story alone is worth the price of admission, but each of these stories contained in this gorgeous collection are clear-eyed, honest while still zinging with emotion. Tiphanie Yanique is blessed with an electric imagination, an expansive heart, and an unflinching gaze. I can't wait to see what she does next."—Tayari Jones

"In *How to Escape from a Leper Colony,* Tiphanie Yanique takes as her subject the outsider, the immigrant, the uprooted. A boy from Ghana is transplanted to Brixton, trading his palm-wine-drinking friends in Accra for new football-playing mates. A Gambian priest finds friendship in a coffin shop in the Caribbean; a one-time Pentecostal leaves her birthplace and dons a burka in an effort to win back her Muslim husband. The stories of these men and women, and the extraordinary grace and sympathy with which they're told, serve as urgent, vivid reminders in this age of displacement and migration, of how powerfully and urgently each human heart aches for its home."—Kathleen Cambor

HOW TO ESCAPE FROM A LEPER COLONY

HOW TO ESCAPE FROM A LEPER COLONY

A Novella and Stories

Tiphanie Yanique

Graywolf Press

Publication of this volume is made possible in part by a grant provided by the Minnesota State Arts Board, through an appropriation by the Minnesota State Legislature; a grant from the Wells Fargo Foundation Minnesota; and a grant from the National Endowment for the Arts, which believes that a great nation deserves great art. Significant support has also been provided by Target; the McKnight Foundation; and other generous contributions from foundations, corporations, and individuals. To these organizations and individuals we offer our heartfelt thanks.

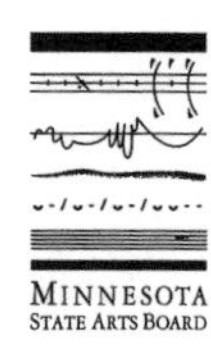

This book is made possible through a partnership with the College of Saint Benedict, and honors the legacy of S. Mariella Gable, a distinguished teacher at the College. Support has been provided by the Lee and Rose Warner Foundation as part of the Warner Reading Program.

Special funding for this title has been provided by the Jerome Foundation.

Published by Graywolf Press
250 Third Avenue North, Suite 600
Minneapolis, Minnesota 55401

www.graywolfpress.org

Published in the United States of America

ISBN 978-1-55597-550-0

4 6 8 10 11 9 7 5

Library of Congress Control Number: 2009933820

Cover design: Kapo Ng @ A-Men Project

Cover photo: "Lover's Tree," Moses Djeli

For the Virgin Islands

“Lead us toward those we are waiting for,
those who are waiting for us.”

From the prayer to Saint Raphael,
patron saint of lovers and travelers

Contents

HOW TO ESCAPE FROM A LEPER COLONY

Introduction

Babalao Chuck said that when they found the gun it was still in the volunteer's pulsing hands. The child was covered in his mother's blood and body. Her red sari redder. The volunteers at the leper colonies were young Trinidadian doctors and British journalists and criminals trading time in jail for time among lepers, and sometimes young people who carried tiny Bibles in their pockets. No one ever told me which kind killed Lazaro's mother. The volunteer was asked to leave and that was to be the end of it.

What evil thing Lazaro will do later we will forgive him for without remorse, because we know his past and because we know he is one of us. For a leper, many things are impossible, and many other things are easily done. Babalao Chuck said he could fly to the other side of the island and peek at the nuns bathing. And when a man with no hands claims that he can fly, you listen. He would return and tell us about the steam in the nuns' showers. About how they had soap that lathered. How they had shampoo that smelled like flowers.

1st Burn the dead

When I came to Chacachacare it was 1939 and I was only a girl of fourteen. I came for two reasons. The first was to bury my father who had lived there for three years and only just died. The second was because I had become a leper. It was in my arm. The same arm my mother held with her own hands, said a prayer over, before leaving me on the dock. Her cotton sari swishing the ground as she ran back to the junction to catch a wagon that would take her to the train that would take her the whole day to get back to Siparia, way down South in Trinidad. I thought of her sitting for hours, her face against the glass, the hole in her nose empty because she had sold the gold to buy me a used red sari and a bag of sweets as a gift to my new caretakers.

I also sat that whole day. I was waiting for the nuns to come get me. I pretended I could hear the sounds of the junction where the wagon driver had dropped us off. The junction wasn't San Fernando or Port of Spain, which we had only rushed by in the train, but it was the biggest loudest place I had ever really been. It was like a wedding in my village with all the food laid out for me to stare at. Men crowded around a small stand that sold raw oysters. They dipped the shells in hot pepper sauce before slurping the meat down their throats. Women reached up for brightly colored buckets and brooms that hung on display. My mother and I rushed by, avoiding getting close to people. We only stopped once to stare at an automobile that roared by in smoke and shielded an African driver who wore bright white gloves. I could not see his passenger. Besides the big work equipment on the plantation, I had never seen an automobile before.

Slowly the festivities disappeared. The busy road turned into a dusty path where there were odd crisscross markings in the dirt that my mother said were from an automobile, like the one we had seen. After hours of walking, and my mother telling stories of her young life in Namakkal, we could more than smell the ocean, we could hear it. And then we were walking along a wood dock with the sea beneath us. My mother sat me down with my legs hanging over the side and pointed to the small mound many miles out into the ocean. That would be my new home, she told me, where the nuns would take me in and bless me with the sacrament of Confirmation when I was older. She did not say, if I lived to be older. Instead she kissed me on the mouth and made me promise not to eat the sweets. And she left. And then it was so quiet, with only the waves and the breeze as sounds of life, that I closed my eyes and pretended that I was back in the junction, eating oysters in pepper sauce, putting them in my mouth with my good hand.

My arm was wrapped and in a sling. When the wagon driver had asked, my mother told him I had broken it and she was taking me to an obeah man. I was ashamed that she had been made to sin, to tell a lie, because of me. Even in my mind I could not forget how my elbow was hurting me in a funny way that wasn't about pain. Even alone on the dock I was too afraid to touch it, to give that arm the healing power of the other one. I was afraid to touch places on me that weren't even private. And I was going to die for it. Die for having those places. My mother held my hand, then left.

It was not a parade of white nuns who came for me. It was a lay volunteer, all wrapped in cloth. Someone doing community service for a crime committed or someone doing penance for a sin confessed. "Get in the boat," he directed. In his voice I knew that he was a man, for nothing in his gauzed body revealed it. I could not tell if he was Indian or African or French. The skin around his eyes was covered in a dark protective salve. We did not speak as we motored the five miles to Chacachacare.

At the Chacachacare dock he told me to go, go. I tucked the sweets under my arm and heaved myself—one-handed—out of the boat. The boat sped off to the safer, healthy side of the island. I faced the intake house. It was a welcoming hue. Not the color of sores or withered limbs. The walls were blue, a mother's color, and the trimmings were green, the color of life. I did not think I would be unhappy here.

I presented the bag of sweets to the young nun who greeted me. She cradled it with her gloved hands and smiled. Then she sent me to bathe in the sea. "Hurry," she said. "Before it gets dark." I did as I was told. I knew that the Caribbean Sea could heal many things. If you have a cold, go bathe in the sea. If you are melancholy, go bathe in the sea. If you are a leper, go bathe in the sea—but on the lepers' side.

He was there on the beach when I came out of the water. Lazaro was not the name he was born with. He was given that name because he refused to die. He was sixteen when I met him that first day, older than me by two years but much smaller in size. I stood a head above him. I had some softness in places, chest and cheek, where he seemed hollow. He had been born in the colony and still showed no signs of leprosy and no signs of leaving. The world would not have him. Surely the leprosy would show soon. In truth, he had nowhere to go. His mother, a dougla, had passed on her mixed genes. One could not tell if Lazaro was African or Indian—there was talk that there was French in him, too. That his father was French. That his father was one of the French priests who came over once a week to celebrate the Mass. Who is to know? The dougla, the mixed race, might be a type of chameleon. They can claim any heritage they desire. They can claim all if they like. Though it is true that not all will claim them in return.

"Is your father they burning tomorrow?" he asked me as he skipped stones into the water.

The sun was almost down. My sari, a lovely red but frayed in places, clung to me, and I felt cold. He wore only a pair of children's short pants. I hadn't thought about my father all day. "I been thinking they would bury him, even though he Indian."

"You thinking wrong. Here we all Indian, no matter how much African we have in us."

We began to walk back to the surgery, where I would spend the night. The nuns, who were our nurses, hadn't decided yet on my treatment. I looked over Lazaro's small body. "Where your leper part?"

"I all leper."

"Where?"

He tugged at the crotch of his pants. "In my head." I expected him to pull his thing out and show it to me shriveled. I waited anxiously. "The next head, rude girl." He laughed loud enough that I grew ashamed I had been staring. He pointed to his temple. "It's in my mind."

On my second day I watched them push my father's wrapped body into the crematorium. The nun who had sent me to the sea, Sister Theresa, stood with her many replicas. Their white faces pink with the heat, their hair covered in veils with blue bands about the forehead. They were all young enough to be my mother—not like the old dogs at my school in Trinidad who wore huge winglike headdresses. I didn't understand why they cremated the lepers when they seemed to have so much bare land on the island. When I asked Sister

Theresa she told me that this was okay because so many of the lepers are Hindu anyway.

But it wasn't okay, not really. Because my mother is a Christian and she told me that if I went to Chacachacare the nuns would feed me better than she could, and give me medicine that she could not, and that I would be buried under a stone like Jesus.

There were two churches. One for the Catholics where the nuns joined us on Sundays and one for the Protestants—who were thought of as exotic. There wasn't any place for Hindus. Though my parents were both Indian, only my father had been Hindu. From him I knew that the Hindu god wasn't so different from the Christian god. One manifestation came in many dozens of forms while the other version came in only three. But the same god. The same jealous god, the same god who fell in love. The Christian god even sometimes fell in love with men, like King David. "God loved King David the way a woman loved a man." My mother would slap my father in the face when he said things like that. Then she would accept his cuffs as her martyrdom. When he showed the first signs of leprosy in his fingers she told him that it was God's punishment. But he would not repent. For me, it was easy to chant about Jesus Christ and slip in a Lord Krishna here and there.

2nd Go to the cinema

For many days the nuns did not know where to put me. I slept in the surgery where they took blood and logged my wounds into a tablet with only my given name, Deepa, in block letters. One option was an Indian woman who had left her child behind with family when she became a leper. She wanted me, but the nuns thought that this might be bad for us both. I, an Indian child, had left a mother behind. It was too perfect to be healthy. The nuns were not keen on putting me with a young man or even with a man and his wife. I could be temptation. Nuns knew about temptation.

They put me in a one-room house with an old African woman. "This your bed," she said. "Yours against the wall and mine besides the door. This so if there is a fire my old leper legs will have less distance to go. Is also so I can keep my eye on your comings and goings. There's all kind of talk of a cure for the leprosy and if you go back to your mother I don't want she to think I been raising you poorly." Her name was Tantie B. I had never known my grandparents, since my mother had sailed over from Madras in southern India before I was born. I knew only southern Trinidad. Tantie B was my grandmother in Chacachacare. And Lazaro was my brother.

For the first months after I arrived Lazaro would take me for walks. The island was green with palm and sea grape trees. It was loud with the howler monkeys that snored all day and mated all night. Lazaro and I often went beyond the fence that kept the lepers to the leper side. We would climb under it, through a gorge deep enough for a body. It had been first dug out by an iguana and now maintained by Lazaro. We would climb trees. We would eat green fruit and spit the seeds out, aim for lizards and fire ants. One day Lazaro took me farther than he had before.

"There," he said, pointing down the hill to a clearing with spots of gray. "The nun burial ground. That's where they put the nuns' bodies. That's where I want to be buried."

"But you ain a nun."

"Who say?"

"You a boy. You couldn't be a nun."

"Why I can't be a nun? Didn't Peter take over the family after Jesus dead, like widows does do? Peter get to be buried under some rock. I want a rock over me."

We climbed down the hill to look at the burial site. The grounds were clean but sharp with ankle-high grass. When we walked we made a swishing sound like waves. The stones over the graves were marked: Sister Marie, Lover of the Lord; Sister Margaret, Lover of the Word; Sister Ann, Lover of the poor and the wretched. We sat among the stones. Lazaro patted my arm gently.

"Soon they going have to chop some of it away."

"I know."

"You afraid?"

"Yes."

"You brave?"

"Yes."

"What you love?"

"My mother."

"And who she?"

"She . . ." I paused. I had not seen or heard from my mother in months. I had not expected her to write because she had had very little schooling. But what was she now? Was she a new wife? Was she going to be someone else's mother? "She a woman who works in the cane field. She does pray to Saint Anne to send her signs." I pushed some dirt around with my toe. "Who was your mother?" I already knew of Lazaro's tragedy from the little things Tantie B had whispered to me at night, and the stories Babalao Chuck told in the clearing when Lazaro was off helping haul in the goods from the delivery boat. I knew, but it still seemed the right thing to ask. I lowered my head so Lazaro would know I did not mean to be bold.

"My mother is the woman who tell me that I was her miracle. I was her sign." With his hand he raised my face so that our eyes met. I felt my skin grow warm and loose. "She tell me a island could be like a world." He spoke softly and I could see that his eyes were heavy with their water. "Try a next thing," he breathed out, so that I realized there had been a long silence. "Everyone love their mother. What else you love?"

I thought about this. I let my good hand run through the sharp grass, feeling the tiny cuts opening on my fingers. "My own-self," I answered at last.

"Then on your grave it will say 'Sister Deepa, Lover of She-self.'"

"What your stone going say?"

"Brother Lazaro, Lover of Deepa."

I sat on a stone with markings that were clear and fresh. I felt the curved coolness though my clothes. It wasn't smooth. It was rough and the thin cloth of my sari did not do much to cushion me. I lifted my feet to try to balance. To try to press the cold stone onto me. "Don't fall," he said.

"I won't." But I got up anyway. "Why we here?"

"Because we lepers."

I nodded. "But why here-here?" I spread my arms wide to mean the world.

Lazaro shrugged. "You don't listen to the priest on Sunday?"

"I never understand what he does say."

"We here because God want somebody to know him."

"Like a friend?"

"Like when someone know you it make you real. Like the tree that fall in the forest when nobody was around. God had want to be heard."

"A tree fall in the forest?"

"All the time."

I could not help myself. Suddenly my body felt heavy. Suddenly I felt alone. I walked over to him and bent into his small chest. I cried loudly. I cried for my mother. "I'm here," Lazaro said. And he said it over and over again.

The doctor dressed in white. He covered his hair and face. Only his eyes showed and I couldn't tell if he was French and tanned, or African but light, or Indian even. I imagined he was my father, whom I couldn't really remember. I imagined this as he leaned into my face and his face turned hazy and then disappeared. I slept as he carved out the muscle around my elbow, which wasn't much muscle to begin with as I was still only fourteen and quite skinny. "They didn't cut your arm off," a nun said to me and smiled when I awoke. And I knew that was something to be thankful for.

I was allowed to watch a movie two nights later at the small cinema that had been built for the volunteers and the nuns. Once a month was leper night—for those of us who had gone to Mass every Sunday and for those of us who had been to hospital. I invited Lazaro and they allowed him to come even though neither the Protestant nor the Catholic church could claim him in their congregation. And he was not ill. He was never ill.

The lepers sat in the front rows. The nuns sat in the very back, like chaperones. The movies that were brought were old movies. Movies that were already old in Trinidad, where my mother was. They weren't even talkies, most of them. Silent things with caresses so passionate they made even the nuns giggle loudly.

Movies are like so much art. They can start a revolution. This was not a movie about war. Or about race and oppression; no one talked about those things in 1939. A man loved a woman. A woman loved a man. They were willing to do bad things for that love.

3rd Kill a nun

I was not yet sixteen when we made the biggest decision of our lives. Lazaro was almost eighteen. Appropriate ages for independence. We went into the jungle of the island to build it. We stole wood meant to steady the leper houses. This was more important. Tantie B did not know what we were doing. I was still alive. She was still alive. Babalao Chuck was dead. I did not go to see him cremated. I believed his stories. I believed he had flown away. He said his Orisha had taught him. I told Tantie B that Lazaro and I were going to build us a house, separate and away from the other houses. And because all every leper wanted was a world that was the same as Trinidad, just with limbs that were fragments of the big island's, a vacation home in leper town didn't seem unbelievable. "Every young couple need some privacy for when they wed," Tantie B mused. And I imagine she thought that Lazaro and I were in love. I cannot blame her. I thought the same.

But we were not building honeymoon quarters. We were going to build an altar to the goddess Kali. Kali who dances and spins this Kaliyuga world. Bringing the destruction we asked for when we didn't know what we were asking. "Dear lordess," I said as I nailed and Lazaro carved. "We is your servants. I drag this wood on my back to show you that we ain no better than dust." For by then I was resigned to the fact that when I died I would not be buried.

It felt as though we were playing a game. But I knew it was not a game. We would be punished, though we would not be lashed or starved. Hurting our flesh was not something our nuns would ever do. They were of a peaceful order that believed in punishing the mind. We would be forced to do penance. Perhaps we would be separated. Perhaps we would have to spend days in church, he in the Protestant, me in the Catholic, where we prayed and prayed all the prayers we could remember and then were forced to learn others. This was not a small crime. This was blasphemy. They would tell us we were building false gods; though I knew Hindu gods could not be fake, since they were around before Jesus. But my mother had washed my mouth with soap when I said such things. Even she had wept that perhaps my leprosy was a curse, for the things my father had taught me.

From my mother I learned that Christians love leprosy. Christians are not so passionate about polio or cholera. But Jesus had touched lepers. Jesus cured lepers. Leprosy gives the pious a chance to be Christ-like. Only lepers hate leprosy. Who wants to be the one in the Bible always getting cured? We want to be the heroes, too. We want to be like Jesus. Or like Shiva. Or like whomever you pray to.

And then we were caught. We had built Kali out of wood. She was rough and less attractive than we knew her to be. But we painted her and a little color made all the difference. We took flowers from the graveyards and placed them at her feet. I did not know how to worship her. I only knew a few Tamil words. My father had taught me the names of the gods and had taken me with him for Diwali celebrations, but both he and my mother spoke only English to me. My mother, I believe, did not want me to learn Tamil. She did not think there would be any need. Perhaps my father felt that since I was Madrasi I would know my language as I knew myself. And yes, I knew some things. I knew how to say please, auntie, and thank you, uncle. I knew how to ask for water or the outhouse. I did not know how to pray.

Though his mother had been half Indian, Lazaro also knew only English. First we prayed the Hail Mary. Then we chanted some words in Ibo that Babalao Chuck said were holy. "Sometimes we going call her Yemaya," Lazaro said. "I want she to have many names." Then he went on his knees and swept the dust from her feet with a son's tenderness.

We were caught one night because we had not returned to our huts. We were caught because we had decided, without really deciding, to spend the night with our Kali. We took our bedding and slept at her feet, under the same one blanket. I had grown taller in the almost two years I had been in the colony. Lazaro had remained small. I wanted him to hold me but it was uncomfortable and awkward. So I held him. We slept with his back to my chest. I was aware of my breasts breathing into his shoulder blades. I tried not to cough or sneeze.

To the rest of the colony, lepers and nuns and volunteers, it would be okay for us to marry. But to release our bodies to any pleasure without God's blessing was a sin. They came for us with torches. We awoke to what felt like a dream. We saw the light before we saw their figures. Sister Theresa, a covered volunteer, and Tantie B.

"It is worse than we thought!" whispered the young nun loudly. "It's the occult." She backed away—her skin darkening with the night.

Tantie B looked around at what we were. Two young people. An altar. The forest. She shook her head but said nothing.

"Better if you had just been fucking," said the volunteer quietly as he leaned his torch into Lazaro's face. His body was covered in a white bedsheet. I held on to Lazaro, feeling the heat on my skin and thinking that this was not a dream.

Lazaro blinked furiously. Perhaps he still thought he was dreaming.

"Do it, for God's sake," said the nun.

"Yes," said Tantie. "Then let them come home."

Under the face wrappings and dark salve, the volunteer's face twitched. He looked as though he was smiling. Tantie B and the young nun stepped back with what seemed like instinct. Perhaps the volunteer knew he was completing a history as he flung the torch to hit our Kali with the force of someone knocking down a city's walls. To be certain, Lazaro knew.

Lazaro wrenched away from me. He flew like smoke. The fire seemed to catch him. Then there was a high-pitched screaming and a deep adolescent howling. I saw Kali rock on her base. I saw the bushes go up in flames. Then there was heat and darkness. Someone began a furious Hail Mary. Then there was nothing. I woke up in Tantie B's house, in my cot against the wall.

"You done sleep through the night," she said when I opened my eyes. "You been in the surgery."

I did not think I responded. I was aware that my face was heavy.

"Took the whole night to get the fire down. Then when folks return we find the phone lines all dead. Been cut." She cleared her throat. "And he missing."

"Who?" I asked, and heard my mouth make a noise that was muffled. My tongue felt dry, as if it was coated with cotton.

"They both missing."

"Who?" I tried again.

"Lazaro and the nun."

I lifted myself off the cot and went to the mirror. My face was covered in gauze. "You been burnt, my daughter," she said quietly but without looking at me. "The idol fall on you. Smash your face and knock you out." I did not feel pain, but I could not shake off the feeling of dreaming. "It going be okay. Maybe for the best," she said more loudly. I pinched myself where my neck was exposed. I looked behind me and then quickly looked back again. If what was behind me changed then I would know I was dreaming. When I whipped my head around there was a shout: "The beach!" I looked over at Tantie. Her face looked heavier than mine felt. Since we'd lived together she had lost two toes. I'd grown more than two inches. She nodded at me. We stood and walked slowly to our door.

Some people were shouting, calling to each other. Most were huddling forward in whispers. We lepers all walked to the beach. There was already a small crowd forming a circle at the shore. It was easy for Tantie and me to slip in and see. We were on the lepers' side of the beach and there was Sister Theresa's body—the hands and feet sparkling in pure white. Her nunnery uniform in pieces and sticking to her smooth body in its fuller places. But she was mostly naked. And she was entirely dead.

"Have mercy," gasped Tantie. "Next, he coming for me."

And there was no Lazaro. I thought he might come to me. Give me a sign. Tell me that he loved me. That he was seeking revenge for the injuries I had suffered. I sat on the shore and watched the day unfold. My bandages were due to be changed that evening.

Some of the other lepers sat with me. Perhaps we have a sixth sense. When lunch was cooked Tantie brought it to me and then didn't leave after we had eaten. I faced inland. I mostly watched the trees and studied the howlers to see if any of them was a boy instead of a monkey. I kept alert so I could decipher any signs from him. Anything that would tell me what to do or where to go. But he did not come to me, after all. It was not me he was avenging. Instead, word came that the boats had all been punctured with large holes and the radios had disappeared. Then I began to watch the big island—the continent of Trinidad—and I wondered how anyone would know to come save us.

I watched the first nun leap off the dock at dusk—right after supper. She had made sure she had a full belly. Then they all lined up to jump. Oh, to see them. Their white robes flapping like wings, then their bodies hitting the water like birds hunting a fish prey. Then see them swimming. Swimming as though they were the hunted ones. And Lazaro, my Lazaro, was still missing.

None of us lepers had left Chacachacare since we arrived. An island can be a world. We knew that the Americans had built a Navy base on Trinidad because there was a war going on somewhere. We'd heard that the Marines were there, too. We might as well have been going to the moon. It was as dangerous and as crazy. We did not line up on the dock like the nuns. We just walked into the ocean. Until we couldn't walk and we had to swim. And we took only ourselves. It was as if we thought we were coming back. As though we were so powerful we could go to the moon on vacation. Both my arms were strong enough. I treaded water and imagined I heard gunshots and the dancing of boots on stone. My face bandages came off in the water. The sea seared into my cheeks and mouth and the soft part around my eyes. Tantie did not come. She stayed behind on the shore and watched me soak into my real life. "I can't swim," she called and then went to our house without looking back at me.

Now when you sail by on your ships you will say the island is haunted. You will visit the places where we bathed and played our pickup soccer. You will take pictures of our houses, our beds made up stiffly like war bunks. The sheets still on them and the pillows well placed. You will see the plates and bowls sitting on the table, the pots and pans lying dirty in the sink. In the surgery, all the records resting open for any curious boaties to rummage through and know that someone's leg had been chopped off, someone else's penis. Someone's arms were too ruined to hold her baby, someone else had been cremated. Someone had begged to be killed in his sleep. The X-rays will still be up on the X-ray machine. Our medicines, the early salves that only soothed but didn't heal and the more modern penicillin, all exposed. Now the government says they will tear down everything and build hotels and casinos so that your ships have a reason to stay in the region and spend money. Or perhaps you will only walk along the shore and swim in our beach.

But if you go deep, you will also find our goddess, rough and elegant. I left her behind. You may visit her if you wipe the dust from her feet. I left for the sea. I swam in the soup with everyone. Nuns and volunteers holding on to lepers for dear life. The dark protective salve running off their faces and revealing them to be of every race. Lepers hoping a shark would come and eat their leg off so at least they'd be lighter and their bodies would stop being a dead weight.

THE BRIDGE STORIES: A SHORT COLLECTION

1

The Parable of the Miniature Bridge Maker: as told by an Island that is between things

The people wore little bridges around their necks. And when couples married they hopped over a little bridge. Everything was good.

There was a bridge maker. He made bridges that people put in their earlobes and around their fingers. Tiny little bridges. Decorated and beautiful and perfect. He decided that when he died he would request a thin bridge fixed to his casket helping to connect him to his dead family under the ground.

His living family insisted that he leave a real legacy. He was famous for small things. They wanted him to be known for big things. So he built a real bridge. Paid for by the Yankees—not to honor his memory, but really for their own convenience. Like everything new. Huge and stretching from Guyana—the place in the world most south—to Miami—the place in the world most north. Before allowing the public to walk on the bridge he gathered all his family onto it for a picture. But the bridge was built like his others, the only way he knew how, delicate and pretty but not able to bear weight.

When the picture flashed—a big, beautiful, blinding light—the bridge fell apart. And not only in that spot but in places all over the Caribbean, so that the many families who had gathered to take pictures (without express permission) also went into the ocean. And though they were surrounded by the sea no one in any of the communities had bothered to learn to swim. The water never seemed as important as the land.

2

The Story of the Burka and the Habit: as told by a Catholic Lady in a big hat

Margo was a kind of ghost. A living ghost. She'd been living in St. Thomas for a decade but she had just up and sailed back to Dominica years ago. She couldn't continue to suffer the lack of dignity she faced here in St. Thomas. Oh, yes. Right here. Her husband, Rashaad, living in St. Thomas like a proper Muslim man. Working even now that their children were grown. Their grandchildren almost grown. It was a sham.

Back in Dominica their house was small and old and rolling down the hill inch by inch every year. No plumbing, she pissed in a pot. She did her business in a hole. Cooked her own food and withered away. This was okay. This was living. Going to mosque every Friday—walking all the five miles on her own. She passed waterfalls and rivers and waterfalls; symbols of life, she knew. She walked fast—she felt she could live forever. In St. Thomas she'd felt she would die. In the small mosque in Dominica there was no separate place for men and women. And women could speak. Ask the Imam questions in Patois during the middle of his speeches. Margo asked the same question every Friday.

"Does a woman sin by not living with her husband?"

"You should do nothing that hurts your family. Always doing what is best for them is best for you."

She was never satisfied. I wouldn't be either. Seems like Imams and priests aren't so different.

What was best was for her to stay in Dominica. Her family had moved on. Her son was Rasta and had exactly three wives—two of them were Ethiopian Orthodox and the other was a teenage devotee of an Egyptian faith long dead in Egypt. Her daughter had converted to Christianity. Her husband had become more devoted to Islam as his children were swept away. But now Margo was returning. She'd heard about the bridge. Who hadn't? All of the Caribbean was talking about it. The next stretch was planned for the British Virgin Islands, though the ferrymen complained and complained that they would go out of business. Proposals were in motion for the Bahamas and the ABC islands. A bridge soon to be under construction between Trinidad and Tobago. Next St. Kitts and Nevis. Bridges connecting the whole region.

She would see the bridge. Then she would go back to her husband. She was ready for the indignity. Urinating in a pot and moving one's bowels in a hole was not indignity. Indignity was her husband's house that was so ornate when there were so many poor in St. Thomas. Indignity was the black curtains he'd laid over all the windows to hide his shame at having children gone astray. Indignity was the burka he suggested she wear even in the hot Caribbean sun.

Their house in St. Thomas was at the very top of the island, at the tip of the highest peak. They'd bought it from the government. How, she'd never know. They'd left their nuptial house in Dominica, left it to slide down the little hill. Dominica was where her son had been born. Then her son had left and finally her daughter. And then she too, gone back to Dominica for eight years.

Margo walked to the corner store—two miles down the small Dominican hill, leaving her door unlocked so that anyone could get in if needed. She begged someone for money to buy a calling card. No indignity in being a beggar—Muslims were required to give alms.

"Rashaad?"

"Margo."

"I am coming home."

"Good. I have been waiting."

"Are the curtains still black?"

"They are more of a dark blue."

"Is there another woman?"

"Never."

"I'm coming soon, then."

"Come soon, then. Come soon."

She'd left for Dominica on a whim. Just walking by the cargo ship of bananas in her burka. She'd been a shadow as she climbed aboard.

Eating the sweet bananas as the vessel island-hopped, dumping its fruit cargo, filling up with parcels of books and clothes from aunties in Tortola to favorite nieces in Grenada. With the new bridge, of course, these waterways would be obsolete.

But what had kept her away all these years? Was it really Rashaad's fanaticism—something he used to steady himself as his children converted? Islam so in vogue, every kid in St. Thomas wearing a "Go Aya-tollah!" T-shirt. Was it her son with his eleven children? No. For mothers it's always the daughters.

Ayana was engaged to be married when the Catholics got her. Yes, we Catholics are always where the blame falls. She was engaged to a good Muslim boy whose parents were from Atlanta. Ayana said she was visiting him after school. But that was a lie. Margo knew that now. Ayana was actually staying after school in Catholic classes. All was revealed one Saturday evening.

"Mommy, come with me."

But what does that mean, really? Come with me down the street? Come with me so I can show you something? Come with me into the bosom of Jesus?

It was a trick either way. Unfair, really. Margo had to sit in the back pew as her daughter let go of her hand and walked down the aisle. And the priest placed a white square on her waiting tongue. "I'm happy, Mommy. Be happy for me." And then Ayana kneeled right beside her mother and prayed. The indecency of that child. Didn't even think of her mother.

Poor Margo had breathed in deeply, that horrible incense filling her nose, and kneeled beside her daughter. "Darling. Jesus never said he was God. You mustn't pray to him." Ayana didn't even nod at her mother. She seemed to have turned to stone. Margo left her daughter kneeling in the church. No energy to drag her out. Ayana was an adult in the eyes of God now anyway. Margo spat on the steps of the Cathedral. And cursed out loud the day that she'd sent her daughter to the parochial school.

"She'll find her way," said her son. "She's just exploring." But what did he know? He was lost too. His dreads all down his back. Dozens of illegitimate children swinging on his legs.

Her husband had taken her head to his chest. "Trust in Allah." But Ayana did not come home. Rashaad put his trust in Allah and darkened the windows; buying the burka Margo refused to wear, praying five times a day. Attending mosque every Friday, at least. And they heard nothing from Ayana. Nothing. Until she arrived one day. No longer stone—now habited. Nunned! In the full nun regalia, a brown rope hanging from her side. Oh, darling. Even I don't trust those costumed types. Well, Margo slapped her at the door. Ayana turned the other cheek. Margo slammed the door. She wore her burka after that. Always ready. Ready to face her daughter on even terms if she ever came back. But she didn't. And then Margo, burkad, had slipped onto a boat headed for Dominica.

Now she was flying back to St. Thomas. Rashaad had insisted on flying and not hitching on a barge again. He'd even sent her the money. The plane was small but it took a long route, circling the north side of the island so the passengers could see the bridge. Steel and cords and everything known to man seemed to have gone into it. It could hold elephants, a whole tropical jungle. It looked so strong. Like the hand of God stretching over the sea and saying "come, come." Margo began to weep.

Her plane arrived late and at the airport she had to wait a long while for her one bag, which couldn't be found at first. When it was finally unearthed it was clear that it had been opened. The wood carving of a rounded thinking man with his head in his lap had been stolen. She had brought it as a gift for her husband. Now she was going home with nothing but herself. She took the burka out of her luggage and put it on right there in the baggage claim area. This would make Rashaad happy. She was being watched in such a way that putting on this extra cloth felt oddly as if she was stripping naked.

It was quite late and the airport was almost deserted, but as she walked to the taxi stand the remaining drivers looked uneasy on their bench. She was a woman, but she was also a ghost gliding toward them. She announced her destination in her French island–accented English. The two older men slapped the younger one on the back and pushed him forward.

The house was out Northside and they drove in silence through town where there were lights on and bars still open. There were no lights on the country roads. Just the occasional high beams of another car. When they reached the hills the young driver began to talk.

"They opening the bridge tomorrow. Well, today, seeing as it done past midnight."

"Yes, I have heard."

"Tomorrow is Emancipation Day here. You know? The day the slaves get free when Buddoe blow his conch shell."

"Yes, of course."

She didn't want to talk to this boy. She wanted to get home and talk to her husband. Start a new life before they died.

"The bridge is that way." The driver turned away from the direction he pointed and made his way up a steep hill. The car revved angrily, jerked and obeyed. They made their way slowly. She hadn't seen the house for eight years. But it was still too large. Still too ridiculously ornate. Three stories on an island where two stories was already an excess. There were lights coming from the ground, lighting the driveway as they made their way. The columns at the entrance were emblazoned with light, making them look even more stretched than they were. There was darkness from the windows.

Margo opened the passenger door. The young driver carried her one bag to the steps of the grand house. Together they waited as she knocked. As she rang the doorbell. As she screamed out her husband's name, causing wings to flap and a distant dog to respond.

"Maam. I have to head back to the airport. My dispatcher is calling." And perhaps he was. Perhaps that sputtering from the car was the boss. Perhaps it was a lover or his mother. Or perhaps it was just static.

"Young man, you can go. This is my house. My husband will come home soon. He's expecting me."

"Yes, but I need to get paid."

She couldn't pay him. She'd counted on her husband being home. Rashaad had Western Unioned only what was needed for the plane.

"Well, money or no money, I can't just leave you here at night. You like my grandmother or something."

Margo stared at him through the opening in her veil. He could see the wrinkles around her eyes. "I'll find you tomorrow and pay you. Now go." She watched the young man walk backward, get in his car, and then drive slowly down the hill. She wasn't afraid of the dark. She'd lived without electricity for eight years. She wasn't afraid of loneliness. She'd lived alone on a little hill for eight years. She was afraid that her husband was not coming home. She walked down the big hill. Still hearing the very end of the taxi's growl in the night's silence. It was a very bright night. The half moon was out, and the house was so high up that the only thing above her was the stars. She would see the bridge up close. She would walk on it. Perhaps she would walk all the way to St. Croix. Live there. Where the land was flat and there were no hills to walk up or down. Where people had to face each other on level ground.

Gravity helped her along, pulling her down the hill toward the magnet of the bridge. She had once felt unsafe in a burka. No peripheral vision. No easy way to get hands out in defense. But in the days that she'd worn it, ready to face down her daughter, she'd found a safety. A safety to be hidden. In the dark now, rushing toward the sea, she felt unseen. The walk was a long one and she kept expecting the sky to get lighter into the morning but it didn't. She thought about her children when they were little. How smart they'd looked in their Catholic school uniforms with dark blue socks pulled up to their knees. She thought about her husband when they first married and he'd built that house in Dominica with his own bare hands. He had promised her he would install plumbing and electricity. But then their son had been born and moving seemed easier. She thought of her own mother, who didn't trust Rashaad because he wasn't Pentecostal. How she had told her father that she loved Rashaad, even though she'd only brushed hands with him in the Juan Diego burial grounds where each had gone to mourn a different forgotten family member.

How could Margo have known then that she would leave behind her own faith and become Muslim to marry him? She'd only been seventeen. How could she have known anything?

By the time Margo reached the bridge she realized that she had seen her whole life in her mind. She was grateful. Now the bridge was towering above her, dwarfing the house on the hill that she had hated for so long. She stepped onto the bridge; there were sidewalks for pedestrians and she ambled along these for some time. Aware that she was high above many things. She paused to lean over a railing and then consider the distance she had walked. She could still see where she was coming from, but where she was going was lost in the darkness. Far below her was a little boat with two figures lying languidly beside each other. One figure was a bit larger than the other.

She knew what it was. Margo leaned deeper over the railing to get a better view of her husband and his other woman. They did not see her. She placed her feet on the railing, one after another until she stood there and screamed, her arms flying about. The young girl much farther along on the bridge watched the woman tip. Heard her screaming: "You said you were waiting!" The couple in the little fishing boat saw Margo as a sparrow in flight. The bridge began to shake. Margo had the flighting feeling that she had been a little wrong, but as she soared she could not remember what she was wrong about. The water rose to meet her life like a wall.

3
The Fisherman's Tale:
as told by someone's grandfather in a corner rum shop

Pour me a greenie. I like my Heineken in a glass, damn it. I'm a gentleman. And I tell you here and now that Tony Magrass wasn't no cheapster. He never weigh down the scale by leaning on it like some does do. His fish always fair and always fresh. He love the water. I mean is love he love the water. Spear fishing and all of that. The little wife is a waitress for a tourist food shop. She old now, but still good looking. Not wrinkle up at all. She the type that too pretty for she own good. She been horning with the manager of the restaurant where she work for years. Years! Salli, that's she name, wasn't even sure that she and Tony son was really Tony son. The manager wasn't good looking, now. Just rich. Just keeping she in she job. Just helping she send Pete to Catholic school.

Pete make alright grades but he fish with his father more than he study books. Giving his teachers fish for free on Sundays. Going to Mass out Northside like good Northside Frenchies. But no one had been fishing on the north side for two years. You know, because of building the bridge and all. Less fish for the locals. Less fish for the tourists. Less fish at Salli restaurant. Tony had taken to fishing in town with the Frenchtown boys. They tease him but they pity all the Northside Frenchies. Their piece of the ocean take away by the bridge that supposed to help everybody—connect all the islands. St. Thomas to St. Croix goin be just a car drive away. Set up a toll in a year when it get popular and needed. Bring in money for the government. Money for the islands. Right? Well. On July 3 the bridge would be opened. On July 3 people would be able to walk even to their sister islands. But to Tony July 3 don't mean bridge open, don't even mean Emancipation Day, don't mean the day before U.S. independence. It just mean he could fish again. But now it was March still.

He wife calling him. "Tony. Tony, baby. I leaving."

He come home and meet the house half empty. The mahogany short leg table, for coffee she'd told him, gone. The rusted beveled mirror that her father self had brought during their first year of marriage, so they could hug up and stare at each other as she belly grow, gone. The art books that she buy secondhand, hinting and hoping for the easel and paints he *never* buy she, gone. In the kitchen there was food in plastic containers they didn't own before. Meals done cook and freezing in the freezer. She'd gone shopping. She'd cooked. But the coal pots and iron pans that her mother had hand down, gone too. In the bathroom her little soaps. Her sweet smelly shampoo. The towel with Minnie Mouse from their trip to Orlando back when money was good—gone. Only the Mickey Mouse one hanging alone.

Salli was in the bedroom. The linen bedspread that he parents had give them arrange neat over the bed. She lying on top of it. Fully clothed. Heels and stockings. Calf length skirt. White blouse. A nice purse at she side. Clothes he ain never seen before. That's a woman for you. She turn her head just so when he enter and watch him in the face.

"I goin with Mr. Kenny. I can't live off a fisher man's salary no more."

"And Pete?" Tony look at he wife, too pretty and lying out on their bed. He wanted to walk to her and unbutton her shirt slow. But he smell of fish. He know she hate that. She watch him hard.

"Pete's a grown man. Going to college in the States soon. He'll stay with you or us. No matter."

Tony leave the room before she did. If I were he I woulda swallow some cold Heineken. But Tony just walk out to the dining room where dinner for he and Pete sitting in plates covered in aluminum foil. He sit down at the tail of the table and begin to eat. He hear her heels clink behind him on she way out.

Pete didn't come home that night. The next day was school but he turn up at eight in the morning to he father's house. He find Tony in bed, wrap up in the linen bedspread, bloat up and sick from all the food he eat. Not just the dinner Salli leave but enough food for at least three days. Pete stand over his old man.

"Ma say you not my real father, Dad."

Tony roll around in his linen cocoon. See the man! Flinging heself onto the floor, onto the tile he had lay he ownself. The tile she had picked out. He fighting now, tearing the linen and old lace until he get free. He son watching from the doorway.

"Dad. Let me know what's true."

Tony reach a hand to he son and together they get Tony onto the bed. Pete sit down beside him. Tony look into he son eyes.

"Your mother is the devil."

"Don't say that, man."

"She a lying devil."

"Chill, Pops. Chill out."

Tony thought they should go fishing. At times like these that is what a proper Frenchy father and son should do. But Tony can't take Pete to Frenchtown—it already crowded down there. So they decide to wait until July 3. So long aways. And Pete leaving two days after that. He get into a nice-up school in the States but they require him to do some summer classes cause he ain so good at maths.

So the father and son wait all that time. And at four in the morning of July 3 they roll up their pants. They have their spear gun and dagger just in case, but really they only want to do some leisure fishing. Maybe bring something home for dinner so they don't have to eat the cooking Salli keep bringing in plastic tins. They push out their boat, and the bridge there gleaming. They see it stretching out across the ocean. They have nets and poles and flashlight and a bag of small live bait.

At the docks there weren't no other men. The other Northside Frenchies thinking to wait, thinking that the fish wouldn't come back so soon. Thought maybe the fish would never come back. Some had already moved from Northside permanently. You seeing them in town. Haunting the place looking for sea jobs, land jobs—anything. But those don't have a son going away. They don't have a wife who leave them for a better man.

The boat engine make a soft noise and though they just heading out to sea it seem like they heading toward the bridge. They wasn't. Not really. It only seem so cause the bridge feel like it everywhere. Like it a haunted rainbow, hunting you round the city. I have felt the feeling. The moon was out and shape funny, like a smile almost. They even see one or two people on the bridge.

"Yeah, Dad. I think we goin catch something, man. I think the fish must be curious to see a boat like ours after all this time."

"We counting on it." But the father didn't really think so. Not really at all. He only want to be with he son like this. Pete been living with his mother and Mr. Kenny all this time because Mr. Kenny could drop him to school while his father went fishing first thing in the morning. But Pete was still his son and Tony love-love he son. More than fishing even. More than life.

"Jesus. Pops, look." Pete was staring past he father shoulder. "Pops, she's frigging jumping." And sure nough. A woman standing on the railing of the bridge with her arms spread wide.

She tip forward and Pete scream—like he mother's own son. A high-pitch thing. And the woman above them spread her black wings and begin to fly like a crow diving to the ocean. But Tony ain even see she cause he busy going blind from a light bright like a saint. It was just then that the bridge begin to collapse. And the water around their little boat begin to swell. And their boat itself begin to shake. And boulders of the bridge crash into the sea causing waves that lift highhigh. And then the sound like hell opening its dirty doors—loud like it coming from inside the chest somehow. The boat rip apart before it could capsize. Son holding on to the one half and spinning off into a whirlwind. Father grabbing on the next half rushing toward ragged land.

Tony Magrass knock on Mr. Kenny door that very morning. The easel hard and heavy under he one arm. The palate of paints dainty in he other. Salli open the door and look at her husband of seventeen years. The father of she dead son. She don' know for sure yet that she son gone, but she know this man ain come cause he hungry. Mr. Kenny not home as yet, so she watch the art ting hard. She look again at she husband and they lock eyes even harder. Despite their distance, there never been a thing but love between them. "Set it up in the corner, Tony."

4
The Lament of the Queen: as told by a seventeen-year-old schoolgirl in patent leather shoes

Guadeloupe did it for love. *Obviously.* As they say in all the movies, nothing else is enough. Of course she wanted to kill herself. Attempted suicide is, like, so in vogue now. Though she did more than die, of course. Juan Diego was a real man who knew not to ask about her past. About how she really won (well, *almost* won) all those teen pageants. He knew not to question anything that had happened before him, not even to question what was happening while she was with him. If it did not stop her from loving him, if it did not rack her with guilt, if it did not make her different, then how could it matter to him? Yes, girl. Guadeloupe was a little whore.

When she said she was a virgin, he agreed. He accepted her with the illusions she presented. Loved her and didn't care about the lies. You know the type. He was a real college guy, mature about that kind of stuff. Dark skin and tall. Those sweet ones are hard to find, and then the wrongest girls are the ones who find them, yes.

Anyway, she wasn't like him. She wasn't mature bout those things. Still in high school and one of those stupid girlie girls. *I* would have known better. Anyhow, she found a love note, dated like three years before she'd even met him. And she just crumbled from the thought that he'd loved someone besides her. Stupid, hey? Crumbled from the realization that he too had a past, that maybe she was not his greatest love in the whole wide world—I mean he had saved the note for *three years* and she would have been like a freshman in high school then. And like all girls who don't know how to forgive themselves—she could not forgive him. So she decided to win the crown, a tiara really, without the usual aids of her body and obeah-magic.

But it would be hard. Because she was Puerto Rican and light skinned and straight haired, though at least her hair was brown. Miss Emancipation, the biggest title in St. Croix, was supposed to be a woman who celebrated the freedom of slaves. Guadeloupe decided to win the crown for the few slave-descended ancestors she had. To show Juan Diego that she could be whatever he wanted. Because when she found the note, she realized that he didn't think her pure, did not think he had her virginity, did not think her a girl who'd first-runnered-up pageant after pageant by her own merit. But that he'd known all along that she was a fraud. And he'd loved her a fraud, when she'd thought she'd had him loving her pure. Thinking that his love made her pure, because he said he loved her as if she was like the Virgin Mary herself. *Anyway.*

Well, you saw it. She won. She'd sung for the talent competition something about God, and our people love that. And for the historical segment she'd been the bridge, the thing to connect us; friends to family. While the other girls wore masks of famed teachers and religious leaders on all sides of their heads or boxes of the legislature building around their waists, the judges and the audience thought Guadeloupe was so innovative to bring the present into such significance by making it history. In the question and answer portion she talked about connectivity, diversity in unity. Despite her light skin, despite the obviousness that more of her ancestors had owned slaves than had been them, how could she lose? We're open like that. We like to know that people love us; we don't care how they look.

She'd competed without aid in pageants before. First with Carlos McEntire, when they'd been Carnival Prince and Princess. You remember that? Then in middle school she'd been Miss Junior May Fair Queen. Who could forget that one? She mimed for her talent. She was good, too. But then winning became serious, the prizes became substantial. She'd done what was needed to place first runner-up in Miss Talented Teen, Queen of the Band, Miss Parks and Recreation, Lady Alpha. Incantations, meditations, all kinds of *tations* to win, to *not lose.* She competed in things she didn't even qualify for, like Mistress of Housing, though she didn't even live in the projects. And now she'd won Miss Emancipation. It wasn't as if she hadn't prepared, like, her whole life. All the singing lessons, and the walking lessons: until she figured out that learning to walk and learning to sing were the same. (Both required breathing and a straight back and hands clasped before the torso. Like so. She could tell a singer by the sway in the hips, though if you ask me you can tell a slut by the same thing.) Finally, she'd won all by herself.

They sat the skimpy little tiara on her head and her first walk as Miss Emancipation was announced. Her blue gown was covered in sequin stars and she really looked good, as if she was a piece of the sky. Her arms shimmered with the glitter her chaperone had applied carefully before releasing her to the formal gown segment. Strutting down the catwalk she was only aware of herself. The spotlight does that. It blinds you, you know. So bright she couldn't see the audience, not even Juan Diego, in the front beside her mother. Both of them looking at her so proudly. She could only clutch the red roses tight in her hands, letting the few thorns prick her fingers but not the delicate dress. She felt her chest swell with heat while the darkened faces below smiled—well, they seemed to smile.

Backstage, the other girls congratulated her stiffly, their lips not touching her face at all. And somehow winning without seducing a judge or casting obeah on the other contestants still felt fraudulent. Maybe, like being a fraud might be her *true self*? She got kinda crazy thinking about that then. She took off her heels in the changing room and put on her sneakers, still in the panty hose and sequined dress. And she ran. No joke. The people parted as she ran by because no one recognized her without her tiara on. She ran to the last place she should have. The Bridge. She had no food and no water but wanted to make it to the other side. She didn't know how long it would take. She didn't know why she chose this as a symbol. She didn't know that when you don't eat or drink for a whole day you *forget* to be hungry. That hunger doesn't matter. Only thirst. It rained the morning of the second day; this is the Caribbean after all. She tilted her head back and kept walking. The worn makeup streaking down her face, then off her face completely. She realized, once the rain had stopped, that her face hadn't been so clean since she was *seven years old.*

A full day on the Bridge. Not on the land, not in the sky, not in the water. She saw the sun set and then rise on this limbo life. Between the night of the second day and the morning of the third she could see the other side of the bridge. The land of the other island just there past the length of her tongue. The thirst for it like, I don't know, like mother love. Scratching at the back of her throat. There was a black sack figure crossing the bridge too. There were two figures in a boat just below. It was late, dark. The moon was high and crescented. She wanted to be on top of that moon. She wanted it at her feet—like a boat to get her across anything. She was such a frigging drama queen. She couldn't know what she had in common with these three figures. But she felt she had to choose one set or the other. The weight of her absent crown solid on her head. She knew that if Juan Diego was with her he would hold her up with his two hands like the angel he was until she became something holy, something to make these lands pure and able. His Guadeloupe.

Anyway. She walked toward the figure on the bridge, but the black-sack woman actually seemed to move farther away, climbing the railing away from her. Perhaps Guadeloupe looked a little off, mad you know, a beauty queen in sneakers, hair looking like crap because of the rain and the ragged days of walking. Guadeloupe looked down where the woman was looking and saw the moon below, at her feet. Saw the little brown boy in the boat stand up to hold her. She felt the tingle of the glow. The halo covered her entire body. Not like a tiara; not even like a crown they gave the boys who won for Mister this or King that. The halo coming from her very bones and protecting her. She was pure. She could save lands. She was the most pure and the most good. A human bridge.

The other woman on the bridge looked now like a huge black crane steadying itself for flight. Guadeloupe, this mixed-up girl who was just getting to know herself, watched on in her new state of grace, and the lovely crane leapt into the air, with its wings wide and open to the wind. Guadeloupe pressed her hands together so gently that her pinkies crossed and missed each other—she felt something glorious come from her and go out into the world. And, *I kid you not,* that was when the miracle of miracles happened. The bridge began to crumble. She was not afraid as the air opened and took her in.

STREET MAN

Let me tell you how I meet this sweet thing. It's Christmas time so the place fill up with people from the ships and the resorts. She walk into the Sun Shack like she one of them tourist. She even talk all Yankee. I don't really bother with she because I don't want to be all Stella get her groove. I let the white lady help she. But Yolanda walk over to me on her own and then her voice change up and she sound like any island girl all the sudden. She want to know about the Maui Jims behind me, so I take them out for her and tell her she look sweet when they on her face. She don't buy a piece of shades but she leave me her number and I don't even self pretend to not watch her ass as she leave.

For two weeks we spend some big amount of time together every day. Sometimes I just drive my four-runner to her house on my lunch break and park in the middle of the street. I tell her jokes about the red-faced tourists who come into the shop—how the women does tell me my accent don't even sound like English, but some exotic native language. How the man them does lean in and ask me quiet-quiet where they could get some weed. Yolanda does laugh so hard that she have to sit down on the pavement and lift her legs scissor-like into the air. She tell me that in college they asked her where she buy her sneakers because they didn't think Nikes could sell anywhere but the U.S. But when she talk about that kind of stuff, it's not funny. It's all serious. And I think that it's a real good thing that she have a sense of humor and some maturity to boot. When we talk serious it does make her want to kiss right there on the sidewalk. I let she. I let she all the time. At the beach in the water. On the couch in my living room. I never let a girl do that before.

One night we sitting in my car, parked in the middle of her street. Since the last hurricane St. Croix don't have no streetlights in this neighborhood. If you get too close to either side of the road the house lights shining right into the car. So we was parked in the middle where it dark. We ain having sex yet but since I a lot older than her, ten years older, I cool that she keeping cautious. I ain no young boy. I cooling. Yolanda's on my lap snaking away—getting her nut. I kissing on her neck and thinking how this young girl have me acting like a schoolboy. She wearing tight white pants and because it's so dark that's all I could see clearly, and her teeth when she laugh and the white in her eyes. At this point we only been seeing each other for those two weeks and I already know she like to laugh and kiss and even do both when we fooling around. I like foreplay. I good at it. I mean I good at the whole shebang, but a older guy know foreplay is sweet. Just doing it is for dogs. I too old for that.

Now a car is coming down the street and I have to drive around the block with Yolanda in my lap and me having to look under her arm to make the corners. She love that stuff. Laugh so loud I had to give her a hard stare. "Hush, no, girl. Your laugh will wake the dead."

When we reach back in front her house she go to me "I have to tell you something." I know what she going to tell me just by how her eye them all small and her mouth all slack, and I don't want to hear it yet. So I say "Get off my lap." When she sitting there in the passenger seat, I try to relax my heart and my dick cause the blood in both is slamming away. "Don't tell me," I say. "It's too soon." But we been dancing all night and now she been on my lap for almost a half hour. "I have to say it cause it's true," she say. So I let her. "I love you, Slick." Damn. Leave it to a young girl. A college girl. To fall in love and have to tell you the minute it friggin happen. I pissed but I don't have no choice but to admit it back. "Okay, Yolanda. I love you, too. Now I gotta say something." And I tell her about what I do on the side. How I deal sometimes. How I have a gun under my seat. I take it out and show her. She get all quiet like she gonna cry and right then I don't know if I want hold her and tell her I going be done with that shit if she will just be my shortie for truth and I'll move with her to Tallahassee where she in college. Or if I just want kick her out the car for being such a damn softy, tell her I need a ride or die chick and not some goody-goody college girl that don't know nothing about the street. I ain gonna change for no man, woman, or child. But she don't cry. She just rest her head on my shoulder. "Shit, Slick," is what she say. And her voice is so sweet and she seem so for real that I decide then that I going wait this girl out cause she could be the mother of my youths. And so I tell her, "If you gonna be my woman you can't be calling me Slick. It's Anton. But don't be screaming it in the street."

For the months Yolanda's away at college I screw out on her, but not really. I thinking about her when I doing it and I wearing a Magnum so I don't give her nothing when she come back. On the phone I tell her I just slapping my stuff when I look at her picture. She thinks that's sexy so sometimes that's what I do for real and I let her listen. I make more noises and stuff than I would if I was by myself, so she could feel she a part of it. I think it's practice for when we really do it for the first time. I mean, I love this girl. I have some secrets but they in her best interest. I is a street man. And a street man is the sweetest man. Them goody schoolboys don't know what to do when they have a lady on their hands. They tell everything and make their woman miserable. They worry about career and shit before they worry about pleasing their woman. Not I and I.

My last name is Colter and that's a good name on the island. Only my pops is the black sheep so we don't have no money like the other Colters. But Yolanda's moms is forgiving. She a black sheep, too. Her husband dead in some American war and now she live down by the seaplanes. So she okay with a street man for a son-in-law. I polite. I say goodnight when I enter. I wash the dishes when they have me over for dinner. And while Yolanda is gone I still visit her moms. Sometimes do her shopping for her. I never bring my piece in their house. I always keep body spray in the car so I don't smell like sensimania when I knock on the door.

I pick Yolanda up from the airport when she come home for summer vacation. First thing she tell me is that she miss me and then in the car she all over me. I call her moms on my cell and say that the plane is delayed but it coming in an hour or so. I take Yolanda to this house on a hill that get blow away in the last hurricane. It don't have no roof and only one wall but it have a flat for the car to drive up and it have a view of the ocean—which is hard to come by on St. Croix. I know this place because I used to deal to the white folks that owned it. They didn't like to come around the park so I would drop it off during my lunch break. When the hurricane hit they run speeding back to Texas. They had want to set up some long-distance thing but Fish and me can't be doing that. We small time and I plan on keeping it so. The place ain been sold yet now so it's kind of my place. I go there to think. Think like how I might one day own my own Sun Shack place. How I would sell shades to all the local roughnecks. Expensive stuff and good quality, like Fendi or Dolce. I think about greeting the customers and putting the things that don't sell on sale. I think that I'll always do my own books so no one even have a chance to mess with me. I think even Fish will come to my place with respect and I going give him a deal. I think maybe I could even have the shop here at this blown-away house. How if someone spare me a loan I could set it up.

I ain never brought anyone else up here. And now I bring Yolanda. We do it right in the driver's seat. I open the car door so there's more space. Her back keep hitting the horn and making her laugh. It's so good, but I don't want to come too quick so I think about my moms who left the outside light on for me and about how she gonna cuss cause I ain washed her car in a week.

When we done I ask Yolanda if it's okay if I smoke. She says it's cool. I don't offer her. I don't like ladies smoking. It's a bad habit and it looks even worse on them. But for fun I blow the smoke toward her and she open her mouth to catch it. I think that yes, this is my woman. My woman is home.

It's summer so we go out constant. Sometimes we hit the beach before it get dark and the sand flies come out. Sometimes she and her moms want to have family time so I wait until midnight and then roll by. I just sit in the car in the middle of the street. Sometimes I park right there, turn off the car, and wait with the radio on low. Yolanda knows my ride so it don't take her long to come out. Then we go to my house and watch a flick with action and a love story—something we could both be into. In my bedroom with my mother snoring just on the next side of the wall, I tell Yolanda that I don't eat pussy but she only laugh as she guide my head.

I don't deal in front of Yolanda because I know she won't like that. If we in traffic and some guy come up to me with his hand open I look at him hard and say, "Partner, you don't see my woman with me?" I never bring Yolanda to the park and she know she better not show up there looking for me. If she in downtown and she want to find me she only need to text me and I'll leave my post by the kiddie swings long as I ain in the middle of nothing.

But once I left Yolanda in the car for almost two hours while I went into Fish house to get a gun put in my mouth. That was his punk ass way of asking why I ain make no profit. And though I could have just told him that I smoke it up myself, so send me to rehab already, there was a gun in my mouth and all I could think about was Yolanda outside in my four-runner, reading her book. I done this before. Gone inside to some nigger's house and stayed longer than I should. Told her I'd be back in a few minutes but then I gone for a hour. This though was the worse. What Yolanda thinking out there all that time? That I's a real waste? Or maybe she ain thinking of me at all.

When I get back she in the seat reclining way back with her feet all up on my dash like she just here in the island vacationing. The thing is Yolanda never complains when I make her wait, but if I'm sweating she look at me all suspicious like she think I been screwing or something . . . but she know I ain been doing that. She does wear me out. She younger than me, so it's no big deal. I'm the one who should be worried really. I mean she not even with me half the year but it seem like she want to do it all the time. I have to keep asking her: "Do you love dick or just my dick?" and she laugh with that mampie laugh and tell me "Just yours, Anton, just yours."

Yolanda is a good girl. And I done decide that a street man like me need a good sweet thing like her. It's a balance. She's not about "keeping it real" and all that fake shit. She's not going hold my gun for me. And I don't want her to. I is the thug in this. I don't want no chick I have to worry might sell me out or turn me in because she know too much. Yolanda know I work for the Sun Shack and that I's a hard worker even when I been smoking a lot. She the kind of girl don't want to know everything that goes on in my life.

That summer she had a job teaching computers. And sometimes I used to bring her lunch. The other girls would look all cut eye at me. Once I see a big bush of roses on the front desk and only for a second do I wonder if they for her. But then I get my stuff together. The next day I bring she flowers. The next day a stuffed bear. Why not? I smoke a little less, add more fronter to my spliff. I save some money because one day I going buy this girl a ring. She start wearing my hand chain around she wrist and it so thick and bulky that everybody must know that it's a man own. That she mine.

At the club I buy her friends drinks and they smile at me and tell she I is the cutest guy she ever been with, loud, so I could hear. On the dance floor when she there tongue-kissing me, like the white tourist girls do the Rastitutes, I make sure our hips don't press cause I know she hate to feel my gun in her waist.

Some of the guys in the park probably think I is a punk. That I sprung over this girl that's cheating on me when she off island. That she too young for me. Too educated. Fuck them. She ain cheating cause I'm digging up in her every single night—enough to keep it in her dreams when she away. And yeah she young, but so what. I still hustling and I almost thirty. Plus, she ain had no pops in her life for a long time. She need a older man. I did two years at FAMU but then my pops disappeared and I had to go home to take care of my moms. I can still go to UVI, but I'm old now. You know. When would I have time? Between selling shades to the tourists at the Sun Shack and sitting at the bottom of the park slide with my pockets full of dime bags. I mean, I know things. I read the entire newspaper every day. And sometimes Yolanda and I shout each other down over politics. We teach each other stuff. This is love, son. The real thing.

One day I up by Fish and as usual Yolanda waiting in the car. This time I have my gun and I open my shirt to show him. "Listen," I tell him. "I ain smoking it all. It's that shitty skunk weed come in from Jamaica. It making everybody sick. Even I can't smoke it. Either I sell it cheap or we go in the hole." He want me to sell some coke to make up. I tell him I'll come back for it cause my lady in the car and it's bad enough I carry my gun around with her. I don't want her caught up in nothing. He give me a hard time but I remind him that I been his partner for years. I'll come the fuck back after I drop her off. I hate that Fish nigger, but he my cousin on my mom's side—so I suppose to know that he won't really kill me. And he's suppose to know that I won't really sell him out.

I've been up in Fish's house this time for only thirty minutes when I get back to the car. Instead of legs up on the dash, she hunched forward. When I open the car she jump and hide her arms. That messes me up. See, once I dated a girl who started shooting. I saw her arms all scarred and blue and it frig me up so bad I never sold heroin again. I never touched her again either. So now I'm freaking out, thinking I done turned my angel Yolanda bad and we in the car right in Fish's driveway struggling. She thicker than me but I still stronger and taller than her. She forget that even though I skinny, I could still pick her up and slam her on the bed.

I get her arms in front and see words written on them. It freaks me out. But it's just words. "Stop looking," she says. "Stop reading." Lord Harry the Judge. I lay back in my seat and I just ask, "This is stupid. You couldn't find no paper?" She shakes her head, "I left my notebook." I open the golf and show her the roller paper, like a small notepad. "I didn't think of that" she say with her voice going all Yankee now. And then she crying like I hit her or something. She sit on her hands the whole drive back. Keep her arms tight by her side. Tonight, I think, I going kiss those arms. I going lick every word if she let me.

When we at her gate I stop her and say, "Why won't you let me see what you write?" And she just shrug. I ask if she let anyone see and she look out the window like she talking to somebody in the street. "I got some poems published in the college magazine." I nod. "Anybody on island read it?" And she look at the roof of my car. She reach up and pick at the felt that's coming loose. I don't have a drug dealer's pimped-out ride. I just have a regular four-runner. She look at the roof like it's falling in and it is. She say, "I sometimes read at this open mic down in Frederiksted." I pull her face close to mine. I kiss her hard like I know she like it. She does call it "the I love you kiss." I say, "Next time, I coming with you." Only when I on my way back to Fish's do I wonder when and how she go there without me ever knowing. When I get to her the ink is all washed off.

For two weeks she forget to tell me about the open mic thing. I act like I don't care. Instead, I do a little investigation. I hit up my crew in the park. "Like Def Jam on HBO?" they ask. I say yeah, but still they don't know nothing. I ask my moms. I check the paper. I ask the lady I sell shades with. Nothing. So I do something bazadie. I stake my girl out. I borrow one of Fish's cars and I park down the street, watching her house in the side mirror. On the fourth night she come out around nine. She suppose to be hanging with her moms. I suppose to be picking her up later for a movie lime.

And yet she standing there waiting on the corner like she frigging selling. Only she dressed up like I ain never seen her. She ain wearing makeup and her hair tie up in scarf. Arms bare and clean for everyone to see. And she ain in a tight pants that makes her ass look juicy. She in a dress down to her ankles, the kinda thing my moms wears around the house. I want to get out and scream to her that she look like a sweetheart, because really she does. I want to hear her mampie laugh. But I don't move. I wait. Like I'm waiting for a hit. Like I'm doing those things we don't talk about. An old Volvo drive up. She walk around and get in. I turn away when the car drive by.

I know how to tail a car. I know how to hold back. How to cut into a gas station and let them get way ahead. I know how to take a parallel street and keep an eye on them at the crossroads. I track the Volvo way to the next side of town. I park in the small lot, because we already here. If she see me now it don't matter. Let she see me.

The spot is a Rasta restaurant. Ital smelling up the place. Making me wish I had bring a beer or eat some meat before I come. I never sell in this part of the island. These cats grow their own ganja. They say it religious and the cops leave them alone. I think that's bullshit. So, if I just grow some locks then I'd be legit? I don't want weed to be legal, anyhow. Then the feds would control it and the profits wouldn't be made on the streets. You don't change a good thing, you keep it so.

It's a small place but I squeeze in the back. I order a sea moss. I ain had one of these local drinks in years. I don't use the straw because that look punky. I sip it from the cup itself. Sea moss does strengthen the back, they say. I don't mind the extra boost because Yolanda does keep me spent.

I drinking down all the nutmeg and coconut as I stare at the back of Yolanda's head. I know my girl, she sitting way in the front there like she must do in school. The restaurant has a stage with a mic and even this announcer guy who's telling crap jokes and singing. A dread is up there now scatting like a fool. There's a pickup band that keeps repeating that it will do backup for anyone who want.

They introduce her as Landi. And I cringe cause I never know she go by this name. I always tell her I think her whole name is sexy. She say she love to hear me say it. "Yo-lan-da." And I say it for as many times as she want. She say that it's a symbol that I love all of her, but now I don't know. The crap announcer take her hand to help her onto the stage, even though I can see she don't need no help.

The guy next to me point his chin and say something bullshit like "Is she I come for." When I just watch him hard he suck his teeth and say "Wait and see" then turn away to sip his energy drink from a tiny can. As soon as Yolanda up there she holding the mic like it my dick or something and she whispering into it and shouting into it and everybody pumping up their fists. She controlling the backup band just by moving her wrist or nodding her head, like they know her body and her ways. There's a spotlight on her and I wondering if she can see me. I the only dude in the place with a ball cap on; without dreads or a nappy fro.

Then I realize that Yolanda ain wearing my hand chain. Maybe she lost it. Maybe it slipped off somewhere outside. Maybe it home safe in her drawer. I leave my sea moss. I thinking I just going check the small parking lot and see if the hand chain dropped out there. I get into Fish's car and turn it on so I have a light. But then I don't look for the hand chain at all. I press the clutch and the gas. I driving away. And I hear Yolanda's voice in the mic, screaming something messed up like: "Change, nigger, change."

THE SAVING WORK

1.

A church is burning down. On a Caribbean island, in the countryside, up a road that might lead to a saving beach, but does not—a church is burning down. Everyone who is associated with this church will later think "my church has burned down." But for now there are only two women there to look at the fire, and blame each other.

They are both white American women in the middle of their lives. They and their families are members of this church. They are each married to a local black man, both of whom are skinny and frail of body. These women want to be the strong ones. They have always been the strong ones.

Deirdre Thompson has brought the garlands for the church stairs. She has brought the pew pins and the flowers for the altar. She was the first to arrive and see the bright flames. She is already dressed in her gold silk suit. She saw the smoke from far away in her car, but she imagined some filthy native was burning garbage in his yard. The smoke seemed to disappear as Deirdre drew near the church. This was an illusion.

Her car had lumbered its way along the narrow cut into the land that is the church road. The men of the church laid the road, and, as a result, it dips erratically. The arms of thin trees scraped at the closed windows of Deirdre's car. She wondered why no one had cut them back. She thought, with some worry, about how the limousine would make its way. The road opened into the clearing where the church crackled in the center. Through the windshield Deirdre saw what she thought was just a smallish fire, more smoke than anything.

Nothing to alert the people in the nearby houses, some two hundred yards beyond the bushes.

But now Deirdre knows what she's seeing. She's seeing the end.

Deirdre Thompson has always been a negative kind of woman. She has one child because her womb had been stingy. And perhaps also because she left her husband once when their son was two. They did not reunite until the boy was twelve.

Her son is called Thomas—after the island of his birth.

Deirdre's husband is an insurance salesman. He owns the business and has other men do the work of selling by foot. He stays in his office downtown and lets his faithful customers come to him. He does well. And his small family does well. But what Mr. Thompson really wants is to be a preacher. He knows he could lead the common folk. He knows he could get better pews for the main room and better robes for the choir.

During the week Deirdre Thompson works as a dental assistant. In the office and outside, as she walks on her lunch break, she wears a white coat and allows patients and passersby to call her Doctor.

On Sundays, when Deirdre teaches the high school religious classes, she does not tell her students that marriage is challenging and a thing to be careful with—like a baby. She tells them instead how much Mr. Thompson loves her and that love saves everything. She tells them that when she met Mr. Thompson she had blond hair down to her ankles and that is why he fell in love with her. She makes them turn the thin Bible pages to Sampson and study the strength that was in his hair. She makes them memorize passages from the Old Testament that demonstrate beauty as a woman's greatest honor. The girl students are mostly of African descent and native to the island. They could never hope for blond hair to their ankles. They look at their teacher with envy or hate or pity—the last because they suspect Deirdre is lying.

Deirdre's son does not attend his mother's Sunday school classes. He was the crossing guard aide in middle school and the student government president in high school. He has always been a ruler of sorts. Thomas is besotted with a girl named Jasmine, the eldest daughter of Violet de Flaubert. He is a year older than the de Flaubert girl but she was skipped ahead, so she and Thomas Thompson had been in the same grade. The de Flaubert girl is brilliant and shy, and Thomas has been in love with her since he was twelve.

Deirdre stands a few safe yards in front of the burning church, watching it creak and break. She hears an engine sputter and knows it must be Violet de Flaubert's car graveling up behind her. Deirdre does not turn to greet her. Now that Violet has arrived she wonders about her own inaction. Wonders about her own ability to simply watch the church crack, and crumble into ashes.

Violet de Flaubert sees the smoke and thinks it must be a campfire. This makes no sense. There are no campgrounds. Then she thinks maybe it's a barbecue, but people don't barbecue much on the island. She thinks on anything but a burning church. She is fighting not to think of a burning church.

Violet has five daughters who are each named after flowers, and with all those girls she somehow still feels virginal. When she teaches middle school religious classes on Sunday, she tells them, truthfully, that she was a virgin when she met Mr. de Flaubert. She makes them turn to passages on the mother of Jesus. She makes them act out the Christmas story. The girl students look at her with respect and adoration, for they are at the age for such things. The boy students look away from her with shame, because they are wishing they were *Mister* de Flaubert. The students don't think Violet is white from America. They assume she is Frenchy and native to the islands because she talks with native inflections and because she's been on the island since before they were born.

Mr. de Flaubert works for the government in the tax system. He is a cog, but he tells his daughters and his wife that he is an accountant. He makes decent money, but with all those girls the money does not last. He, too, wishes he were a preacher. He knows he could give good sermons. He longs to reach out and put his hands on people and speak in tongues and see flames of Jesus spark on their heads.

Violet de Flaubert is a teacher in the school where her daughters and Deidre's son are enrolled. She teaches high school because her daughters are in high school. Before that she taught middle school. And before that she was a teacher's aide in the elementary school. She is a teacher because she is a mother. To her they are the same thing.

Two of her daughters are students in her Sunday school class. All five of her girls are strangely beautiful and brilliant. And they all have a saving flaw. One is overly shy, another is overly bookish, another cares only for her violin and practices incessantly, one is prone to fits, and the last is a bit of a tart. But even this last one reads science fiction and is friends with the oily-faced girls.

Jasmine is the eldest. She is the shy one. She has a debilitating crush on a boy named Moby. Moby is the shortstop of the baseball team and during football season he is the quarterback and during basketball he is the tall center. Many girls are fond of Moby, and quiet Jasmine does not stand a chance. Though Moby has every now and then complimented her on her outfit during free clothes day or asked her about calculus, Jasmine hasn't said more than a few sentences to him during their entire middle and high school years together.

Jasmine is unaware of Thomas Thompson's adoration for her. She thinks of him as the brother she never had, and in high school she went to watch his soccer games. But this island is American and soccer isn't yet popular. No one thinks that the soccer players are valiant. Jasmine doesn't understand the game at all and thinks the players look like overgrown squirrels fighting for a nut.

Despite the friendship of their children, Deirdre Thompson and Violet de Flaubert hate each other. They act, of course, as though they are very good friends.

2.

Violet is already crying as she eases out of her rotten station wagon and feels the heat of the fire. She knows what a burning church means. She was a child in the America of the sixties. She doesn't understand how this hate has followed her. How her father's Klannishness has found her on this island of black people. She wonders if somehow her father has burned down the church. Somehow he has hunted her down, and this is her punishment for marrying a nigger and having half-nigger children. Beautiful amber-colored children—the kind she had hoped for to save her father's sins. Daughters her father would have adored if they had just been lighter skinned and straighter haired. But then Violet remembers her father is dead.

Violet thinks of all her daughters as strong. She calls them "tough as nails." Her girls' shyness or bookishness or violinness is their armor to face the world. A girl's kind of trick armor. She doesn't know her daughters very well—there are just so many of them. She doesn't know that their armor is insufficient when battling the world.

Only four months ago Deirdre's son, Thomas, and Violet's daughter Jasmine went away to college in America. To the same city, but not to the same college. Violet didn't think much of this. She thought maybe the two would meet up for coffee every once in a while.

Deirdre hoped that shy Jasmine, with her slutty name, would disappear into the sewers of the city and from her son's mind. She hoped the girl would end up on drugs or pregnant, and that her son would end up married to an Ivy League coed with professional ambitions and cooking skills. That would show Violet—but then Deirdre would whisk away these devilish thoughts with a little prayer. She does not wish to be so evil. She was only thinking of her son. Deirdre knows Thomas wants to be president someday, but she believes that sons are fragile and in need of their mothers.

What happened with Thomas and Jasmine is common but not simple. They did meet for coffee in a chain café with a French name.

"It's cute in here, Thomas. I like it. I'll be coming back for sticky buns."

Thomas frowned thinking of Jasmine here without him. This was a public place. There were many people around. He thought that this should be their place now.

"Thomas. Stop making that face and get me some sugar, no. Brown, please."

He got up. He loved that she could barely speak to anyone for her shyness, yet she could order him to get her some sugar. She could demand brown sugar.

While he was gone Jasmine watched the other people, who all seemed pleased with their organic orange juice or chai lattes—things she had never known before. She could hear their private conversations clearly. They spoke carelessly, as though it didn't matter who was listening. Beneath Jasmine's new fall jacket was a silk blouse that Moby had once told her looked nice. She shifted now so she could feel it slide across her shoulders.

Thomas rested half a dozen little brown packets beside her cup. "So," he said. "How's chemistry?"

"I'm not taking chemistry."

"It's a joke. You know, like chem is so hard, so that's all that anyone really cares about." Perhaps this was only a joke on his campus or perhaps just in his dorm among his new friends. "So what are you taking?"

Jasmine chewed a sticky bun and sipped on her coffee. She began her list and leaned across the table so the others wouldn't hear. "Intro to Women's Studies. Intro to Psychology. Race and the Essay. The History of Math."

"Aren't you taking English comp or, like, Biology 101 or the regular stuff?"

"Yes, stupidee. Race and the Essay—that's a composition class. The psychology is for my science credit."

He thought to make a joke about women's studies but then thought against it. "Race and the Essay. What you learning there?"

She sucked her teeth with annoyance. "I don't know. We only been in class for a month or something." She sipped her milky coffee. It was the color of her skin. "Theory and history, mostly. You know . . . how ethnicity marginalizes the experience with the world and is reflected on the text . . . and all that. The stuff we didn't learn at St. Mark's."

Thomas sat up straight now and stirred his Earl Grey. He wanted to ask what "the text" was but he suddenly felt defensive. "St. Mark's was good to us, Jasmine. I mean, I feel it really prepared me for college. Like, I know all about Plato's cave and, like, no one else in my comp class does. I mean that's education . . ." But he realized that she wasn't paying any attention. He tried again. "Tell me about your roommate. You get along?"

He watched her face as she talked about her roommate, who had a new college boyfriend already. It seemed Jasmine didn't care for her roommate because the girl had pushed herself onto the dorm committee. Jasmine said this might be a sign that the girl was arrogant. Thomas had to force himself not to watch Jasmine's mouth. He thought to look into her eyes but that often made his own eyes well with tears. So he watched her forehead and her cheeks and she looked out into the street and then back into her cup of coffee.

Though Violet and Thomas are both a combination of white American and black Caribbean, they are different in color. He is a kind of yellow color. Almost like gold. Her color is muted and therefore more mysterious. This is not something that Jasmine thinks. It is what Thomas thought that day in the café as she talked and talked.

From her dorm room phone Jasmine called her mother. "I met with Thomas Thompson today."

"Well, that's nice," Violet said. "How are you doing making new friends?"

"Fine. I mean I haven't made any. My roommate is frigging annoying."

"And a boyfriend?"

"Yeah, she already has a boyfriend. Not even a month of school yet. Can you believe it, Mom?"

"I mean you, baby. Is there a nice smart boy in your science class maybe? Remember, you want a smart man. One with a bright future."

"Oh, Mom. You know you're harassing me. My roommate is so . . ."

"She's just having fun. Fun is okay."

"Okay, Mom. Okay."

Jasmine hung up without speaking to her father, but she was left wondering about him. She wondered about her mother's insistence that she search her science class for a boyfriend. She wondered about her father's inadequacies. She felt bad for him and mad at her mother.

But Jasmine also felt that her mother had made a mistake in her choice of a husband. It was not a mistake Jasmine would repeat.

3.

"My father killed himself just like this." Violet says this in a screechy voice though she has only meant to think it. It is not something she has said to anyone and now she has said it to the fire and to the figure ahead. She is almost hysterical with tears. There really is a church, her church, burning right in front of her. Right here on this island that was supposed to be brown skin paradise. The suicide is a secret Violet has kept from her husband and her daughters. Her parents are dead. Her children are told honorable stories. They do not seem to mind that they don't know their white cousins, and Violet has been grateful for that indifference.

She sees with disgust that it is Deirdre Thompson there ahead, standing before the church as though just watching is serious work. As though the burning was her own doing. Deirdre who is chubby and unhappy and dangerously insecure. Violet focuses on the back of Deirdre's head, with its short, sharp hair. She cannot help but finger her own rolling curls thankfully, and then feel ashamed for her blessed endowment. Violet cannot remember ever touching Deirdre, even in the peace during church services. But now she thinks that the goodly thing would be to move toward Deirdre, closer to the flames, so they can work this fire out as a team.

Violet hugs the ring pillow to her chest protectively, the bands sewn gently on. She gives her voice as an offering. "My mother died in the fire, too. They never said suicide, but it was." And though she is crying, the words are very clear.

But Deirdre does not move at all, and for a second Violet thinks she should step forward and hug the thick woman. Then it comes to her like a pinch that Deirdre is the arsonist. That self-righteous cow would love to see Violet's daughter sullied. She clenches her jaw and takes a breath. Deirdre can burn for all she cares. Instead she asks, employing her slight island accent for strength, "Can you at least fucking tell me if our babies are inside?"

Deirdre feels her shoulders and neck tighten. What is Violet de Flaubert carrying on about? Her dumb racist roots? And she has the nerve to ask the question that Deirdre herself should have asked. Deirdre hadn't thought about anyone being trapped inside. She hadn't thought about anybody but her son at home waiting, and now Violet is about to do the saving work. But then again, perhaps Violet has just gone mad. Deirdre wonders if this insanity is connected to the fire and why. But Deirdre knows why Violet would want to bring down the church. It is easy to know why. She has always been jealous of my family, Deirdre thinks.

Between Deirdre and Violet there is more than a fire. There is something more destructive. It is something like history and the future converted into flesh. They have children between them. And now they have their similar histories and their common futures like a leash from one to another.

Jasmine's face went hot under her skin when her roommate explained to her that if she ever arrived at their door and saw a hair scrunchy on the doorknob she should go to the lounge and watch TV for an hour.

But the first time Jasmine saw the pink scrunchy, she sat in front of the door and waited for the animal noises to calm. Then she opened the door with her key and got in her bed—shoes and all. She could hear them in the dark talking about her. Whispering about what to do now, until finally the boy slid out of the door like a thief in the night.

The second time the pink scrunchy was ringed around the doorknob Jasmine sat in front of the door and cried. She sniffled loudly until another girl walked by in a towel and asked if she was okay. Jasmine nodded and buried her head. But the girl wouldn't go. She sat next to Jasmine and put her arm around her. Then she offered to make her some tea. She had a forbidden electric teapot in her room. The two of them sipped green tea until past midnight and the other girl's roommate came home.

The third time Jasmine came home to the scrunchy, she thought about barging in and demanding that the boy get out. She thought about calling her roommate a slut. But then Jasmine thought on her own sister. The youngest, who was just fourteen, and the only one of the sisters who had gone all the way with a boy. Instead of barging in the room again, Jasmine went to the girl with the teapot. But that girl's roommate was in, and Jasmine was too uncomfortable to stay there with them both and drink tea. She asked to use their phone. "You have a great accent," the other roommate said. "Are you from Jamaica?" Jasmine nodded her head to avoid conversation. She was calling Thomas.

The subway station was emptier than usual. The café where she was meeting Thomas was only three stops away but the ride took a long time. Jasmine was a little afraid as she sat on the train and the few people got on and off. She didn't risk even glancing at her books. She held them to her chest and thought about the best ways to use them as a weapon. The train rumbled like a can and creaked to a stop. Her sneakers rubbed and squeaked on the ground of the dark station. She pushed her way through the turnstile and began to run. There was no one around until she burst out of the stairway and into the street. But there was the café and there was Thomas standing at its entrance. He took her books and held the door open for her.

At their table he laid the brown sugar packets on her saucer without her having to ask.

"Are you okay?"

"Fine."

"So, what's up? I mean, I'm glad you called and all. We haven't talked for a good while and you didn't return my calls, but I was just wondering . . ." He was doing it again. Rambling on and complaining.

"What are you?" Jasmine asked.

"What?"

"You know. White or black? What do you feel more?" It was question from her Race and the Essay class. It was a question about passing. About being something you were not or becoming something you were not meant to be. But it was also a question that she and Thomas had been thinking about all their lives.

"It's different." Thomas didn't want to say the wrong thing but he wanted to be honest. He always wanted to be honest with Jasmine.

"How so?"

"At home, I feel mixed. Everyone knows my mother and father. They all know what I am." She nodded her understanding. But he continued. "Here I feel more white, I guess. I mean, I think some people might think I'm all white even. I guess I'm white in America."

This was the wrong answer. "You should take the class I'm taking. You'll think more about the responsibility you have to be true to yourself."

He slapped his spoon clumsily around in his cup. "Well, what do you feel?"

"I feel mixed here." She stared into her tawny coffee. "Everyone asks me what I am and where I'm from. They assume I'm from Jamaica whenever I say anything. Don't you hate that?"

"People say they can't hear my accent at all. I have to pull out my driver's license to prove I'm not from right here." This wasn't right either, so he stopped. "What do you feel like at home? Since you're mixed up here. Do you feel black at home?"

"I just feel like myself at home. I just feel like Jasmine." But as she said it she knew this wasn't all true. Jasmine. What kind of name was that? Her sisters were Rose, Lily, Iris, and the youngest, fast one was Daisy. Rose and Lily seemed dignified, Iris seemed sharp and tidy, and Daisy was, well, lighthearted. But Jasmine—what a name. A little, ugly flower that gave off a strong, whorish smell.

Thomas held Jasmine's hand as they walked back to his dorm. He didn't let go even when he had to pull out his school ID to unlock the main entrance and then his keys to open his door. His was a suite with a common room and kitchen. The common room stunk of sweat and corn. Thomas only noticed it now that Jasmine was with him. The TV in this room belonged to one of the suitemates. Its light flashed onto the face of another suitemate, asleep on the university-issued couch. Thomas opened his door and hesitated before turning on the light. They had to wade through his T-shirts and jeans that lay on the floor. His bed was made, thank God. A habit his mother had instilled in him.

He poured Jasmine a Coke that had gone flat and offered her his cleanest T-shirt and a pair of boxers. They had undressed in front of each other only once, but that was in her parents' station wagon at the beach and it had been a claustrophobic, platonic thing. Now he left the room.

In the room alone, Jasmine still felt as though she were being watched. She wanted to take a shower, actually, but she imagined the bathroom might not be very clean. She thought about removing her underwear. She took the panties off but then didn't know where to put them. She hadn't come with a purse. Only her books and her keys that she'd stuffed into her pockets. She put the underwear back on and felt a little dirty, but also less so in another way.

4.

Because Deirdre hasn't moved or even acknowledged her presence, Violet begins to skitter around the church and call out, "Anyone inside? Anyone? Inside!" She knows this is ludicrous. If there was anyone they would be screaming or dead already. Violet cannot even get close. The heat is so heavy now that it seems to burn her. She waves the white pillow in the air slowly like a flag.

The church is a small two-story, surrounded on the sides by a wide clearing of gravel for cars to park. Beyond the clearing, endless trees. Behind the church, the edge of the mountain. In front, the small road that leads to the main road. At the main road is the sign *Christ's Mission Evangelical* with an arrow pointing up the road less traveled. At the end of the road is the church. A simple structure. The bottom floor for worshipping and the second floor, with its outside staircase, for the offices and children's classes. But now as Violet steps closer, the church makes a screeching noise and seems to implode, as the upstairs crashes down into the first floor. Violet runs back to where Deirdre stands sweating.

The women still do not trust each other. Now they never will.

Because Thomas had his own room he didn't have to signal Jasmine's presence with a scrunchy or a tie. His naked doorknob made her think of their sleeping in the same bed as an innocent act. They lay down in the extra-long twin bed and faced each other. She smiled to show him she was grateful, but he only looked at her, trying not to blink, until his eyes teared up. He touched her face. He kissed her forehead. And though that could have been just a brotherly gesture, they were, after all, in a bed together. And though they were clothed, though they had known each other for so long, they weren't really siblings after all. And so they kissed, and Thomas, who had kissed a few girls, tried very hard to be sweet and gentle. Tried very hard to not be forceful, but his whole body was in it. To him it was the beginning.

To Jasmine the kiss was kind of nasty, but thrilling. It was her first real kiss. The first with tongue. She let him explore her mouth and press against her body. It was a curious thing to her and she imagined it would stop and then they would go to sleep and then never talk about it. But then he whimpered, "Oh shit," and popped out of bed as though burned. She saw that something milky was seeping through the crotch of his boxers and had smeared on her thighs where they had been rubbing. "Oh shit," he said again and seemed as though he would cry. She looked at him, fascinated and disgusted, as he bit his lip and pressed into a corner of the room.

"I made you do that," she said without thinking. "I mean, I made you do that without us even doing it for real." Thomas didn't nod or address her observation in any way. He grabbed a towel. He turned his back to her when he took his shorts off.

"I'm sorry," he said, when they were back in the bed, new boxers on them both. "That's not how I wanted it to be."

It wasn't anything, Jasmine wanted to tell him, but couldn't. For a long time she didn't sleep, but finally her dreams were filled with images of her own feet climbing over walls of water.

Early in the morning, she edged out of the bed. She took her clothes into the common room and dressed there with the sleeping roommate and the blinking TV as an audience. She left and took the train. She felt bold and brave, and other things she had never felt before.

She rode the subway back to her dorm room and packed her backpack with things to read, things to eat, and clean underwear. She e-mailed her teachers to say that she had to go on a trip and would miss class and to please let her know what the homework was. She got on a train and then transferred to a bigger, sleeker train where the seats were soft and personal. She finished a luscious collection of short stories during the three hours the train took to get to the next city. When she arrived she caught a yellow cab. Only then, with the cab slamming through the city streets, did she marvel at herself again. She thought of her fast roommate and her loose sister and then of her own sluttish power over Thomas. "The new me," she said to the audacious skyscrapers around her.

But when she arrived and knocked on the dorm room door, she thought that this was all very crazy. It had taken her almost half the day to get here, but only now did she really consider what she was attempting. She started to run back down the hallway, her one small bag like a hump on her back, but by then Moby had opened the door and called to her, "Jasmine? Jasmine de Flaubert, is that you?" And she had stopped running and turned to him. "Yes, Moby. It's me—Jasmine."

5.

Church ashes are not like any other. When this fire has cooled perhaps Deirdre will return and find a golden chalice that had refused to melt. Or the ruby from the preacher's wife's favorite ring. Deirdre will return and take the ashes in her palm. She might wonder if the New or Old Testament is sifting through her fingers. Perhaps it will be the Christmas story, there on her fingernail. Perhaps it will be Revelation settling on her shoe.

But now, facing the fire, Deirdre has thought of what to do. Finally, now that the church is doomed and her pew pins a certified waste of money, she pulls out her cell phone and calls the police, who connect her to the fire station. They have no idea where on island she is and now the church is shuddering with the growl of an earthquake. It is making such a racket that Deirdre has to walk farther away to give directions to the fire station operator. And now Deirdre notices the trees and wonders if they will catch and she says slowly into the phone that the church is close to Crossroads and to take the road to

Fortuna. But they must look for the church sign. They must look . . . and as Deirdre says it she looks at Violet de Flaubert, who is crying in front of the fire as though she is about to become a sacrifice. Deirdre wonders whether perhaps Violet has pulled down the sign the fire trucks will need in order to find them.

Deirdre leaves the operator on the phone to back away from Violet and run to her car. Violet might be a madwoman, but she's smart. Deirdre knows her. She knows that Violet keeps liquor in her fridge and jokes that Jesus drank wine. She knows that Violet lets her youngest daughter wear short skirts and calls it "finding oneself." She watches as Violet's face grows panicked but smaller as Deirdre reverses her car all the way down the long path to the main road.

Now Violet is there alone. Alone with the maniacal fire. She must pull herself together. Where is her armor? Her mind moves frantically to thoughts of her eldest daughter. She looks down at the sooty lace of the pillow in her hand. It is made of the same material as the dress. And then she is running, the gold rings loosening, loosening. Violet runs a wide arc behind the disappearing church. She runs to look for Jasmine.

When Thomas called home to his mother, he said that he had news. Difficult, but wonderful news. Deirdre knew, from the tension in his voice, that the news might be those things for him but a tragedy for her.

"Jasmine and I are getting married."

As Deirdre's hand stiffened around the phone, she noted that her son did not say, "I want to marry . . ." or even "I have asked to marry . . ." He said it as though it would happen any minute and without his mother's say. Deirdre's hearing became very sharp as she listened to her son breathe. Finally he said, "It will be okay, Mama. We'll live in her school's married dorms. Neither of us will have to quit college or anything. I mean, Jasmine might have to take a semester off, but . . ." and then Deirdre began to scream. She poured her muted Christian obscenities into the cavity of the receiver.

Thomas knew his mother. He knew she would get over this because she was tough. He rested the phone down quietly. He wasn't scared at all about getting married to Jasmine. This was what he had always wanted, and now it had been granted. He couldn't disparage it because it happened differently than he had hoped. It had happened. Now he would fast-track their future together.

Jasmine called her mother. She held her breath and listened to Violet say, "Hello. Hello? I'm sorry, I can't hear you. Try again." After a few minutes Jasmine called back and heard the same sweet voice say the same thing. It took the fourth call in a row for her mother to pronounce calmly into the silence, "Look here, you cow, stop calling my fucking house." And finally Jasmine announced into the phone, "Mommy, I'm pregnant."

The wedding was hastily planned for Christmas break. They were only freshmen in college. He was eighteen and she was still seventeen. The church folk would whisper, but Jasmine wouldn't be three months gone when Thomas made her honest.

With money his father sent him, Thomas bought Jasmine a diamond ring. He told his roommates that he was moving out to be a father and a husband. He told his academic adviser he was getting married and so would have to speed up his coursework.

Jasmine only wore the ring when Thomas reminded her it was supposed to stay on her hand. She didn't tell her roommate anything. She did not tell Moby anything. She only thought on the way Moby had said her name, Jasmine, again and again in the dusky light, as though it was something holy. The musk of their bodies had made her feel safe when she lay there with him afterward, but now she could not seem to wash it off. She feared people could smell it on her. That time with Moby was not something to tell a sister or a friend. It was not something to write in a diary. It was something to keep to herself, simply to know she was capable of it.

Thomas bought their tickets home on the same flight. They held hands in the airport as they window-shopped and as they sampled the camouflage of Lancôme and Chanel on her wrists. Jasmine thought, yes, I can do this. I can be this woman. I can love Thomas like a woman would. They still hadn't had sex. But now he kissed her in a way that was all gentle—like he was calm now. And he whispered a little joke as the plane took off: "I can't believe you're so fertile. When we do it for real we'll have to use the rhythm method so you won't get pregnant again too quickly." She gripped his hand and tried to smile as the plane lifted. She wondered if he really believed himself.

At home on the island Jasmine's younger sisters were either embarrassed that their sister was pregnant or eager to ask her questions about sex. The violinist sister didn't seem to care either way. She practiced and filled the house with her music—the same desperate song again and again. It was the song she would play for the wedding.

Jasmine sat on the bed that was still hers in the room she shared with Daisy. She clenched her stomach to see if she could feel something that was more than herself. I'm not ready, she said in her head and hoped the baby could hear. I want you, but not now. Not in seven months either. Come back another time. I'll be good to you then. She lay back and pressed her fingertips into her stomach. Then she made two fists. But Daisy, the youngest, walked in. She sat on the bed at Jasmine's feet.

"So, why didn't you and Thomas use protection?" The violin screeched from the next room, but then resumed its melody.

"I didn't have sex with Thomas."

"Oh." Daisy had been the first sister to do it and so knew a lot despite her age. "Well, then you're the Virgin Mary. And when she got pregnant she got married."

Jasmine touched her stomach with the flat of her hand. "I haven't talked to the other guy since. I just wanted to do it. It was just a one-time thing. Just one brave thing that I did. And now it's done. Okay?"

Daisy took Jasmine by the arm. She dragged her to face the bottom drawer of the bureau that they had always shared. Below the holey socks was a string of little square packets. Daisy pressed two condoms into Jasmine's hand. "For the next time you contemplate bravery."

The Thompson and de Flaubert houses became places of bustling activity. The wedding colors were purple at first, because that was Violet's name and she was the mother of the bride, but Thomas's mother insisted purple was a funeral color. So Deirdre picked out the pew dressings and the tablecloths and even the official color—a yellow that was almost gold. Deirdre's husband tried to offer that the color might be gaudy, but she wouldn't have it. "My son is a prince," Deirdre spat, as if they hadn't made Thomas together.

Anyone would have thought that Deirdre was the mother of the bride, what with the fuss she was making. The floor of her living room was strewn with invitation samples and yards of tulle. In the kitchen, stray Jordan almonds rolled around like tiny rotten Easter eggs.

Thomas stepped over things and tried to be patient when his mother asked his opinion. "We don't need all this, Mama. The only reason we didn't elope was that Jasmine wanted her mother to be there for the wedding." Sometimes Deirdre would look at her son as though he were a stranger and then go back to her catering menu. Sometimes she would look at him and then pull him close, as though he were just born. Either way, he would leave her shaking his head and marveling at his mother's passionate strength. Then he would call up his beloved to check on her, but often Jasmine was sleeping or out or sick. They had not seen each other since they'd arrived on island and their mothers had taken over.

Violet sat before her sewing machine like a convert and in two days she'd made the bridesmaid dresses all in purple, despite Deirdre's choice of gold. There wasn't time to sew a wedding dress at all, so one afternoon Violet and Jasmine went to a boutique. There among the pretty things, Jasmine grew excited despite herself. The dresses were so lovely, she felt like a princess. Maybe she could get married after all. Maybe it wouldn't be so bad. She thought that maybe she would talk to Thomas. Maybe he would say something romantic and her chest would swell with love, instead of the doughy feeling that filled her throat now when she thought of having to consummate their marriage.

The dress they chose was too expensive, but they bought it anyway and put it on Mr. de Flaubert's credit card. With a corset Jasmine's stomach became totally flat and no one would ever have to know. The gown ballooned into the backseat of the car when they drove it home. The skirt of the dress was wide and fluffy, like a ballerina's tutu.

6.

And so it is easy for Violet to find Jasmine behind the church, the smoke curling around her like a lover, standing at the cliff, her tutu of a dress flapping about her as she rips it off and releases the corset and finally her belly. By the time Violet grabs her from the edge, the girl is only in her underthings. The wire of the can-can like a guarding loop around her.

Violet holds her daughter until she herself stops crying and the smoke begins to burn her own eyes. She guides her daughter, can-can and all, to the car. They leave the virginal white dress and the useless pillow in pieces behind them. As they are leaving, the fire trucks come screaming. The road is so narrow that Violet has to reverse her vehicle back to the smoldering church—and since they are there, they now have to stay so Violet can answer questions and lie that she has no idea how the church fire began. No idea at all. And she doesn't even pass an incriminating look at her half-naked daughter sitting like a stone in the passenger seat of the car.

The firefighters don't address the almost-bride because they think her devastation is too precious to disturb. But really Jasmine is sitting there feeling the thing in her womb churn like a fist of fire. "Another time," she commands it. And finally the blood burns out of her.

When Deirdre walks into her living room she sees her son and his father ready in their tuxedos. They look at her with their eagerness and excitement, but Deirdre's face gives something away because Thomas stands as though ready to fight the thing that has hurt his mother. "Sit," she says. It comes out dry and smoky. The boy sits slowly. Deirdre looks from the father to the son and sees, only now, that the two look unmistakably alike. All she has contributed, it seems, is a slight lightness in color, a slight thinness of the lips, a slight narrowing in the nostrils.

She gestures for them to make room on the couch. "I have something to say." She takes their hands into her lap. But then all she can say as she looks from one to the other is, "Marriage isn't everything."

The future leader of corporations and civic clubs and maybe even the free world stares at his mother as though she is mad, because there she is crying, and he has never seen his mother cry. "What are you saying, Mama? Pop, what is she saying?" Thomas clutches at his groom's boutonniere until he feels it come loose.

This family has never thrown a Frisbee around together at the beach. They have never sat in a circle and told each other stories. They have never even prayed together except at church. They have never before talked to each other about the divine risks of love.

CANOE SICKNESS

for Kodjo

We had moved to the mother country from Ghana when I was six. I'd learned English. I dated white girls. And Chinese girls. And one memorable Italian in fourth form. I played football on the junior national team, even though I still didn't have a British passport. I'd done everything my friends back in Accra talked about over stolen swigs of aktpeteshie. I was going to be a hero. I would play football, representing Ghana in the elite British clubs. Those of us on the junior national team hoped for the World Cup. The chaps looked forward to playing for their nations: England or Ireland. Only a few of us looked forward to playing for places like Cameroon or Jamaica. But we were all mates. Joined by the sport we loved. Singing songs about Margaret Thatcher's private parts on the bus to games.

Every morning in my parents' flat in Brixton, I'd wake up before anyone else. Before I brushed my teeth or sipped hot milk, I'd go running in the crisp morning air. Our coach didn't tell me to do this. I just did it. Sometimes I ran when I didn't want to. Even when I was sick or tired from studying. I ran. Discipline—I chanted to myself as I passed the kiosks only now beginning to fry johnnycakes for the morning breakfast buyers. Though the smell of dough frying would follow me around town, I was never distracted. We on the junior team were being trained for greatness, but I had a special mission for myself.

My mother didn't know I ran. Even my nosy know-everything sister didn't know. My father knew, but not because I told him. Sometimes when I was running out, he was just coming in. We acknowledged each other and he went toward his bedroom, I went toward the front door. He knew discipline. Going to graduate school, working full time. Often, he wasn't home for dinner. Sometimes when I came back from running, the sweat cold on my neck, he'd be in the living room on the couch. His body deep into the creases, the couch sinking into the floorboards. His shoulders and head leaning into a textbook.

I ran even in the winter. The cold shooting like nails into my nostrils, cracking at the skin of my face. I'd have to rub Vaseline around the corners of my mouth and nose. I ran in the summer and hated it most of all. I had to suck hard on the air. I was sweating before I'd even gone a hundred yards. And still, the air would claw at my insides, burning the place where my throat and chest met. My father always said I should love the summers, being from West Africa. I have always hated summer. I ran because I had to be good. I needed to come to the kitchen table and sit with my parents and sister and know I was the firstborn, the only male child, done good. I wanted my father's eye of approval. The slap on the chest from my mother's two hands. Her lovely face, laughing when my team won. My sister asking me for help in maths, calling me Elder Brother, despite her having cursed me for chatting up her pretty friends earlier in the day. Even in Brixton we were always an African family. There was no reason I should contract Canoe Sickness. There was no reason I should find myself emulating a people I had never known. In St. Vincent the Caribs, like Africans, were taken over by the Catholics and other colonizers. Unlike Africans, the Caribs are almost gone.

A Carib often sits in his canoe waiting in quiet, being as still as possible. This is the way they hunt shark. Sometimes the stillness takes over and the man, the husband, the father, the breadwinner realizes that he cannot move. His spear across his lap is sterile despite the poison at its tip. His quiet becomes him and he cannot shout or even whisper. The only way he can fight through this paralysis is by leaning his mind into the sea breeze or breathing into the shadows as they move across the canoe.

Recovering movement takes a long time. Often the sharks have circled and gone. Sometimes the hunters will die of starvation, their entire families starving behind them.

It happened to me. Not in the West Indies, but in London. In my parents' closet in Brixton, to be precise. For those who suffer from Canoe Sickness, precision is the only way to be saved.

I did do one thing that may have caused the tide to turn against me—made me more susceptible to illness or ill will. I dated Sally Brune. My mother had warned that if I dated a British girl, I might eventually marry one. A British woman wouldn't know how to comb our young daughter's hair. My mum would raise her eyes subtly to point out the half-British/half–West Indian girls in the supermarket with knots in their heads. My father said my half-British sons might not respect me. It was hard enough to get sons to look up to their fathers, he said. How much harder if the son had the colonizer's blood in him? I had dated other British girls before, but Sally Brune was different. A little plump. Blond hair. Brown eyes. A little short with smooth legs that she shaved every day. She was smashing, really. Sally was different because she and I weren't just talking, I wasn't just chatting to her. Sally was my girl. I'd asked her after a game—that's always when I felt most bold. And she'd said yes. Just like that. She started coming to my football practices. Imagine. Hot babe Sally Brune with her little tagalong friends yapping over her head, while she stared out at me.

She wasn't shy. She was bold, like I like my girls. Sometimes she'd ask why I didn't run after the ball. Why I let other guys get the goals. I explained to her that I was a defender, not a striker. And she said she figured I was too sweet, too nice and giving. I wanted to tell her I loved her then, but I didn't. I never did.

My father was rarely at my practices or at my games. But I still respected him. He was a big man. Not so handsome, but he had an air. He was a lecturer by habit and I knew that when he got his PhD he'd be one of those long-winded profs who ramble on and lose people, cracking jokes that the students don't get. He worked so hard for that PhD. He never got it, though. His visa ran out and they wouldn't renew it. And we all had to go back to Ghana. But he worked hard. All night out. Mum would leave his dinner in the pot and send us to our studies. She was strong. She raised us, really. It wasn't until I was already a grown man that I realized she was young as well. That she should have been pursuing dreams, breaking hearts, discovering the world. Not raising us.

Then one evening my father did a weird thing. He came home early. Dinner hadn't been served. The tomato stew on the stove wasn't even the dark red my mother said it needed to be before she could add the canned tuna. My sister was putting her hair into curlers. I was trying to study my European history but I kept thinking of feeling up Sally's tits. Sally wasn't a slag, she wasn't letting me go all the way. Which was good for me, 'cause coach warned that shagging before a match could be bad news and I know for sure that some midfielder's screwing had cost us a game before. So I'm there with Sally's knockers and Churchill, and my dad comes bursting in.

We're all surprised. He does a spin. He calls to my mother "Woman, fix my dinner!" in an exaggerated way that makes her kiss her teeth and giggle a little. He calls to us "Offspring!" and he waves his lecturing hand into the air. "Today your paapa is a star!"

There should have been a sound track, someone should have banged a gong. Instead, there was silence. I'd never seen him so emotional. "I finally made it to a film. Children, go to the theatre and watch me. I'll be there. Representing Africa!" My mother placed a slice of bread and a square of cheese on the table. She smiled boldly and told him to sit. He winked at me as he bit into the sandwich.

I was the eldest so I asked. I didn't ask well. I didn't know how to ask. "Paapa. Why were you in a movie?"

"It's my job, son. It's what I do to bring money home." He chewed for a while and we all waited. "I'm an extra. I'm not really a star." He nodded and chewed. "Perhaps one day I can take the family to a film. Yes?" He looked over at my mother. But her tomato stew had turned dark red. She was dumping in the tuna.

It was a long time before he came home early again.

After he went to bed that night, one of the few times he went to bed before the rest of us, my mother told us that Paapa was working hard. It wasn't easy finding a job when he wasn't legally allowed to work. He was in the country on a student visa. All he was supposed to do was study. My sister lowered her eyes. "Can you imagine Paapa out there in the middle of the night, waiting in line in the cold just to get some small part in a foolish movie?" I couldn't imagine. My sister shook her curlered hair and it made a clattering sound. I felt ashamed of my father, not pity or pride. I looked at my mother to see what she felt. She looked at me and nodded.

My mother was beautiful. I knew that even though I was her son. Not beautiful the way other sons think of their mothers, but beautiful the way a man thinks of a woman. Which is why when Sally told me what she told me, it made my head go loopy for a while.

Our team had just won a friendly and I was feeling strong. I was in my old Puma trainers but my new football boots were slung over my shoulder. I thought maybe today she would invite me to her house to meet her parents, and today I would say yes.

"Your pop said he was in a movie?"

"Yeah. My old man is a joker."

"Have you ever seen him in a movie?"

"He's just mamaguying, I think. Giving an excuse for never coming home. He's studying all the time."

"So your pops is never home?"

"Nah, babes. But Mums is, so no private place there. Don't be getting no ideas."

"So your pop doesn't even sleep at home?"

"He sleeps all right. But sometimes on campus, you know. He's a student. Gonna be a doctor of philosophy."

"Doesn't your mum get lonely? For a man, I mean?"

"Nah."

"It never crossed your mind that your pop got himself a little tart on the side?"

"What you getting at?"

"My pop's got a whole other family. How you know yours en't?"

Imagine what that did to me. My best girl revealing what should have been in front of my face. I left her and my soccer boots there and walked away. I ran away. I didn't hear Sally scream after me. She knew what she'd said. She was a smart girl. More mature than the other silly biddies. She made me run. Running, you should know, is a kind of stillness. I ran away from Sally and I didn't feel like I was moving. The music shops blasting out a bass-warped zook and highlife, the restaurants painted in red or yellow, the loud ladies haggling for imported mangoes and yams; they were all being swept away by some mighty force. I was standing still and that mighty force was me.

I ran through the park where some of the blokes smoked weed after school. I ran past the rosebushes where I'd once kicked a girl when she called me a black coon. I ran toward my house. My thighs were quivering with a weakness I had never known before. It hurt. I thought about how foolish I would look to Sally the next day. I thought about my dad out all hours. Not working a real full-time job. Studying more than I did. I'd never seen him touch my mother affectionately. I imagined him now, touching some cow of a woman. I pushed through the pain.

At the door I stopped to sit on the steps. I leaned over. I thought about throwing up. I thought about it hard because I wanted to do something like that. I wanted to heave and grunt and be sick. It didn't come. Instead I went in and sank into bed. When my mother called for dinner I pretended to be sleeping. My father didn't come home until it was almost morning. Until it was the time when I would normally run.

That morning I did something I had never done. I did something little children do, the kind of thing that scars them for life. I went into my parents' room when I began to hear my father snore. It was morning. My mother was still sleeping. My sister wasn't even up burning her hair with the curling iron for school. I hid in the closet. I sat down among my mother's shoes and wondered if I was ruining them as they crumpled quietly. I leaned into my father's trousers, knowing I was wrinkling them. Knowing I was taking out the creases. I made myself still and quiet. I did not sleep. The smell of starch and leather was heavy. I stared out at their sleeping bodies, wrapped up in their light blanket. I realized for the first time that they'd given me the heaviest comforter we owned. I wondered if my sister's was heavy enough for her. Perhaps I wanted to cry with the weight of my parents' marriage on my shoulders. The weight of my manself lying there in my father's skin. My mother was on her side, facing me in the closet. Even in her sleep she was beautiful and strong.

Their room was not a place in our flat I was familiar with. It was the same size as mine and my sister's, with one big bed instead of our two. My mother hadn't made the peach-colored curtains. She'd bought them on the street a long time ago when we were shopping together for provisions. I had to hold my sister's little hand as Mama and the bejeweled woman went back and forth over prices. Mum had said it reminded her of home. She'd said sometimes memory was better than food. That was back when we'd first come. I could see now that the curtains were almost white with fading.

My knees were drawn up to my chest. I held them in place with my hands. A little of the dawn came through the slants in the closet door. It made lines of light on my arms. I was there because I wanted to see if he touched her. They never kissed or held hands in front of us. I thought this was just their African modesty. If he loved her, he would touch her in private. Kiss her when they woke up. If they began to even look like they might have sex I'd burst through the closet. I'd be embarrassed, maybe I'd never get the image out of my head, but I'd know my father wasn't giving it to another woman. Wasn't out with some British hussy.

Perhaps I did cry. But I was still. I wanted them to be natural. I wanted them to be unsuspecting. Eventually, my father shifted. It was such a sudden thing that I wasn't sure if I had seen it. Then he leaned over and kissed her temple. He didn't wait to see if she awoke. He rolled back over onto his back. Then she opened her eyes. She looked straight at me. From behind the closet door my heart moved more than a beat. I wasn't excited or scared. It was if I had already witnessed something that really would ruin me. Her hair was wild around her face. I thought I would jump. But I didn't. Of course, this was because I couldn't.

My mother didn't smile. Her eyes were open but nothing else had changed. Damn it, shouldn't she smile? What else was smiling for? Then my father's hand came around and tugged at her hair. Her hair was thick and strong and he didn't caress it like I caressed Sally's. He grabbed a piece of it in his fist and pulled her toward him as if he was simply tugging at her hand. She rolled over and settled into his shoulder. Her back was now to me. I could feel one of her buckled shoes digging into my thigh. They didn't speak. They seemed mysterious and foreign. I couldn't tell if they were okay or not. I couldn't tell what had just happened. They stayed like that for a while. I thought maybe they had gone back to sleep. But then I heard the door open to the room my sister and I shared. Then my mother rolled over and sat up. She pushed her feet into her house slippers. As she walked away from the bed my father's hand trailed along the back side of her nightgown. He held on to the edge of the silky fabric until she finally smiled and smacked at his hand as she pulled away. I could hear my lungs and my heart and even the pulsing in my leg because it had fallen asleep.

And still I couldn't move. It was as if I had become nothing. I didn't even exist there in the closet. That's why I couldn't move. I wasn't a body anymore. I couldn't feel a body. Was I dead? Was I dying? My father grunted. I wanted to hear the grunt again. Perhaps the sound would move me. My sister was yapping loudly. My mother was cooking red-red. Discipline! I said to myself. To what existed of myself. Move! Run! I knew my body. But my body wasn't supposed to do this. Perhaps I was dreaming.

I thought about movement. I contemplated it. I tried to imagine the smallest part of myself. My arm. My forearm. The hair on my forearm. If I breathed heavily maybe the hair would move. Move, hair. Move, damn it! And then one single hair shivered under my light breath. I saw it move, though I never felt it. As suddenly as I'd had that success my entire body collapsed from the fetal position I'd wrapped myself into. My head hit across my mother's heels. My feet slammed against the closet doors. I stood up quickly and pushed myself out. I saw my father watching me as I ran toward the shower.

I didn't wait up for my father again. Sally didn't bring it up again, though she did bring my boots the next day. My sister started dating a Nigerian boy and that caused my parents some agony. He wasn't from our tribe. He wasn't even from our country. Yes, he was African. But a Nigerian? She might as well have dated a Brit, or worse—a Jamaican. I was spending less time at home. So much practice. To be honest, I was taking Sally to the movie theatre on a regular basis.

Using the money Coach gave us as allowance. Somebody might say I was looking for my father in the films, but really I was looking to get under Sally's skirt. I'm not a bad guy. But, like I said, Sally was hot. I respected her, don't get me wrong. But she was my girl and that's what couples do. I could never afford popcorn but Sally would buy the sweets and soda without even making me feel less of a man. She was good like that. We'd usually watch something fruity that she wanted. Though sometimes we'd watch an action flick. We were watching *My Sunshine Boardwalk* when it happened again.

I wasn't being very cool. I had one hand around her shoulder, which was a good move. But I'd leaned over a little and I had my other hand in her knickers. I had popcorn butter on my fingers so they were sliding around her hair down there. She was staring at the movie screen as if nothing was happening. Even from my twisted groping position, I was staring at the movie screen as if nothing was happening. Then I saw my father. Right there in the same jacket he wore when coming home. His very own schoolbooks under his arm. He stopped right in the middle of the screen. He looked far away at something. How did I see him? He was in the middle of a crowd. Other people were looking up, looking at their watches, taking out their umbrellas. But there was my father. I remembered my mother not smiling for so long. Him pulling at her hair. Her nestling into his shoulder. Everything without words. Without sound. Almost as if they hadn't moved. I took my hands off Sally. Then I froze. I felt myself incapable of moving. I wasn't sure if I was breathing. It was like I was on the roof's edge and I wanted to jump. You know the feeling. But I couldn't. I imagined myself moving. I imagined my feet lifting off the cinema floor. Nothing. Something sad was happening on screen. Something devastating. I couldn't move. Sally wouldn't touch me. She wouldn't reach out to push me, make me move. My eyelids fluttered. I could blink. But I couldn't move my mouth. I couldn't whisper. "Move," I said in my head. My father had left the scene. He'd walked off the screen into the city. Did he walk toward our house? Did he walk to campus? Did he walk to stand in another line where they would ask him to look at something else in the distance and walk some more?

The main character died. The leading lady was in mourning. And I was burning with stiffness. I felt as though I had run too many miles and my muscles had grown loose and liquidy. The leading lady was waiting on a busy London pavement. All these people were rushing by her. Going places. Many of them were in dark grey suits. There weren't any saris or kente among them. These were movers and shakers. They were hunting down their destinies. I couldn't remember what the leading lady was waiting for. But she just waits there. With all the other people rushing around her. I wanted to go to her and tell her, "Lady, get out of the street." Tell her that she should move on. Her lips are quivering, she's looking like she could melt under all the rain, because she's got no umbrella. And then he walks behind her and pauses. Just like that, as if he doesn't know that this is the same bloody movie. My father looks at her as if he would tell her, "It's okay. This waiting isn't okay but you, you are okay." And then he walks off the screen. The leading lady is crying now. Her crying is like a child's. It has a rhythm. I begin to lean into the rhythm. The movie ends with the woman still waiting and crying.

Then the credits came rolling up and I felt myself leaning. I felt myself about to lose balance. About to hit the floor. About to feel an impact that would shake me loose of the stiffness. Then Sally smacked my leg and I stood straight up as if she'd slapped my face. I guided her out of the theatre as if nothing had happened.

I couldn't get the last image out of my head because it seemed as if my father had looked at a stranger and understood. Or perhaps because it was as if my father was there in the movie theatre right when I was feeling up my girl. Or because my father was suddenly larger than his true self. Or just because my father was something I didn't know he was. There was nothing so grand in these things. Nothing really. But I didn't go with Sally to a movie ever again because I was afraid that all I would see would be him big up there. Him sitting down to a meal in a posh restaurant. Him driving a minicab like any poor foreigner. Him in a world he wasn't supposed to be in.

I've had the sickness since. At a game. When as I went to tackle a striker, I suddenly saw my father on the sidelines, making a fist and yelling. Suddenly his voice was all I could hear. The ball went by me.

If I hadn't been kicked to the ground I would have stayed there and stared at him. Unable to move toward him. Unable to move toward the goal. When I got up and looked around he was not there. Perhaps he was ashamed that I'd let the ball go by me. Perhaps he knew that I wouldn't want him to pity me. I'd rather pretend he was never there, then he could congratulate me afterward and skip the lecture about the importance of staying alert in this country.

Now I fear the sickness. I fear it will come on me when I'm teaching my fifth form history class to the students in the Accra Day School who dream of Britain. We will be reviewing the years between 1940 and 1960 when the colonized world clamored for independence. We will turn to civil movements and we will discuss the decay of small economies and indigenous family structures. I will pass out a *National Geographic* that features the Caribs whom my pupils insist on calling Indians. The students will gawk when they read about catching sharks with spears and bare hands. But even that will not do it. I will be telling them about the movement of African and Caribbean immigrants to the U.K. I will say a word like *Brixton* and then I will be unable to say anything else. My students will look at me quietly for a minute, maybe many minutes because they are polite. Eventually, they will move into mayhem. They will throw things and laugh and I will be at the head of the class hoping that something they throw will hit me. That their laughter will grow into a thing that can reach out and pull me down.

I fear that the sickness will take over when I am sitting down to dinner with my wife and daughters. My wife of twelve years will serve groundnut soup and gari with the spices that my mother could never get in Britain. I will remember how my mother would explain all the cooking to me, not just my sister, because she felt a man should also know how to take care of himself. I will be thinking of how I love my mother but of how my wife's cooking is better. Then, without being able to help it, I will be wondering about Sally. I will be thinking about my fingers in her flat slippy hair and I will feel bad for thinking this. I will say out loud that I am glad we do not have sons. Then I will be staring into the bowl unable to move. My daughters will go on chatting and I will be hoping the soup will steam up at me, push into my skin and move into my pores. Move me.

After my family was sent back to Ghana, I decided against becoming a professional football player. I had the sickness that I felt wouldn't really ever let me play. I had to concentrate on my studies so I could have a chance at university. A chance to still fulfill the role of the firstborn and the only male. During the A-level exams I would whisper to myself like a mantra—Discipline. Discipline. In Accra it was hard to run. People would shout at you as you went past. You were a spectacle. Instead, I would juggle the football in some dusty corner of our neighborhood park. Reciting lines of Shakespeare to the beat of the ball hitting the ground.

I got an upper-level degree in college. A lecturer had encouraged me to go on but then my sister married an African American and my parents moved to live with them in Ohio City. It wasn't so easy for her to get her brother over, so I had to get a job in Accra. I married a Ga woman my mother and father would have approved. Now I look at my daughters, their hair processed straight like my wife's, and I think that someday I will tell them the story of how I was going to represent us in the World Cup, as a star defender on the national football team.

WHERE TOURISTS DON'T GO

Mason spots the Downtown Little Catholic Chapel during his first month in Texas. "That's strange," he says out loud and tugs at Robin's hand. But Robin sees the train ahead and tugs harder in the opposite direction. Mason looks back at his discovery. The so-called chapel is connected to the buildings beside it like so much of American downtown. A CVS on one side and a bakery with a cartoon of a baker making an OK sign on the other. It's not even a stand-alone. Mason is thinking that it can't really be a Catholic chapel at all, as he and Robin board the Houston Metro without purchasing their fare. They sit toward the front and try to act natural. The conductor doesn't come aboard to check anyone's ticket.

Mason is an architect and he has always wanted to be an architect. He works for a large firm that promoted him with this transfer from New York to Houston. His new employers seem to like him—they smile at him a lot, though he hasn't been given a raise. He works hard, he does. He doesn't join the other guys for happy hour on Fridays and he only smiles and says thank you when the women ask him to join them instead. He's never been a bar kind of guy so the first rejection is easy. But Mason is good looking and Americans croon over his Jamaican accent, so passing on the women is harder. But of course there's Robin now.

Two months after the move an acquaintance is passing through the city and Mason agrees to meet him for a late lunch. Mason and the friend hadn't been close when they were in college in New York and they hadn't even known each other in Jamaica. The acquaintance, however, would have called Mason a friend because they studied together often and were in many of the same classes. They'd played some dominoes once at a house party but that was early in freshman year before Mason's father had called him long distance to ask about his grades. Though the friend is from Jamaica, he's from the countryside and not the big city of Kingston like Mason. Mason has always thought the friend was a bit naive. The guy had been the only male on the Caribbean dance squad. Mason remembers cheering him on as he bubbled on stage. Even through his whistling and whooping Mason had felt a little bad for the guy, up there making a poppy show of himself. But he'd also been a little jealous. He'd never learned to dance like that.

Now they are eating what this café calls a po-boy, but previously in New York, Mason had known it as a sub and back in Jamaica it was just a sandwich on French bread. The friend tugs gently on the coming in of a beard. Mason puts his hand to his own smooth face as if in demonstration. The friend tells him he is into clean energy consulting.

The friend leans forward over his po-boy. "I building a house back home in Portland parish. Totally solar powered. My wife with a pickney on the way."

"No joke?"

"No joke, man. It's an experiment. The house, I mean. I designed it myself."

The friend pulls out sketches and lays them like a gift across the table. "This is my newest thing, right here."

Mason looks at the sketches but he can't see it. He turns them slightly at an angle but it doesn't look right. He shifts them again but now it looks upside down. Mason nods, trying to place himself. "So, why you branching out into architecture now?"

"Well, I did engineering *and* architecture in school." The friend smoothes his sketches protectively. "You don't remember?"

"Yeah. I remember now."

"And you? I don't see no ring." The friend holds up his left hand and wiggles his ring finger to emphasize his own gold band.

"I have me a little sweet thing." Mason shifts and considers putting his suit jacket back on. It's tailored, something he'd gotten in Kingston. "She's a good woman," he says finally.

"From Yard?"

"Nah, she's from Chicago. We met in New York after school. But a good woman, you know."

The acquaintance had finished every bit of his sandwich and fries. Had pinched up the straggling pieces of lettuce. Had slurped down his cola until there was no ice left to rattle. Now Mason stands to shake the friend's hand as the friend leaves with his drawings, promising to look Mason up when next he's in Houston.

Mason heads toward the train. He is eating and walking—something his mother has always scolded him against. But it is something he has come back to since moving to Texas. Like reading at the dinner table. Like talking on a cell phone in a restaurant. It is the kind of thing he would never do at home. But Robin, his girlfriend, is an inadequate mother. And now Mason should be looking for the train but instead he is letting the liquid mayo drip onto his suit jacket. "Look you there," he whispers out loud.

The banners stretch down from the narrow third floor to the first and spell "The Downtown Little Catholic Chapel." The banners are a dark red and the letters are in black. There are windows big enough to stand in.

Mason has not once desired to attend Mass since leaving Jamaica years ago; his family is part of the rare race of Kingston Catholics, but now he wonders what's behind those windows. Is it really a chapel? Maybe it's a nightclub with an exclusive guest list. In New York there had been things like that. Maybe the third floor is the champagne room and there are strippers there on Saturday nights. Behind Mason water shoots up from the fountains, announcing the train's arrival. Houston is not like New York. People don't jostle Mason to get out of the way. There is space here. Wide open space. Mason walks backward for a few steps, without bumping into anyone, until he feels the grid of the light rail under his feet. He throws the remains of the sandwich into a garbage can and boards the metro without purchasing a ticket. The metro goes only goes north and south. It is the end of a workday and so Mason is headed south toward the apartment in the manicured Museum District where he and Robin have set up house.

As the train glides through the city Mason thinks of the black leather couch that Robin has chosen. She is looking for white accents. She wants them to have an Asian-themed living room. "This is stupid," Mason had said. "We're not Asian."

"So what? I'm African American and you're Jamaican. You always remind me that those are two different things. I'm not having this place all islanded out and you don't want my African American things . . . so we're choosing a neutral ethnicity."

"What are your so-called African American things?" he asks.

"The African shawl. The praise woman sculpture . . ." She begins to list off her prized possessions.

"How does African *imitation* become African American?"

"And the Caribbean is so perfect? You Jamaicans just imitate everything black Americans do and put a reggae beat on it."

Mason wanted to shake her but he shook his head instead. "Your sculptures are tacky."

"You would say that. Your parents' little prince. But we're a couple now, Mason." And she twirled her wrist to the ceiling as though casting a spell. "Asia is a compromise."

So they had compromised. But now he wasn't sure they had it right. The bonsai tree and the little water altar. It all seemed so adopted. No, worse—it felt stepchildish. But these analogies weren't right at all. Robin would yell at his insensitivity if he said them out loud. She's a teacher. High school. And she thinks Asia is very enlightened. Since moving to Houston she's also discovered that she likes fajitas and tacos—so the kitchen will be in Mexican style.

The metro stop is so close to the apartment that Mason can walk. It's even closer than his stop was in Brooklyn. His suit is stained now and so he carries his jacket over his shoulder. He puts his free hand in his pocket. It's hot but he still walks with his back straight and he doesn't relax until he's in the door. "Robin, baby. I'm home." He knows she's there. Her car is parked out on the street. But she doesn't answer him. He passes through the living room where his architecture books are laid out like art pieces on the coffee table. Her books for school, things like *Jane Eyre* and *Robinson Crusoe*, are lined by height on the bookshelf.

When Robin is mad at Mason she says things like "my friends warned me against dating crazy Jamaican men." When she is happy with him she calls him "my little island boy." Mason feels oddly proud of both accusations. Today she's in the bedroom watching a vain reality show too loudly. Mason goes to the kitchen and pulls out a beer. He holds it to his neck like he sees in the commercials. Then he pops it open on the counter. This, too, is something he gets from TV. He drinks the entire beer right there, standing. He lifts two more from the fridge and goes to the bedroom. Everything in there is flowery. Robin even has a purple imitation silk canopy that she wants him to install properly. Right now it is spilling ungracefully from the bedposts to the floor. She chose a violet canopy because it was a compromise—she'd wanted a black bedroom and he'd wanted white or orange. But now he hates the whole thing. He pushes the canopy aside and sees that she's grading but that she's also in her nice underwear . . . not the kind she wears to school. Her hair is wild as though she's washed it and just let it go without pressing it straight or blow-drying. He sets the beers down on the plastic side table that looks like wood. He takes his pants off. She giggles and calls him her little island boy.

But Mason hadn't been able to finish his po-boy. And here now with Robin he isn't able to finish up either. She had. She always did. After some time he just keeps moving and pushing until she grimaces and holds him tightly. "I'll be sore," she says with apology. He relaxes. It's all too much work anyway.

They had been in Houston for three months when the I-Festival came around. They'd seen the billboards: "Come back to Jamaica!" But Mason thought that his country was doing a vigorous tourism campaign and ignored the signs.

"I-Fest," says Robin like a local. "Every year they do it. Last year was China. This year is Jamaica. We should go."

"Some fakeness, probably."

"Well, I want to go. I want to see what Jamaica is like. The place you're from . . ." She goes to touch his face but he pulls away. She pushes up her mouth and balls up her fists. "Just hit me," he thinks. "Just give me a reason." And then he can't believe what he's thinking. He takes her fisted hands in his. "Okay, baby. We'll go." He feels the madness in him slink off to the walls like a ghost. The walls are still white.

They go on the last day of the festival. When Mason holds the schedule in his hands he only stares and stares. He'd waited. He'd procrastinated. He hadn't really wanted to come. And now look. He'd missed out on two really big and really good Jamaican bands. Bands he hadn't seen since he was in high school and had snuck out for because his mother had scoffed when he'd asked permission. Now he wants to rip up the schedule. He passes it to Robin instead. She looks it over. "I know you probably don't want to see 'fashions of Jamaica' but that's all that's on stage right now." He nods, wanting to scream. There is still a crowd and they have to meander through. They are downtown, not far from where he works. He can see his building. That's his window way up there at the top like an attic. He turns from it.

It is the smell that he recognizes. Jerk and curry. He hates to be a stereotype but he's missing food. Food-food. Food from home. They buy their tickets and stand in the long line for jerk chicken and curry goat. He searches for a Jamaican accent among the others in line, but mostly Texan inflections come to them. He thinks with amusement that some of these people must be tourists to Houston—visitors from San Antonio or Austin or even more exotic places like Waco or El Paso. Mason wonders now if the food will be authentic. He longs to taste Jamaica.

While they stand in line Robin moves so that she leans into his chest. They inch forward in the line like one body. His arms wrap around her shoulders. They don't talk. He stands there with the smell of Jamaica and the longing for home and his woman in his arms. At that moment he loves Robin more than he ever will.

They move toward the fashion show with their Styrofoam plates of food. They pass the booths that claim "History of Jamaica" or

"Fortune Telling—Rasta Style." The food is already a disappointment because it isn't much and now Mason is almost afraid to eat it. They rest their food on a wall and watch the show that isn't a fashion show after all. It is a dance routine. Young people blasting the latest dancehall and bucking and rolling in "100% West Indian" T-shirts. The crowd is too thick for Mason to see below the dancers' waists but he imagines that the girls wear batty riders and the boys pedal pushers. That would be Jamaican fashion maybe. All he can see is their heads snapping and their hands flaying like whips over their heads—*common,* his mother would have called it. He is lifting his fork to his mouth when Robin makes a face.

"I can't eat this."

"What's that, Robin baby?" He rests his fork down.

"It's too hot. Too much pepper."

"Here. Drink some coconut water. Cut the curry spice."

"Are you listening? I can't eat this at all. I can't even taste anything but pepper. My mouth. I can't taste my own damn mouth."

"So, what you want me to do?"

Robin turns away from him and walks her dish to a garbage bin. She dumps it with aggression. Mason watches her do this then turns away toward the dancers—his chest inexplicably tight.

"I'm going to get some funnel cake."

He nods to show that he's heard her but he doesn't look her in the face. Her hair is pulled back so that her cheekbones stand out.

When he finally turns she has disappeared into the crowd. She looks like everyone. He eats his jerk chicken without tasting it. He leaves all the sauce on the plate without sopping it up with the cocoa bread like he would have if things were different. He goes to throw his plate away. He touches his waist to feel his phone. It's on buzz. If Robin needs him she can call. He walks around.

He passes the clothing stands and the booths of jewelry. Every stand has a boom box and they all compete into the air. A brackish noise follows him. Every booth boasts a true-life Rastaman doing the hustling. But when the dreads call out to him to come check their goods their accents sound like New York or maybe one of those small Leeward Islands. They're selling perfume oils and shea butter and "Come Back to Jamaica!" T-shirts. Mason fingers a pair of mini-boxing gloves. They are rearview mirror ornaments. Things to swing back and forth as you drive. He buys the ones with the X of the Jamaican flag and daps the dread as he moves on. But then he remembers that the car is not his but Robin's. Then he buys a real flag. A huge green X in a black bed. But he thinks that it won't fit in with any of their décor. So he buys a workout wristband with the Rastafari colors, but then he knows he will never wear it. And so he buys a sticker, and a T-shirt and a ball cap all with "Jamaica" sprawled in red, yellow, and green. He keeps walking. He moves past the platform shaped like a boat's hull: "A Tribute to Piracy and Port Royal." Past the kiddie stage where there's a puppet show going on—one of the puppets has dreads. The other is a dog. The dreaded one might also be a dog. He goes through Artists Lane, which leads to a roped-off exit. There he stops to look at the photography wall. "Emerging Artists of Jamaica." The one that he stares at bears only an honorable mention ribbon. It is a black-and-white close-up of a young girl. She looks as though she is pretending to be angry—as though any minute she will burst into laughter. *Vex Pickney*. That's what it's called. The sign above all the photos reads "Originals available for delivery from Jamaica." Each print is stapled into its mounted wood.

Mason wants to own this picture. Not after delivery but now. He thinks that maybe he can tear it off gently. If he can do it with confidence everyone will assume he belongs and think nothing of his theft. But he's too scared. He leaves it behind and goes to the exit rope that separates the festival from the street and ducks underneath it with all his booty. The slack guard there even holds up the rope a little to make Mason's escape easier.

Mason heads toward the train. He feels his cell phone buzzing in his thigh pocket but his hands are full. He sees the red and black banner and the CVS and the bakery. "It's a blasted sign," he says out loud. He pushes open the door to the Downtown Little Catholic Chapel and the a.c. stings his face.

There is a desk there as in any office building. Perhaps it's the offices for the diocese, and not a place of worship. A man in a postal worker uniform rushes to hold the door for Mason. The man has a thick wooden rosary around his neck and Mason wonders if this is a joke of some kind. Perhaps this man is the priest. Perhaps this isn't a Roman Catholic place at all, but some odd sect. But no, there is the priest, an old man all in black with the white checker boxed at his throat. He leans on the desk as though it is holding him up. The postal worker leads Mason to another set of doors where Mason sits in a back pew and rests his goods besides him.

The old priest, now in cream and gold robes, wobbles around the altar with an ugly orthopedic cane. Mason stands and sits and kneels on cue and without thinking—it is a dance he's been doing since he was a child. There are only a few other people in the congregation. Mason is in shorts and cotton button-down shirt, but everyone else wears work suits, though there is the postman assisting up on the altar. It feels as though they are all on a stage.

The old priest rasps through his sermon. It seems as though he is on his deathbed imparting final strained words and not up in front of them serving Mass. When Mason walks up for Communion he grows nervous and can't remember which hand is for receiving the host and which hand is for putting it into his mouth. When he reaches the priest, Mason opens his mouth and allows the old man to place the wafer on his tongue. It is the way Mason's parents receive Communion.

There is no singing at the Mass and in all it lasts just twenty minutes. Mason sits when it's over, not knowing what do. Everyone else sits. The priest ambles out a side exit, and still everyone else sits. Mason doesn't remember this as part of the Mass. In Jamaica everyone exited in song and rushed to shake the priest's hand outside. Now everyone just sits or kneels and faces the altar. Mason looks to the postal worker for guidance but he too is just sitting now—though his arms slump over the back of the pew as though he is on a couch watching TV. Mason looks at the huge crucifix behind the altar. The gaunt Jesus struggles on his cross, his head hanging down in what looks to Mason like helplessness. Jesus's knees bloom red on his pale skin as though he's been begging.

Mason looks up at the ceiling. It's blue. Blue-blue like the beaches in the prettier parts of Jamaica—the places that as a Kingston boy he's only seen in tourist brochures. The places where he thinks the tourists go. The ceiling is crisscrossed with white rectangles that swell at the middle and look like canoes. He thinks of Caribs and Maroons. People he has never seen but studied in school. He stares at the beams and wonders if he can design them himself with slits for the Caribbean sun to come sliding in. Then he notices that still no one has left the chapel. He thinks maybe the people are, in some way, waiting for him.

He picks up his loot. It jingles as he gathers it in his arms. He walks up the aisle as he had done as an altar boy in his Kingston suburb and places his boxing gloves and flags and T-shirts in front of the vase of flowers that was perhaps someone else's offering. He bends his head at the bright gold halo that bursts out of the Eucharist bowl. Then he turns to leave, trying in vain to catch the face of one of the other worshipers. He walks into the foyer but then back to dip his hand in the holy water and make the sign of the cross.

The old priest now smiles and reveals a set of real but worn teeth. "Can I help you?" He seems unaware of what Mason has just done. Mason shakes his head. He cannot explain himself. He thinks to make an escape but there in the wall beside the desk is a sculpture, a bust. And instead of leaving, Mason goes to look at it. The sculpture doesn't seem to have a face. It's a man with his hands cradling his head and his shoulders rounded into the shape of a heart. Mason leans in close and thinks he recognizes something. The sculpture is called *Man of Sorrow #2*. Mason blinks. Who is #1? He turns to the priest who is looking right at him. "I would like to go to confession," he says.

The priest gestures for Mason to go on ahead and Mason ambles down the hallway. Mason opens the door marked "Reconciliation" to a closet of a room. He kneels at the metal mesh in the wall and looks through it to see if he can see anything on the other side, but he can't. He sits back. He's not sure what he's doing at all. He's not sure why he doesn't want to marry Robin. He's not sure why he doesn't want to go back to Jamaica. He's not sure why he's jealous that his friend ate that entire sandwich and fries.

Though small, the room is lit and on the wall Mason notices a simple little crucifix, half a foot tall, with a Jesus made of dark wood that looks like mahogany. Jesus doesn't have straight hair hanging from his thorned head. He has short tight curls like Mason, like "the wool of a lamb" the priest back home said was the biblical description of Jesus's hair. Jesus's face is stern in this crucifix even though it is bent to his shoulder; even with that gentle nose that isn't pointed or narrow. This Jesus is carved lean but does not look gaunt with a suffering of starvation.

Mason opens the door but the old priest has finally made it down the hallway and the door almost swings into him. "That crucifix in there," Mason begins hurriedly, "where can I get one like it?" The priest follows him and then holds his chin as he looks at the mahogany Jesus. "I don't know. It looks like it might be an original." Mason nods; he knew that it would be so. His phone rattles in his pocket but he doesn't answer it.

"Would you like," the old man begins in his slow rasping voice, "to confess, my son?"

"I don't know."

The father nods as though this is acceptable. "I will go in and wait."

They go in separate doors and appear on opposite sides of the dark screen. They cannot see each other, really. Only outlines. Mason sees the priest as a mass way in the distance. The screen a kind of horizon. He kneels and leans his chin on his folded hands, but this is uncomfortable. He puts his forehead on his hands but this is no better. He stands and wonders if this is an appropriate posture for confession. The wooden crucifix is at his eye level now. He looks back at the form beyond the screen; like any land, it hasn't moved. Might even be sleeping or dead finally. Mason touches the Christ. It is a little unstable on its thin steel platform. "I'm going to fix this," he says out loud even as he's unscrewing the bolts with his fingers. When he releases it from the wall the wood splits a little and leaves a wedge of itself behind. Mason, crazily, stuffs the crucifix down the front of his pants. As he leaves the confessional he knows the old father is alive and awake and watching him.

Mason passes *Man of Sorrow #2* but doesn't stop. He leaves the Downtown Little Catholic Chapel. Outside it is burning with Houston humidity, but Mason wants to feel the fire. He walks back to the festival. Back, perhaps, to Robin. With each step he feels the wooden Jesus hard in his crotch.

THE INTERNATIONAL SHOP OF COFFINS

For Peter and for Rachel

I. Simon Peter Jatta

The shop does not smell of death. In fact it smells very much like soap. And wood maybe. And mothballs. The ocean, too. The shop is close to the ocean. Anexus Corban perches on a stool behind the display case. Above his head is the sign: "Custom Made Coffins Available w/ at least 3 months notice." The door opens with a jingle from the bell that's tied to the door's handle, and Corban gets his smile ready. He smiles at everyone who comes into the shop. Smiling too broadly is crass and unsympathetic. But no smile at all makes him look grim and funereal. Like an undertaker. Corban sells coffins. He is not an undertaker. His shop is not a morgue. It is not a funeral home or mortuary. He dresses in black because he has his own things to mourn, but this is a coffin shop. A coffin shop only.

Importing to the Virgin Islands is not easy but Corban imports his favorite pieces. The children's coffins are from West Africa. Corban imports their shapes and then paints them himself. His technique with the wood was never very good but he loves the painting. The coffins are in shapes that a child's body would be happy to lie in living or dead. One is shaped like a sneaker. It sits in the middle of the room as though a giant lost it in his stroll through the building. It is white and has a Nike swoop on the side. The laces are made of cloth, but the rest is made of wood. There is also a lollipop one, the candy part painted in blue and green and yellow swirls, the stick—where the child's legs would go—painted an authentic bone white. Corban's favorite is the treasure chest—a baby's coffin. It is mahogany and in fact it is a treasure chest in every way. Only that the inside is lined with bright gold satin, and when it closes it is airtight.

The windows of the shop are large but Anexus Corban didn't make them so. When he opened his shop, fourteen years ago, he opened it in this building. The building is old. Perhaps in the last century grain was stored inside. Perhaps in the century before that slaves were held inside. Just last night Corban had glass installed in the window holes and now he can keep the big wooden shutters open. He can see outside and still keep the air-conditioning on and still keep the noise and mosquitoes out. And this morning he also realizes, with joy, that the sunlight shines right in, brightening the whole shop. This is an additional bonus. So now Corban cannot help but smile too broadly.

When the door opens with a jingle it is okay that Corban is smiling with some teeth showing—so unlike his usual practice. It is Father Simon. Simon is not a customer. He is a visitor. He comes to look at coffins. It is the place on the island where he feels most comfortable. For him the shop is an art gallery. A place to stroll through with hands clasped behind the back. Father likes the children's coffins best. They remind him of home, of Gambia. He always spends considerable time with the car—it has a sun roof for an open-casket viewing—glass in the sunroof is optional but recommend by Corban. People like to kiss the body of their departed, but this is not what Corban fears. With his coffins people like to touch the coffins themselves. Someone reaching into the hood of the roof can be very distracting at a funeral or a viewing.

Father Simon comes in often and Corban enjoys his company. Corban knows that Father Simon recommends his finer caskets to families Father is counseling in grief. The finer caskets are very expensive. These Corban gets from Europe. One is in the largest shop window today. Its debut. It is a casket of pure white marble. Inside it is lined with down pillows covered in Tibetan white silk. It has pallbearer handles but they are vestigial. The coffin is too heavy to lift or carry. One can also purchase the special Dignity Deluxe carriage for its transportation. The casket is an artisan piece but the Dignity Deluxe carriage must be ordered from a catalog.

The store is never crowded, so often when Corban and Simon are there they can talk openly. They talk the way men might at a rum shop or on a corner, but more quietly. Corban goes to rum shops on some nights after the store is closed, but Father Simon cannot do those things because of his profession. "Do you have anything new in, Corban?" But before Corban can respond that he has installed glass in the windows—just look at the light—two girls in school uniforms walk in. They have notebooks. "School project," the blond one says as she waves her book at him. He knows they are lying. He knows that though he is running an honest and important business, for some his shop is just a curiosity. They too are attracted to the children's coffins, but the darker one slinks away shyly to the Mexican coffins that are closer to the counter, where there is less light.

These are shiny, waxed like a new car, in colors like amber and magenta and burnt orange. There is an image of the Black Virgin emblazoned on the side of one. On another the Virgen de Guadeloupe takes up the entire outside cover and there is another replica of her on the inside of the lid as well. Corban makes a mental note to move one of them closer to the window so it can catch the new sunlight. He also watches the girls. They want to touch things. Corban has to come from behind the counter, where he displays small things like votive candles and marigolds, to ask them if they need some help.

"We're picking our coffins," says the brown-skinned girl.

The other opens her eyes at her friend. "For a history project," she interjects.

The girls wear ties. They are seniors in high school. Private school, by the uniform colors they are wearing, but Corban can't tell which one. He leans on a plain pine coffin. It has been nailed with wooden nails, as the Jews in the Virgin Islands most often request. It is not the kind of coffin Father Simon would ever suggest. He leans on it more heavily. It is strong despite its simplicity.

Simon looks the girls over. "What is the topic of the assignment?" He does not know them. They do not go to the Catholic school.

"Death," the fair one says.

"The history of death?" asks Simon with what sounds like disbelief but is actually heavier with intrigue.

"The history of mourning," the Indian-looking one interjects. Father Simon nods. Now he knows they are lying but the history of mourning would indeed make a decent field of study.

"Well," says Corban, looking askance at Simon. "This is a place that celebrates life."

Father Simon snaps in. "Not life, surely, Mr. Corban," giving him the *mister* because the young people are there. "Perhaps *lives*. Perhaps many individual lives." He runs his hand delicately over the treasure chest.

Father Simon has brought Corban more business than any other single person. Every family he counsels for their grief he also counsels them to go to Corban. And Simon always counsels for wealth. His form of counseling always encourages spending: "Take a trip." "Buy something for yourself." He takes his own advice often. There is nothing humble or modest about him and he is quite un-Catholic in this way. Father Simon wears two fine gold chains around his neck—one in yellow gold and the other in rose gold. On one wrist he wears two thick yellow gold hand chains, one in the popular puff Gucci link and the other in a more traditional rope. On his other hand he wears a ring on each finger. This is the left hand. This is also the hand he proffers when he is shaking hands. This is an odd thing to do especially since where he is from the left hand is considered the dirty hand. No one here in these American colonies takes offense at the left-handed shake. It seems to everyone only that his right hand is always busy, holding up his robes at Mass or scratching at the corner of his eye. Parishoners feel dismissed perhaps by the disinterest suggested by a left-handed shake but no one suspects that they are being soiled.

Father Simon is below the Western average in height. He had been slim when he first arrived on the island as a young priest a decade before, but he has grown thick. He is balding and has a great big head, so that balding seems quite natural as you never can imagine hair making it across the entire skull. The balding is most prominent at the back of the head and at the temples. But never does Simon appear short and fat and balding with a big head. He walks and speaks and gestures as if he is a very handsome man. This is learned. And this is a sign of an inescapable past.

In Brikama, the city where his parents still live in Gambia, Father Simon Peter is a very important man—even there where his past is known. As a young boy he had worked as a carpenter because his father wanted all the sons to have a trade.

The thing about working wood is that wood changes. It breathes. It shrinks and tightens and buckles and sheds. All depends on the kind of wood. Some wood needs glaze. Other wood needs paint. Some wood doesn't take paint well—makes the color look garish when you meant for it to look gentle and soft. Once a tourist bought a sculpture that Simon Peter himself made. But this is not why he is an important man. He is an important man because he is a priest. How Simon Peter went from woodworker to priest is the drama of his life.

The name of the shop was Jesus Saves Wood. It was a big shop at the edge of Banjul. In Banjul the ocean did not yet turn into the ocean-fed river that split the country. It was still the ocean and it blew salt into the shop. Simon Peter often took the long way home from school so he could watch the water. Before Simon, one of his brothers had been sent to Banjul to learn the trade of fishing. This brother was much older, in his twenties, whereas Simon was a teenager. Simon never saw his brother, who was engaged and working hard to make money before the wedding, but still he looked for him along the roads that led to the beaches. In Brikama, Simon Peter had never seen the ocean or the river.

The shop had been written up in some tourist book so besides the usual few Germans and Brits now many Americans bought their carvings from the front part of the store. The Americans would walk among the stools and walking sticks. They would pick things up and touch them as if they owned them already. If any of the assistants, Simon Peter included, were in the front this would make them nervous. They could see this touching made even Uncle Omar tense. It was such a violation. To pick things up, to touch them, to treat them like your own when you hadn't yet paid. But the Americans were allowed. They were allowed because they did it with such authority that no one knew how to tell them to put a piece down without insulting them. Then they would leave with only one small piece and smiles on their faces as though they'd done the shop, and perhaps all of Africa, a favor.

Later when Simon's carving was touched and picked up he would understand what a violation it really was. He had seen the American tourists haggle and haggle as if it was a game. They would laugh or look hurt alternatively, as though this wasn't a livelihood. As though they didn't have more dalasi in their purses than the entire shop had in its safe.

In the back was what Uncle Omar called the studio but everyone else in the town just called it the workshop. This is where the assistants sold things to Africans. Bed frames, tables, shelves, and coffins. All these things were made to order. Back there Omar trained the three boys, all like brothers in the art of wood. Omar's wife and children were in England. She was working and it was said that the children were going to school. Sometimes his wife came home with fancy clothes and gifts even for the boys in the shop. Things like soaps and creams and T-shirts. Omar's children never came home.

Of the three boys, Simon Peter was the newest addition. He was still learning to make shelves when the senior boys were making coffins and fancy tables. Only Uncle Omar made the carvings that the rich people bought for decoration. That, he said, was art. Simon was in awe of it. Uncle Omar, as he told the boys to call him, didn't use the big graceless tools that the boys used for tables and shelves. He used little dainty knives, he caressed the pieces, he spoke to them. Simon would pocket little pieces of wood and try to copy Omar's designs. Copy the "We All Are One" and the "Brotherly Love." Those were his favorite. When he went home on the holidays he presented these crude interpretations to his mother, who passed them around to her co-mothers before giving them finally to his father.

The shop was like home. Simon Peter went to school in the day and came home to the shop at night. He worked in the shop and Omar paid his school fees and fed him. In his first and only year with the shop many things happened to Simon Peter. One was that he did very well on his exams and was offered a scholarship at a Catholic boarding school in the country. His brother had been offered a scholarship before him. This kind of thing made his parents proud, but his brother had not been able to take the scholarship because his parents did not want their sons taught by the white man. They had seen what it did to other young men. How they learned the European ways and forgot their own. They had decided that Simon Peter would teach and run a wood shop in their village. But they did not have their wish. Simon Peter ended up going to the boarding school even before his year of apprenticeship to Omar was over.

He had done so well on his exams that the school would be willing and pleased to take him mid-semester. Besides, the schoolmasters were happy to save the boy from the drudgery of the wood shop. At the boarding school the Catholic priests will notice his quiet piety. Notice his love for art and nature and encourage his path to seminary. He loved art, it is true, but he will avoid the other young boys for reasons unrelated to piety.

His brothers in the shop were Kebba and Valentino. Valentino was allowed to put the final coat of paint or varnish on tables. He was in charge of dusting and polishing the carvings in the front room. He was the boss of them. Kebba was happy to have someone younger. Someone whom he could show around and be more important than. And Simon Peter was happy to oblige. Valentino was so talented and so lucky, and though Omar made it clear that his sons would inherit the shop it was easy to see how Valentino might manage to usurp the never-come sons. That would leave Kebba and Simon Peter as Valentino's servants. But now at least they had each other. Though never completely.

On the first day: "This is your bed, Simon Peter." Valentino showed him to the floor in the corner. Kebba looked away as he made his own bed by laying down a piece of cloth over a bed frame. He smiled a small shy smile when he looked at Simon. But he did not offer any help.

In the morning Valentino was already up. Not bothering to wake them so they could impress Uncle Omar. Kebba went to Simon Peter and shook him from the floor. "You have to make your own bed." Simon Peter thought he understood and started to fold the clothes he had laid down as cushion. "No, no. I mean you have to build your own bed. You sleep on the floor until you learn how to make a bed frame. Then you can begin to save for a mattress."

"But I won't be getting paid. Uncle Omar is using my money to send me to school."

"Then I don't think you'll be getting much good sleep."

Simon hadn't wanted to cry but he recognized in Kebba a small kindness that made him feel a burn in his chest like he might cry. They worked side by side that day and every day. School was only until 1:00 p.m. and then Simon went to the shop. The other boys would have been working all day already. They wouldn't even seem to notice when Simon slipped in beside them to watch. But then they would mutter to him to fetch this or do that.

"Like so," Kebba said. Showing him the mechanics of a coffin. "It's the easiest thing we do. You get their height, their width, and their weight. Then you know how to cut. Always leave more room because sometime the body bloats, depending on the cause of death. Sometimes it shrinks. But we don't always know the business of the corpse. Always give at least three inches all around just in case." Most often the coffins were made for Christians, for secular Muslims who thought coffins sanitary, or for those from mixed families like Simon's.

Two months into Simon Peter's assistantship, the body came. Simon had already been home and given his mother the miniatures. He kept his favorite one in his pocket at school and caressed it as if it were a pet mouse. After the body came, that one time, all their lives were changed. The coffin was made by Valentino. When Simon came home from school he found Valentino sawing at a large board of mahogany. For an entire three days Valentino had put aside his normal duties to make a coffin. Simon didn't understand why thick heavy wood, usually for stools or walking sticks, was being used for this. When Simon went to the front there was Kebba gently polishing the "Seller Woman with Basket" and "Thinking Man" with a reverence that Simon envied. Simon caressed the little figurine in his pants pocket. It looked at though he was touching himself inappropriately. Kebba pretended not to see.

The shop was in confusion because the premier assistant was not doing the premier work. When Simon went to the front room Uncle Omar barked at him. "Boy. Go finish that table for Mrs. Anidiye. And ey, don't disturb Valentino. He is building his father's coffin." Finishing the table was a huge promotion. The table was a fine one and the end nubs of the legs still needed to be carved out. Then the legs had to be attached. Then the whole thing had to be sanded down and varnished. Simon went to the workshop and sat down before the table. He daydreamed as he worked. He thought about his mother and his sister sitting at a table this fine. As he worked he gritted his teeth. It was easy to forget Valentino working only feet away.

Valentino did not weep. He did not shake. He made the coffin with quiet care. It was a magnificent coffin. Not like the ones the shop usually made. This was like the ones they made in the capital. It was like a little shed for just one person. The lid was a door. With a handle for you to open. "The House of Valentino Bodji Sankareh, Senior" was painted on the door with a fine brush. "Private property" on the next line. And it was no normal door. It was like the door to the rich people's houses. It was like the doors in the expatriate neighborhoods. Thick with sheen over it so it would last and resist termites. With designs on it. Intricate things no one knew Valentino could do. Swirls like on walking sticks. Two swords crossing at the blades. After Valentino fell asleep on the third night Kebba and Simon Peter peered at the coffin that was really a mansion's entrance. They stood above it, open mouthed, in awe and jealousy of its craftsmanship.

All three boys slept with the coffin that night before the body came. But Simon Peter did not sleep well. It seemed as though the door would open and a family would come crawling out, not sure how their front door ended up in the middle of the workshop. He dreamed that he knocked on the door. No one answered and so he opened it. And when he walked in it was a big white house with fancy paintings right on the walls. Angels flying around. And he walked the halls and he was wearing shoes. Rich grown-up shoes that clapped on the ground and made a loud dignified noise. When he woke up Valentino and a group of men were bringing in a large body that was stiff and stinking. It smelled like rotten flowers. Kebba and Simon pretended to stay sleeping even though the men were quarreling loudly with each other. It was still in the middle of the night. They opened the door and Simon, peeking out from a pair of pants that were his blanket, almost cried out. He looked over at Kebba and Kebba was looking at him. The men rested the body down. Then with more loud quarreling they hoisted the coffin out. And then Valentino was gone.

The shop was quiet and for a minute Simon thought he'd go back to sleep since tomorrow was school. But Kebba climbed out of his bed and went over to the full bed where Valentino had slept. He patted the mattress. He sat on the bed, a transgression he would not have attempted just earlier in the day. Then he watched Simon right in the face as he lay down on the bed and pulled the light cover over himself. Simon wanted to climb onto Kebba's bed frame which was nicer than the floor. But Simon didn't dare. Not yet. He had a transgression of his own.

The next day Simon arrived from school and dropped his bag in the corner of the workshop beside his pile of bedding. That afternoon Uncle Omar was distracted and heartbroken at the loss of his most promising assistant. He had kept the shop closed for the day, with a purple wreath at the entrance. Inside, Uncle Omar was instructing Kebba, his new lead assistant, in the making of something that days earlier Kebba had only dreamed of making. Simon slipped by and went to the front room. He had been in there before. He had helped with customers. Smiled at them. Carried their heavier purchases to their cars. It smelled like wood polish. It smelled like Simon imagined wealth smelled like. It was dark. The tall "Wise Man with a Stick" seemed as though he would reach out and hit him. The "Washer Woman with Baby" seemed poised to scold him. The shop did not sell religious pieces. Uncle Omar was a secular type but still he would not make wooden crosses or cedar rosary beads, even though they sold quite well elsewhere. He didn't believe in creating images of prophets or God. Simon Peter pulled his little figure out of his pocket and rested it on a shelf. It stood out. It looked odd but he thought it looked beautiful. It was soft and smooth in unexpected places after weeks of rustling in his pocket.

"Tino is not coming back," said Kebba that night. Simon had exams the next day and all week. "You can have my bed if you want." But Simon didn't go to Kebba's bed. He was afraid that Valentino would come back. Simon wasn't afraid that Valentino would hurt him or that Mr. Omar would be mad. He was afraid of insulting Valentino by participating in this move up. He was also a young man of principles and it seemed wrong to take over Kebba's bed when he had not earned it. He didn't like that Kebba had taken over Valentino's bed. But that night Kebba gave him a gift. Kebba let him study his books by candlelight. Valentino had always said "Lights out" with a gruff and final voice.

For days Simon had the dream again and again. Of opening the coffin door and walking down the glowing hallway. Sometimes he would stop to study the pictures, which were of old wise men. But the hallway just kept going and his shoes kept knocking and if he lifted his hand he could see that he was wearing a black Western-style suit.

"What does the dream mean?" he asked Kebba one night as they sanded down a set of dining chairs.

"It means you're going to be a big man. Someone who travels."

"Really?" said Simon with hope and unease. He dreamed the dream again that night with less foreboding than before.

One Saturday, the boys awoke and took their normal bucket baths, sharing the soap. The tourists came all week but on Saturdays the boys took charge so Uncle Omar could have a break. Today was the first day that Kebba would take money. He wore a new shirt that Uncle Omar's wife had brought from the U.K. It said "London Lover." Kebba was proud of the shirt but the letters were sticky and felt heavy on his chest. They made him sweat so that he often had to stretch out the collar and blow cool air down the front.

That day a black man came in. He was an American, they could tell right away by how he walked in and went to look at something before he even greeted them. The boys stood taller so he could see them. He smiled at them but only waved his hand and said "Just looking" in his clipped English. He was American but in the face he looked like a Malinke. Each boy looked at the man in his silly short pants and close-shaved head and wanted badly to sell him something. Kebba was the seller. Simon was only there to help carry things. He sat in a corner with his maths book but he looked at the man and thought he was a fine-looking man. He wondered with shame if the man had children. If the man wouldn't like to take him and Kebba just for a visit to America. As the man moved silently around the shop this desire changed. Simon felt his stomach tighten. He looked over at his little figure on the shelf and felt afraid for it. Usually, the Americans made a lot of noise. Often they laughed and asked for the address of the shop—promising to tell their friends. Others treated Uncle Omar with a reverence that was fine to see. They would ask for the meaning of each piece and Uncle Omar, who was honorable, would say if there was a meaning and would say "No, it is just for its prettiness" when there was none. This man was different. He didn't touch each piece. He walked around with his hands clasped behind his back. He bent to a stool and studied it closely with his eyes. He seemed to be smelling things. He seemed to be circling around a small ball of two men embracing as for wrestling or camaraderie—it was not clear. It was Simon's piece. The man seemed to be narrowing in on Simon's piece and now he was picking up Simon's piece and touching it and Simon's eyes welled and he felt ashamed as though someone had pulled down his pants and touched him in front of his whole village. His heart pumped hard and he held his breath. His eyes did not leave the hands of the man, wrapped around the thing he had made.

"I would like this and that tall thin man with the long beard," the man said to Kebba. "How much?" Kebba named an exorbitant price for the tall man without hesitation. "And this?" said the man holding up Simon Peter's ball of two men whose heads met at the neck. Their arms disappearing into each other's shoulders and sides.

Kebba leaned forward to look at it, pretending he wasn't noticing it for the first time. "That is special piece," he said, simply beginning his haggling routine.

"How much?" said the man in a tone that the boys were not sure how to read. Perhaps it was impatience, perhaps it was desire. Such nuances of culture interfered in communication even when the same language was spoken.

The man left with Simon's figure and with the tall thin man. He did not want Simon to help him take it to the car that was waiting, and for this Simon was relieved. Simon said to himself that he would not make anything again. Well, he would make coffins and tables and things people commissioned. But he would not make something that existed just for its prettiness ever again. He felt now that this was too much to lose. He did not know how Uncle Omar dealt with the loss, but Simon Peter decided he would not make that kind of pain a recurring one.

He did not dream the dream of the door and the hallways that night but the next morning he woke up in Valentino's bed with Kebba. He did not know how he ended up there, but there he was. He woke to it slowly. He felt Kebba's thing on his bare behind and Kebba's hand wrapped around him and resting without aggression on his thing. Simon hollered. He did not holler because he wanted to incriminate Kebba, really he didn't. But because he had been dreaming of the man who took his pretty thing and when he woke the hand on him felt as though it was that man's hand. Simon thought maybe he was in America. He hollered out of a kind of happiness, then a kind of shock at the removal of his dream, then a kind of disappointment, then finally out of a kind of shame. He tried to pull up his pants and rub off the feeling of Kebba's thing between his buttocks cheeks. He continued to shout.

Uncle Omar came in from the front room where he had been going over the money Kebba made, unable to remember the figurine Kebba insisted he had sold. When he came into the workshop he saw, and knew, and Kebba began saying, "He climbed into my bed. The sinner. The dirty boy." And Simon Peter began saying, "No. He pulled down my pants in my sleep." Omar took a piece of plywood and smashed it against both their heads until they slumped to the floor and saw blackness. Simon was sixteen. He did not know it, but he was older than Kebba by two years.

Simon was saved. The next day he went home to his parents. Mr. Omar drove him, head bandaged. When he arrived at his mother's door he was hurled out like a bag of trash. Uncle Omar went to talk to his father. His father called him to his house. Uncle Omar was there and his mother came with him.

His father spoke with a big voice. Simon Peter did not know his father's voice so well and now it seems a voice of which to be afraid. "Mother Simon you must leave. This is a man's business."

But Simon's mother would not leave. "This is my only son. You sent him to the city and he comes home to me with a bandage on his head. I will not leave. I did not leave when he was coming into this world. I will not leave now."

Simon wanted his mother to leave. He did not know what kind of punishment was given for sodomy but he had read the Qu'ran at his father's feet. He imagined they would cut off his thing, and then it took all his will not to swoon. He knew he could be pushed out into the street to wander—that would be a mercy. He did not want his mother there to hear his punishment.

"He has passed his exams highly. We had intended for him to work here in the village as a teacher. But now that cannot be. He cannot stay here. He cannot teach other children. Our shame will be a secret from the whites. They would like him to go to their school in the hills. A boarding school. It will be paid for. He already has the Christian name his mother gave him, so that is good. He is going. He is going and perhaps they will help him."

His mother did not interject. She did not wail or disagree. Simon Peter understood this all to be a blessing. Even a privilege of sorts. He was going away for school. He would be educated by the whites. But he was going away really for waking up in the wrong bed with his pants down. He was being sent out of the village. This was a veiled punishment.

And he did not see his parents again for many years. At the boarding school the other African boys sometimes held hands as they talked. They sat close and whispered. This was done. This was how young boys conversed. It was pure. It was so because no one could expect it otherwise. But Simon Peter would not hold hands with any boy or girl. He would not allow them to sit close. Because Simon Peter did not trust himself. He never knew what became of Kebba.

But what became of Simon Peter is that he set himself aside and being aside looks very much like standing out and standing out can look very much like standing above. And so the priests noticed him. On holidays he did not go home. His parents did not come to pick him up and so one priest or another would let him stay in the refractory on a big sofa for his bed. And they came to see him as theirs, as one who could become like them. And he became the senior prefect and the other boys called him Senior Jatta. And eventually he was given his own room, which was good because it was hard, very hard to be in the same room with other boys. He was afraid they would see him in his sleep, his face slack, and know. And in his own room he could lie and think of Kebba and invent fantastical lives for them. Maybe he didn't scream that morning. Maybe he should have understood. Maybe it could have been their secret. Maybe together they would have inherited the shop and they would have slept on the same big fluffy bed. And they could have had wives and children who slept in a different house. And he would have let Kebba push up against him all he wanted because Kebba sold the figurine of the two embracing wrestlers for so much money. And though Simon did not see a cent of that money it still felt as though Kebba knew he was valued. Something he made had been valued.

Simon Peter studied to wash away these thoughts. Like so many studious children, he studied to keep from doing other things. He wore black shoes and a black suit, the only one he had. And he carried a small black suitcase, the only one he had. All given by the priest and nuns at his school. He knew he had become what he always dreamed. And before he left on the plane, the priests delivered his parents to him and his mother kissed him and his father stood aside and nodded. When he walked up to the seminary in Surrey there was a big wooden door. He walked down the halls and his feet clapped in their grown-up shoes. He looked at the walls with the distinguished men. He knew he had not left Kebba behind.

And now he sends his parents money. And now his father can brag that his son is a real man. And now when he visits he takes back gifts—soaps, creams, and T-shirts. And no one speaks of what happened.

And now he was in a coffin shop again. The two young girls have left. They left with laughter and talk of what to wear. He knows they don't have a project. He knows they are just in Corban's shop to look. He doesn't mind this. It is the same reason he is here. While the girls were there and giggling, he watched them. He watched how they stood so close and didn't seem shy about pinching each other or pulling on each other's hair. As though they are lovers, he had thought. But he knows they most likely are not. But he envies this closeness all the same. In fact, this relationship he has with Corban is the closest friendship he has had since he was sixteen and living in the shop. He had to come clear across the world. To the Caribbean. A place so distant and different from Gambia. But every week he is here. To talk to Corban about things. Sometimes about Africa. Avoiding Gambia and talking about the conflict in Liberia. Corban loves to talk about Liberia. He is fascinated that its capital is called Monrovia. He comments often that naming an African city after an American president is enough reason for a civil war.

After the girls have left, a woman comes in. She is middle aged and has papers in her arms. She stands in the center of the room as though waiting for someone. Perhaps for her dead person to come wafting in. So Simon walks about the gallery quietly, his shoes clanking respectfully. This is a kind of penance. This is a kind of chapel. He runs his hands along the coffin in the show window. It's not wood. It's made of marble. It must cost ten thousand dollars, he thinks. It might cost more. He wonders if it is the kind of coffin he could be buried in. If he is worth this kind of thing or if he can simply afford this kind of thing—which is sometimes the same and sometimes different depending on whom you are talking to. He feels the thing in his chest. He has felt it again and again over the years. The thing that is like tears. He thinks of Kebba saying, "It means you will be a big man. You will travel."

II. Anexus Corban

Just last night Anexus Corban had glass installed in the window holes and now he can keep the big wooden shutters open. He can see outside and still keep the air conditioner on and still keep the noise and mosquitoes out. And this morning he also realizes that the sun shines right in, casting lovely shadows about the room. This is an additional bonus. So now Corban cannot help but smile too broadly.

When the door opens with a jingle it is okay that Corban is smiling big. It is Father Simon. He is not a customer. He is a visitor. He comes to look at the coffins. It is the place on the island where the priest feels most comfortable.

The store is never crowded, so often when Corban and Simon are there together they talk to each other. Today Corban is proud of his windows. "Do you have anything new in, Anexus?" Simon speaks with a British accent, even though he is from West Africa and only spent a few years in Britain as a young seminarian. This cover-up suits Corban fine. Even endears Simon to him. Corban, who is pure French-Trinidadian, has trained his own voice to give the inflections of an island man rooted in the St. Thomas soil.

Corban wants to tell Simon to look at the new windows but he knows that his friend is less interested in light and the effect of the light. The priest wants only to know about the coffins. Corban doesn't let this dampen his mood. Today is a good day and such days must be savored. Before he can mention the new windows, two girls in school uniforms walk in. "School project," the blond one says as she waves her notebook at Corban. He knows they are lying. He knows that though he is running an honest and important business, for some his shop is just a curiosity. They are both attracted to the children's coffins, but the darker one slinks away shyly to the Mexican coffins that are closer to the counter, where there is less light. He looks at her and his chest tightens. There is something about her. Her face there in the shadow. The resemblance is only slight, but today, with his new windows, Corban is vulnerable to the past's intrusion. The girl reminds him of Usha.

Corban forces himself to come from behind the counter, where he displays small things like keepsake urns and cloth handkerchiefs, to ask the girls if they need some help.

"We're picking our coffins," says the brown-skinned girl with a sureness that is unexpected, and yet all Usha. "Your sign says custom made."

"For a history project," the other one quickly interjects and opens her eyes at her friend.

The girls wear ties. They are seniors in high school. Private school, by the colors they're wearing, but Corban can't tell which one. He knows they will ignore the plain pine coffin held together with wooden nails. That one is for the Muslims; they most often request its strength and simplicity. He wonders if the one with the dark hair is Muslim.

Father Simon looks the girls over. He does not know them. They do not go to the Catholic school. "What is the topic of the assignment?"

"Death," the blond one says.

"The history of death?" asks Simon with what sounds like disbelief but is really intrigue.

"The history of mourning," the Indian one says, and again seems to be gaining a kind of temerity simply from her own voice. Father Simon nods. He knows they are lying but the history of mourning would indeed make a decent field of study.

"Well," says Anexus Corban, looking askance at Simon. "This is a place that celebrates life."

And Anexus knows about life. He knows about an entire life. Because he has lived an entire one already. In a way, this is his third.

The brown girl buys a box of marigold petals and pays for it with a fifty. She must come from money, Anexus thinks. He enjoys seeing it. He enjoys being the victim of it. As she waits for her change, the white friend flirts with Simon—the way young girls like to flirt with priests. Thinking maybe they'll get them to recant their vows, though really young girls wouldn't know what to do if a priest did recant and go to them looking for love. The girl is looking at Father Simon and smiling only a little. When she walks away she makes her hips swing sharply. It looks as though she's testing the priest but really she is just testing out her own power. It's the thing young people do.

Anexus knows about this. He too came from money. A girl once flirted with him and then he rejected his family and devoted himself to her . . . well, that is a story. And though he's lived many lives, in all of those lives he has loved her—Usha. In all of those lives it has been her and only her.

Once the girls are gone Corban and Simon talk. Simon must put his hand up to his face to block sun coming in and that is when he notices that there are new windows that allow much more light. "It's bright in here now," he says and then immediately wonders why he doesn't like the brightness. He decides he is being selfish. This is not his shop after all. He lowers his hand and allows the sun to stream into his face. "It's bright," he says again with forced optimism. Corban smiles his big smile. Yes, Simon is his friend. A friend pretends for you. A friend bends and changes. Corban offers to make some coffee and when he goes to the back of the store to perk it he hears the jingle of the door's bell. He leaves the coffee and comes to the front.

He doesn't say "May I help you?" because he knows that kind of thing is so much what his customers want to hear. In the early days he would say things like that and the customer would say yes, yes, yes, and then not be able to stop saying it. Yes, please help me. For God's sake, help me.

Now when he comes out to the front he looks out his big clear windows at the people walking by and says, "Good afternoon." The woman responds with an echo. Simon begins his slow walk around the shop. Corban doesn't watch him, he watches the woman.

She is over sixty. Around the age that Usha would be. She stands in the middle of the shop and turns one way then the other. Anexus waits for her and thinks: I am waiting. His chest tightens again at the large truth of this. The woman looks at him finally then walks toward the counter. "My husband . . ." she begins. Anexus prepares his face. ". . . is coming." As she says this a man walks in.

The man doesn't say anything but he seems to be making a lot of noise. He is big. His clothes are loose and rustling. He stamps his feet even though there is no welcome mat. He clears his throat and walks to his wife. "Do you see anything the old man would like?"

"I can't do this," she says, though she seems stoic and prepared to do anything.

The big man nods and approaches Corban. "Sir. Can we see your traditional caskets?"

Now Corban would argue that all his caskets are traditional. But he knows what the couple means. He nods and takes them to the Western-style stainless steel selections and then to the oak. "This one has a drawer in the half couch, for letters and mementos." He demonstrates how the drawer can remain open during the viewing and then close securely and for all eternity when the casket is shut. "This one has a glass cover to protect and preserve the deceased." He can read this woman. She wants to make her dead person last.

When they've left, Corban marks the date and house where he will deliver the casket. They chose a cherry wood with champagne-colored lining and a deluxe pillow like in the Virgen de Guadeloupe casket. On the inside of the lid they have asked for a photo display. They do not say why, but Corban knows it is so that if the dead old man should awake, the first thing he will see is images of himself with his loved ones. Corban has told the couple that he will install four oval frames of silver but that they must provide the pictures. Corban does not remind them that if the dead old man should awake he will be stuck under four to eight feet of St. Thomas dirt.

Corban returns to the back and pours coffee into little matching teacups for himself and Simon. He pours the remaining coffee into a teapot that is part of the same set. He brings it all out on a tray. He and Simon sit on stools on opposite sides of the counter.

The friends drink two cups of coffee each as the sun comes down.

"The windows are very nice, my friend."

"Thanks, Simon. That's good of you."

"I think they will bring you more customers."

"Come no, Simon. You are my best customer grabber. These windows are purely aesthetic. An old man shouldn't miss a sunset if he doesn't have to."

"Well, now I suppose you won't ever have to. And me—I should be going now. I have to write my sermon for tomorrow."

"You should do those things on a whim. Like a politician."

"Ha!" Simon smiles and shakes his head. "I think politicians prepare."

"They pay people to do it for them. You're a priest but don't be gullible."

"Yes. I'm a poor gullible priest and I cannot afford to pay for a sermon writer. Sounds a bit unethical, my friend. But if you come across an honorable lad who offers his services cheaply you let me know."

"What's it about?"

"The sermon? Lazarus. You know the story, of course."

"Of course. What position will you be taking?"

"Faith. The importance of faith in life."

"That's hard, Father. That's hard. Women cry and then their brother gets raised from the dead. What kind of message does that send?"

"That faith can raise the dead."

They were both silent for a second before they allowed themselves to laugh. Then they looked around the empty room cautiously.

"Well, you know," began the priest again and more seriously. "It is possible that Lazarus was not quite dead. He may have been in some kind of low coma. The loud screaming and prayers might have brought him around. Or his heart might have slowed or even stopped. It is possible that Jesus thumped on his chest. This might be our first recorded CPR."

"Are you going to tell the congregation that?"

"Of course not. No. I plan to talk about faith over demanding. You know those women did not ask Jesus to bring Lazarus back to life. Everybody has got to die sometime. They were just good and faithful and so good came to them. That is what I'm going to talk about."

"Maybe I'll come."

"It would be nice to have you, friend." Father Simon swirled his empty teacup with a twirl of his wrist. Corban moved to pour him some more. Simon shook his head. "It would be nice to have you, my friend." He started to walk out.

"We'll see, Father," Corban called out to him. "I won't come up for Communion, though. I won't be in a state of grace."

"Your coffee will do." They laughed.

Corban would not go. He did not have anything against the Church; he had been raised Catholic himself in Trinidad. He just did not want to see his friend dressed in elaborate vestments. Layers of cloth—each fold steeped with symbolism. Each color signifying something that no layman could ever really know. Corban didn't want to see Simon Peter wearing a little hat with cloth bells ringing or a big pointed hat with a bit of gold that shimmered. He would go if Simon was a Franciscan. He would go if there was a guarantee that Simon would wear a plain cassock and sandals. Wealth had betrayed Corban once already.

When Simon left, Corban began to close up the shop. He went outside and fastened the shutters. Back inside, the shop felt comfortable and old. He replaced the mothballs in all the caskets. He wiped down all the wood caskets with Pledge and the marble and glass ones with his own purple solution. He ran the handheld vacuum over the baby coffin that was covered with pink fleece. He dusted the urns and lowered his special silver one down from the highest shelf to take home and polish with toothpaste. This one was shaped like an island. An island he had loved and lived on. It was the urn he planned for his own ashes.

Then he did the windows and the display case. Then he walked around. He went to the Virgin casket. It was the flashiest of the caskets—with its golden sheen on the outside. It was solid wood, like all his wood caskets. But it was really the lid with its Virgin surrounded by her own bright blue body halo that made it Corban's favorite. He thought of the Indian girl who had paid it attention and smiled at the memory.

It was a full couch casket and the Virgin took up the entire lid. The length of the dead body that would rest in it. Corban didn't think this design was for the deceased. This design was for the mourners, a beautiful thing for them to reflect on as they said their last goodbyes. He imagined waking up dead in that casket to the Virgin lying on top of him, her face on his face. He had always thought it was a woman's casket but now he wondered.

He felt inside and squeezed the cushioning. It took some effort to heave himself in. It was made for someone slender. Someone younger perhaps. Anexus had been young and slim but that was so long ago. He was pressed tight in the casket, as if it was less of a bed and more of a cradle. He reached up his hand to make sure the lid was securely up. He crossed his arms over his chest. "So this is what it feels like to be dead," he said out loud. Then Anexus closed his eyes and thought of Usha and Jean.

Usha Persaud and Jean Monroe had met on an island called Gasparee, off the coast of Trinidad. It was a small island. He had to jog five or so laps on the developed half just to get a workout. Rich white Trinidadians had vacation houses here that they visited during long weekends. He and his brothers had brought over the sailboat. They were there for the weekend because his brother was getting married and the bachelor party was that night at Gasparee in the Monroe family bungalow.

The party was wild and raucous. Jean saw his father wander off into a back room with one of the African strippers. The Indian one was sitting on his brother's lap; his crotch was sticking up like a tent. Jean watched for a while as the other young men cheered her on, hooting over the little gyrations she made. But then Jean pulled her off because he knew his brother and he knew his brother would be ashamed if he cheated on his fiancée. The young men hooted at Jean and pumped their fists into the air before turning their attention to another female, a dougla who wore feathers in her hair.

The girl led him through the door that was his parents' bedroom. Through the walls Jean could hear the small squeals of a woman. Jean sat on the bed. "This will be extra," the girl said as she kneeled down. Her accent was thick with the South Trinidad village she must have come from. The Indians and Africans his father did business with had more British inflections. Even his family, which was white French on both sides, sounded more British than anything. She had a gold nose ring and a gold chain from her nose to her ear. Jean watched it glimmer against her dark skin as her cheeks tensed and released. Afterward, he handed her more money than she had asked for and said "Thank you" as his mother had trained him. She handed him her business card. "Anexa" it read and then two different numbers but no details on what the business was.

Nothing like this had ever happened to Jean. He touched the ends of the woman's hair as she walked back out to the loud party. He wondered if what had happened was real. If that woman was real. He wondered if he should feel guilty. The throbbing in his groin told him that what had happened was real after all, but nothing else.

The next day Jean Monroe's brother was sent on the motorboat to get ready for the evening wedding. Jean stayed behind to help clean up. He was taking a bag of trash down to the bay where a barge would take garbage and poor passengers to the main island. Jogging back, he saw the woman walking with a big flat package under one arm and a toolbox in the other hand. His first thought was to be surprised that she would be up this early after such a busy night at the party. He had decided that women like this Anexa could not possibly exist in the daytime. His next thought was that although he had paid her, he still owed her something. He ran to help her with the things she was carrying.

She turned her head and he realized that it wasn't her at all. She looked at him with expectation. "Do you need help?" he asked, slowing down and wondering at his own disappointment. She smiled and handed him the toolbox. She was older than the woman from the night before. She was older than him even. She did not have a ring in her nose or a hole where a ring might have been.

"I'm Usha. Usha Persaud," she said. And her accent was refined. And her smile was genuine. She looked at him. "And you?"

"Nice to meet you, Usha Persaud." He repeated her name the way his father had taught him. To help him remember. "I'm Anexus," he lied. "Anexus Corban."

He was nineteen. She was twenty-six.

She had a key to a bungalow that belonged to friends of his father. She offered him a drink and went to the fridge and made him a mimosa. He knew she did not live here. But he accepted her pretense; after all, he had lied about his name. He would let her have her farce. They sat on a fluffy couch. "How long have you lived here?"

"I don't live here," she said.

He hadn't expected her to give up so easily. "I knew that," he said as though he had won a little prize. "I know the people who live here." He sipped his mimosa and smiled. Ready now to give up his true identity.

"I'm the artist," she said and pointed with her glass to the painting still wrapped in its protective brown paper. She leaned toward it and peeled the paper off without ceremony. He looked at the painting. The Indian woman in it was painfully familiar. She had a gold nose ring with a gold chain that ran from her nose to her earlobe. She was at a window and there was a palm tree and there was a shadow so real he looked around to see what might have cast it. But it was in the painting. Jean began to excuse himself.

"Why so soon, Anexus?" Usha asked as he backed out, never leaving her place on the couch.

He thought to himself, "I should kiss this woman. I should kiss her good and hard like in the movies." But he thought too long. "I'll see you around, Usha." And then he ran.

At his brother's wedding Jean wept as hard as the bride's mother and drank more champagne than anyone. His own mother looked at him with worry. She had hoped he would follow his brother to New York University or his father to London University, but he'd been home for a year now and hadn't even filled out the applications. She brought him to sit next to her at the reception and tousled his hair. "My baby," she said and he rested onto her shoulder.

Anexus Corban woke up inside the dark coffin. The lid was closed and there was no light. He was in complete darkness. He could not see his mouth so close to the Virgin's that he could kiss her. He panicked. He began scratching at the lid and jostling his heavy body around. His breathing became a shriek and finally the lid lifted and he sat up and he was there in his shop. And it was quiet. He was sweating. It had been hot inside the coffin.

He removed himself without ease or grace. He sat on the stool that was usually Simon's and drank the last of Simon's coffee which was cold but still sweet. He licked the sugar at the bottom. "Damn it, Usha," he said as he carried the teacup and saucer to the back where there was a sink. He washed them and dried them and then returned them to their set. He had the whole set. The plates and the saucers and the little teapot. It was an early wedding present. They hadn't picked out a china pattern but Usha's friend made pottery and had made an entire set for them. There had been no other wedding gifts.

Corban got in his car and drove into the hills. Up to the humble condo complex where his apartment was. He owned his one-bedroom apartment and he paid nominal fees so it was called a condo. He watched a movie on HBO while eating a pint of ice cream. He changed into his pajamas, which resembled prisoner smocks and not hospital scrubs as he thought, and climbed into bed. He touched the picture of Usha and a version of his younger self together in a gallery. And he spoke to the painting of the brown woman at her window in her bright sari and gold chain across her cheek. She loomed on the wall across from him. "You're beautiful," he said to her and then drifted off to sleep.

Their first date was not their first date at all. Jean Monroe went looking for Usha in the galleries all over Port of Spain. There weren't many galleries and most had Carnival-themed work. None of them carried work by Usha Persaud. He left his number and his name as Anexus Corban. He went back to Gasparee but the Thompsons weren't there. He got the housekeeper to let him in, saying he'd forgotten something. When he went to the living room he stared at the blank wall where her painting was supposed to be. "Oh, Usha."

He began to go a little crazy. He applied to New York University. For almost two months he followed his father around and talked art at all the business meetings. His father began to rest his hand on his shoulder when he introduced him. "My son," he said now. "He knows a lot about art." A lawyer colleague invited Mr. Monroe to an opening at his house for Trinbagonian artists and patrons, but his father pressed Jean to go in his stead. There on the wall was another window but this time a young African girl standing at it. She held up one finger to her lips as if to say "hush." In the lower right-hand corner what looked like "Usha Persaud" was scrawled in gold. Jean could feel his body stiffen. He stood tall and scanned the room for her. He knew she was there. He knew it as if he was dreaming. It was as though he could smell her.

"Have you seen Usha Persaud?" he asked someone casually.

"I don't think she's here tonight." And Jean was filled with the feeling that the people were lying to him on purpose. He felt desperate. He walked quickly around the room trying to seem calm. In every little group there was an artist. He smiled at the people he recognized. The artists were easy to pick out. They clutched their wineglasses like torches. They seemed smaller than everyone else. She was not among them.

Jean went outside to the lawn. And there she was. She was sitting in the grass looking out at the sunset. Her skirt was fanned around her as if she had arranged it just so. He walked up beside her and stood there. He looked down and she looked up. "Hello, Anexus."

"I've been looking for you."

"Oh, I've just arrived."

They stared at each other and his chest was filled again with that desire to kiss her, like in the movies. "Sit down," she said.

"My white pants. The grass." He smiled and shook his head.

"Sit on my skirt. I have it spread out just for you." His neck went hot. He gave her his wineglass and lowered himself carefully to sit on the cotton patches of her skirt. She sipped his wine as though it was hers. The sun was setting, and then she turned to him and kissed him soft and sweet with her mouth still trickling wine. He felt the heat all over his body.

He got into NYU, as was expected. "Come with me," he said to her as they lay in bed. They were in the room that was his parents' in the bungalow at Gasparee. This was the first time he had brought her there.

"Where? To college? I've already done that business, Anexus."

"We could live in Manhattan and you'd be able to sell your work."

"And you'd be a college boy. I don't think so."

"Marry me, Usha."

She looked at him for a moment. Her face grew distant and wrinkled with concern. She looked as though she was about to cry. It looked as though he had ruined everything. "But I haven't even met your parents."

"I haven't met your parents, either."

She shook her head. "That's different."

"Who cares about parents?"

Usha and Anexus had been going to private art openings and making love in the patrons' spacious bathrooms for just over a month. He had been introducing himself at all her parties as Anexus Corban. He wore different clothes as Anexus—nothing tailored. Shoes bought in the regular-people stores. He let his hair fall loosely over his forehead. He cultivated a more rootsie accent. If he saw an acquaintance he would look over Usha's head and put his fingers to his lips, "hush," and the other white man would understand at some conquest level and smile. Only once did someone ask "Aren't you the younger Monroe boy?" but Anexus shook his head and offered his hand. "I'm Anexus." He avoided the patrons and the patrons' sons. He stood with the artists. On so many levels it was a side he had never been on before.

Usha did not know that he was Jean Monroe. That his father was a rich merchant who owned a lumber business. He told Usha that the bungalow was his parents' house. He told her that his parents lived in England and rarely visited. He told her that he was an only child.

"*I* care about parents," she said.

"Usha, baby. Times have changed. We must be rebellious. This is the beginning of a new era. I want you to be my wife and all that. And we're big people. We don't need permission, right, my girl?"

"Anexus, we barely know each other. This isn't real. This is pretend." She had not smiled yet.

"Is this pretend, Usha?" He raised his arms to signal the room and their lovemaking. "I want to marry you. Forget NYU."

"You can afford to live in Manhattan. You can just decide so easily to go or not to go to college," she said. "You must be even more rich than I thought. Is that why I can't meet your parents, Anexus? You know I don't have to marry you to be your lover."

"I want a lover and a wife and a mother of my children and all that. What do you say, Usha baby? Here, I have a ring."

It was not his mother's. It was not a family heirloom at all. He had bought it from a jeweler the Monroes went to often and it was so simple and plain that, despite the solitary diamond, the jeweler did not even suspect that it was an engagement ring.

Jean moved Usha into the bungalow on Gasparee. It was perfect for her because she liked the solitude of the island—it was not the season when the bungalows were in use and most of them were unoccupied. Sometimes she had the whole island to herself. She transformed what he told her was the guest room into her studio. She painted and she sold paintings. At parties on Trinidad or on Tobago for the next month they spoke about themselves as fiancé and fiancée. But no plans were made toward a wedding. Jean felt this was her responsibility. He waited with only a little anxiety for her to tell him when. He waited for her to tell him the date and the place and whether she would invite her parents. He slept at his parents' house sometimes and told Usha that he slept at the office. He did not tell Usha that the office was his father's. She did not question him and he did not find this peculiar. His parents did not question him, either. His mother thought her son was taking time to "find himself." Perhaps his father knew. Perhaps he had a mistress of his own in a bungalow on Gasparee. Jean didn't think on those things. Jean was waiting.

Then one day he walked into his father's study to go over some paperwork and there was the painting. The window and the Indian woman. He stared at it. "Oh, you like it?" asked his father with amusement. "I'm trying it out. Seeing how it looks. I think your mother will hate it, but this is between us men."

"It's okay. I guess."

"From a really beautiful woman painter. Lakshmi. Oh, that's not it. Now what does it say?" He leaned forward to look at the gold signature. "Usha. Lovely woman. Charming, too."

"Did she come here? Did she mount it herself?"

"Oh, yes. This morning. I was thinking I'd have your mother

invite her for tea. Might be nice? Your mother might like the artist even if she doesn't like the art."

"Mother will hate that."

"Exactly!" The elder man looked at the painting and then back at his son. He smiled. "The artist is even more beautiful than the painting." Then he raised his eyebrows mischievously. Anexus dropped the papers he had brought on the desk and walked out.

He called her on the phone and she answered before the end of one ring. "I knew it was your house. I saw your pictures on the wall. You have a brother and a mother and a father. A sister-in-law. All right there in Trinidad. I should have known better. Really, I should have known."

"He wants to invite you over for tea."

"He already has, Jean. I'll be there on Wednesday."

"Don't call me Jean."

"In your fantasy you want me to be your wife, but you don't even tell me your real name."

"It's not my real name."

On Wednesday Jean arranged to be away all day. On Wednesday night when he went to his parents' house the painting was still hanging in the study. He sat there until his father found him.

"Jean, I've bought the painting. The artist charged me a pretty penny. But your mother approved after all."

Jean had that feeling again. The one where he wanted to say something or do something big. He had rehearsed it in his mind. But now he couldn't say it. His father patted him on the head. "Maybe you should rethink NYU. I've enjoyed getting to know you better, but it might be good for you to explore the world and such."

Jean Monroe nodded.

When he went to her that weekend there was a man in the house with her. He rushed at him and started to beat him with his fists. The man hollered and Usha came rushing out with a tray of tea service in her arms. "He's the photographer. What the hell are you doing?"

The photographer stumbled to the couch in confusion. Jean

stepped back and looked at Usha. "Where did you get that teapot and cups?"

"A gift from Patrique."

"For what?"

She rested it down. Patrique was a good friend. One of her friends who had become their friend and visited them in Gasparee and invited them to his parties. Patrique made a lot of money off his pottery. He made entire plate and cup sets for rich white people not unlike the Monroes. "A gift for what?" He repeated with suspicion.

"For us." She breathed. "An engagement gift."

In the kitchen she took out a cigarette and blew out of the window. The smoke came drifting back into her face. "The photographer is just taking pictures of my paintings. So I can show them more easily."

"Am I paying for it?"

"You don't have to."

"I just wanted to know. I just wanted to know how he was being paid."

She put out her cigarette in the sink then passed him a bag of ice from the freezer. Jean took the ice outside to the photographer with the blooming black eye and said, "Sorry, man," but didn't mean it.

When the photographer left, Jean went into their little bedroom and lay facedown on the bed. He had to do something. But there was no movie or novel or anything to imitate for this. She came into the room. He could smell cigarettes and wine. Those were her smells.

"I'm going to New York," she said. He did not respond. He felt dead. He felt as though the bed was a kind of coffin. "With the money from selling the painting."

"I could have given you that same money," he said, his mouth muffled by the pillow.

"Well, I wanted to earn it as a painter." There was silence. He heard her exhale again and again. "I don't know how I feel about having sex with my patrons. You know? I suppose prostitution is a kind of art, but I'm a painter and that's it." He had no idea what she was talking about but he knew she had rehearsed it. He knew she had been practicing it since she'd put up the painting in his father's study and had seen his picture again and again as she walked through the halls of his parents' big house. "Aren't you going to New York University? I'll be in Greenwich Village. They're so close. Aren't they?"

He sat up and nodded. Yes, in the States they could marry and no one would care. No one would even have to know. He could just be Anexus Corban. "I love you," he said. "That's for real."

That night they took the poor people's barge over to Trinidad to see a movie. It was the first time they had been in Trinidad, on the big island, for something other than a gallery opening or a private artist reception. The movie was a love story and Usha cried all through it. He held her but she kept crying. Not just tears but a heaving that made people stare at them as the theater emptied out. "Why are you crying so hard? What is it?" And she shook her head. But still he felt brave. "This isn't a game, Usha. I'm for real."

He didn't follow her to the plane when she left two weeks later. It happened so quickly that he knew she had been planning it for longer than she had let on. But she gave him her new address in New York and he took this as a kind of concession. When she left he went to their Gasparee home and lay on the bed. "She is gone," he said to himself. "You will follow."

The day after Usha left he bribed Patrique, the ceramist, for her parents' address. He was surprised to find out that it was deep in rural San Fernando—a part of the island he had never been to. He went racing down by car. And then he had to go slow. And then he had to ask people, because the directions, he realized, were not specific. But no one wanted to help him. And he had to beg and get out of the car and give money and finally he found the house and the parents were there at the door as if they had been expecting him. And it dawned on him that after all the questions and turnings around that someone had probably run to warn them that a white man was asking about for the parents of Usha Persaud. At the door they asked him, "What have we done?"

"I am a friend of Usha's," he said. They invited him in.

"She never mention you, sir," said the father as they all sat in the tight living area.

"Are you Mr. Persaud?"

"Yes, sir. And this my wife." The wife did not move to fetch him tea or water. She stared at him as though he were something exotic.

"I just . . ." And Jean looked around. It was a small wood house. This entire living and dining room no bigger than the bedroom in the humble bungalow he and Usha had shared. But on the walls were little paintings of windows. Miniatures. "I know her work. Her paintings."

The father did not look impressed but the mother smiled and leaned forward. A young girl child with thick black hair cut short around her face shied in and sat next to the older woman. Jean stared at her. "I bought one of her paintings," he finished but did not move his eyes away from the child. The parents looked at each other and then back at him.

"We ain seen her in almost three months. She does send money. But that's all."

"Do you know where she is?" he said with a sudden panic.

"She's in the U.K."

"Pardon me? I didn't hear . . ."

"Our Usha. She is in London. In the U.K."

Jean went to New York University that year. And he did not look for her. She had lied to him. It was a game after all. Perhaps by now she had sold his engagement ring. But then that would make his heart go soft because he had given her an engagement ring that was small and plain and way below his means. And yet while he was in the city he was filled with that feeling that she was there. That she was close. That if he just walked faster around a corner. If he just got to a bakery a little earlier. If he just went to one art opening instead of another, that she would be there and they could start over. They had only known each other for three months.

He studied for a degree in art history, which his father wrote to him was flippant but okay if it included estate management and museum curatory. It did not. After graduation he did not move home. He thought he would travel. He would study art all over the Caribbean. He thought he would start with the smaller islands, and the Virgin Islands were interesting because half was British and the other half American and he liked being able to visit America by just taking a boat from the British Tortola where he stayed. But he found that much of the art in the galleries of the V.I. was by European and American expatriates and covered Carnival and beaches, but not much else. The native painters there worked humble jobs as carpenters or fishermen and kept their masterpieces on their own walls—afraid of the corruption from the outside world that would settle like a film on their work. They were like superheroes. They taught secondary school English by day and then flashed paint around by night. It was hard for Jean Monroe to study them. It was hard to learn. Whenever he went to a gallery the docents or the owner would take him to look at their new acquisitions. When he asked for native painters, they would shake their heads as though scolding. "No, we don't have that. Everyone asks, but we don't have it. Sorry, Mr. Monroe."

He lived like this for three years. On Tortola, where the art world was very small, only four or five full galleries on the whole rock, he was known and thought to be a kind of eccentric genius. He never bought paintings but he could talk about them for hours over a cigarette and a glass of wine. The expat women flirted with him, but he insisted that he was married and a faithful man. They giggled and never believed him. He survived by writing letters to his mother and father, who thought he had gone mad but sent him money anyway. And then he began to write Usha. He wrote to her again and again, mailing the letters to the rough address in San Fernando. He started them all the same way: "Dearest Usha. If I should die first I will have my ashes sent to you . . ."

And then a letter came from his mother that there had been a fire on Gasparee. That everything had burned down. All the buildings. Everything. The letter stayed in his fist for five hours. First he sat in his small room and tried to imagine the island of his best youth black with soot. Then he went out into the streets where there were bars frequented by tourists and newcomers and he drank Trinidadian rum and told everyone in a loud voice that this is what his wife's crotch tasted like. Then he staggered back to his apartment and lay face down on the bed not knowing what to do, until he fell asleep and the letter slowly unfurled out of his palm.

The letter had not invited him but he still caught a plane that went through Puerto Rico and then directly to Port of Spain. He checked himself into a bed-and-breakfast and for two days he did not call his parents to announce that he had arrived in Trinidad. He went to galleries. On the second afternoon he walked into one and there on the wall was a huge painting with four big windows all open to the sun and shadow. No people in it at all. He stared at it. "Can I help you?" asked the docent and Jean jumped. There was a red dot on the painting that marked it sold.

"Yes," he said. "Yes, yes, yes." But then he could not say anything else.

"She's a native Trini artist," the lady said, looking him over now and wondering if he could afford anything so nice. She offered him a book of Usha Persaud's paintings. It was a hardcover book. He opened it. The woman continued. "We represent her work and her husband's." He dropped the book and then fumbled to pick it up. He was twenty-five years old. In Tortola he had told everyone that his wife was a painter named Usha Persaud.

"Does she have a card? Is there a way that I can get in touch with her?"

"We sell her work. You can talk to me."

"No, no." He considered saying *we are old friends*. Or *we were lovers once*. Or *I am her husband*. "I would like to tell her that I am moved by her work."

The woman reluctantly passed him a card. "Usha Persaud." There were two addresses. One in London and one in New York. He walked out into the quiet street of Cascade. And walked until his legs gave way. "London," he said out loud. "London *and* New York." He sat down on the side of the road and began to weep.

Now Anexus Corban awoke in his condo and saw that it was still dark. He stretched, ignoring the painting as he did in the morning, and went for his shower. At the breakfast table he drank coffee and ate a large bowl of Cream of Wheat, both heaped with sugar.

The first apartment he lived in when he moved from the British Tortola to the U.S. St. Thomas had been in the back rooms of what was now the International Shop of Coffins. His shop. It had been in a place on island where it was cheap to live and when he'd leased it from the owners they had been happy. It was a hundred-year lease. Now the land that the shop sat on was worth enough for a man to retire on and live out his years in comfort. But he would not allow the owners to break the lease and the owners were a big family who could never decide what would be done with the land even if Corban did let it go. He was not often bothered.

When he returned from Trinidad with Usha's painting under his arm, he had thought he would settle in Tortola and open a wood shop there. He would receive the initial wood free from his father's company—now run by his brother. But when he returned to Tortola he had introduced himself as Anexus Corban and the people who knew him laughed and continued to call him Monroe. "Jean Monroe is dead," he said. Some tried because they could see he was serious. The secretive native artists called him Anexus because they understood the need to live more than one life. But the gallery owners and art patrons did not take the Trinidadian seriously. So he left. And when he moved to St. Thomas he wrote Anexus Corban on his lease. He was given a driver's license and he made business cards for himself. Soon the only thing that revealed the existence of Jean Corban Monroe was his Trinidadian passport.

He thought he would make art out of the wood his brother sent. He made boxes and painted them and thought they were very modern. They were splashed with every color to imitate the sunset. He thought they would be like little postmodern metaphors of the home. They opened only halfway or didn't open at all or opened to reveal a wall of wood. He made them again and again trying to perfect his technique. It was not subconscious. He was very consciously thinking that he would take pictures and send those pictures to Usha's gallery and then Usha would see them. And then she would call him and she would fly to St. Thomas and they would commence a lifelong love affair that her husband would never know about—or, if he dreamed bravely and wildly, maybe she would leave her husband and make a home with him.

And then one day Anexus sat down to a *National Geographic*

and there were the coffins of the artisans of Ghana. Coffins shaped like the thing most reminiscent of the deceased. There were coffins like domes with the checkered black and white of a soccer ball. There were coffins painted with murals of the village where the deceased had been born. The custom-made coffin movement had spread to other West African countries. And he looked at his boxes and thought that he had been making coffins and never known.

But these artisan coffins were different. They were plain on the inside. They were not for the deceased. They were for those left behind. He understood this. He drew up a design for an urn and sent the sketches to a contractor in Accra. Three months later they sent back the heavy silver in the shape of a miniature Gasparee island. He ordered two coffins in the shape of houses and within a week they had been sold. He opened the International Shop of Coffins.

After he polishes the silver Gasparee urn with toothpaste and a firm-bristled toothbrush, he sits down at the breakfast table to begin his newest note to Usha. To the address of the gallery in Port of Spain now because he no longer wants her husband to find them. All these years she has never written back, but then again he is not sure she ever gets the notes. He begins it as he always has: "Dearest Usha. When I die I will have my ashes sent to you. You may scatter them over the shores of Gasparee." But then he stops. Carefully, he tears that page from the pad and begins anew. "Dear Usha. Perhaps this will be my last letter. I only want to say, I have only ever wanted to say, that because of you I was raised from a kind of death . . ."

III. Gita "Pinky" Manachandi

The children's coffins are from West Africa. He imports them. They are in shapes that a child's body would be happy to lie in—living or dead. One is shaped like a sneaker. It sits in the middle of the room as though a giant lost it in a stroll through the building. It is white and has a Nike swoop on the side. The laces are made of cloth, but the rest of it is made of wood. There is also a lollipop one, the candy part painted in blue and green and yellow swirls, the stick—where the child's legs would go—painted an authentic bone white. Corban's favorite is the baby treasure chest. It is mahogany and, in fact, it is a treasure chest in every way. Only that inside it is lined with satin and when it closes it is airtight.

The store is never crowded, so often when the proprietor, Anexus Corban, and his friend Father Simon Peter are there together they can talk as candidly as two men with pasts too illuminated for forgetting can talk. This day Simon Peter sits at the stool reserved for him and begins. "Do you have anything new in, Corban?" But before Anexus can respond with a mention of the glass windows he's just installed, two girls in school uniforms walk in.

"School project," the blond one says as she waves her notebook at Anexus. He knows they are lying. He knows that though he is running an honest and important business, for some his shop is just a curiosity. Like everyone, the girls are attracted to the children's coffins, but the dark-haired one slinks away shyly to the Mexican coffins that are closer to the counter, where there is less light.

Corban comes from behind the counter, where he displays things like folded silk shrouds that look like nightgowns and tiny prayer books from every God-fearing religion he knows. He asks the girls if they need some help.

"We're picking our coffins," says the brown girl.

The other opens her eyes at her and interjects: "For a history project."

The girls wear ties. They are seniors in secondary school. Private school, by the colors they're wearing, but Corban can't tell which one.

Father Simon is annoyed at them. He does not know them. They do not go to the Catholic school. They are an interruption from his favorite part of the day. He tries to overcome this. "What is the topic of the assignment?"

"Death," the fair one says.

"The history of death?" asks Simon with what sounds like disbelief.

"The history of mourning," the brown-skinned one interjects. She is thinking that this place is like a museum of death. No, no, a gallery of mourning. She sees the simple wooden coffin, the kind that the Baha'is get buried in because it is all pine. It's all natural and will go back into the land without harm. The girl likes this idea in theory, but still to her the coffin looks very sad.

Her name is Gita Manachandi. That is what her parents named her and when they gave her that name they expected that it would stay put until she married and it would turn to her husband to rename her—last and first name both. A brand-new name for her rebirth into wifedom. But Gita did not stay put. She did not always go by Gita. She would not ever go by any husband-given name either. It was not that she did not like the name Gita. It was just that early on her best friend had begun calling her Pinky because . . . well, because of a mistake, as is the case with the birth of so many nicknames. Perhaps Gita too was a mistake. Pinky became Pinky in the second grade when her family moved from Bombay to the island and Leslie Dockers asked her her name and she said it but with shyness and Leslie thought she said Pinky and that was that. The teachers did not call her Pinky. Her parents did not call her Pinky. In the classroom and in her home (one was only an extension of the other) she was Gita. In the playground and in the street (one was only an extension of the other) she was Pinky. She and Leslie Dockers were a pair. Their mothers had approved of the friendship when the girls were young for the mistaken reason that each family felt the other would help with assimilation to island life. The Manachandis thought that Leslie's family was Creole—the white French they had heard were native to some of the islands. The Dockers thought Gita was Trini—Indo-Caribbean from Trinidad. But neither family was from the islands and by the time each family began to question the need for this friendship, it was too late. The Manachandis were from Bombay. The Dockers were actually from Leeds.

The girls became island girls of their own accord and by the time the Dockers or the Manachandis realized that actually, they did not want their girl children to be islanders at all, it was too late. It was not that she was Gita-Pinky. She did not feel as though she lived on any hyphen or margin. She was both or either.

In the shop Pinky listens to the priest talk to Leslie about what mourning is like in Gambia and the Catholic Church. She doesn't know what grief is like in India, though at her house it means loud phone calls to living family and quiet talks with the dead.

Leslie, who is not listening at all, stoops down to inspect the little car coffin. Pinky wanders over to the Guadeloupe one with her pen and notebook ready. The coffin is open to show the Virgin emblazoned on the inside. She leans into it as though wanting to feel the satin on her face. She is thinking of her mother. Father Simon, watching her, wants to pull her back. He is afraid that perhaps the lid will come crashing down. His body tenses with this feeling but he knows it is not his business to tell her what to do in Corban's gallery. He stays quiet. Pinky peeks over at Corban but Corban is watching Leslie who is lying on her belly on the floor to better see into the coffin car.

"Damn," Leslie says. "It's got leather lining in this bad boy."

Simon watches Pinky put her hand into the coffin and touch the inside. This is allowed but she does it as if she is afraid to be caught. Now Corban sees her. She is squeezing the cushioning. She looks up and pulls her hand out. "It's luxurious," she says. "You could sleep in it. How much does it cost?"

"A lot," answers Corban suspiciously. But Pinky is bolder than she seems. She lingers as though she were a real customer. She asks questions like What kind of people buy these? Where did you get it? When people come in do they shop, do they bargain or do they just buy? Then she pulls out her fifty and buys some marigolds that are in a tiny clear box. They are fresh and soft. They are the same color as the Virgin coffin. Corban feels more warmly toward the girl then.

"It's so beautiful," she says, referring still to the coffin as Leslie pulls her to leave. "It's like art." The girls were on their way to a party.

Gita was pretty smart by all definitions, but no one thought there was anything so special about this. She was a hard worker. She studied with the ferocity of someone in love. And this *was* special. She was respected for this by teachers and sought out for guidance by students. Her parents, who imagined her growing up to be someone's wife, approved because her study habits meant she would be a desirable catch—a woman who could bear smart and studious sons. Gita did not see it this way. She imagined that she was growing up to be an obstetrician-gynecologist. In her dreams she treated immigrant Indian women and slipped them birth control while their husbands waited in the lounge. Because she was darker than most of the other Indian girls who came straight from India, she was often mistaken even by her own for being Guyanese or Trinidadian. To be called Guyanese or Trini was thought to be an insult by some in the subcontinent community. But Pinky did not take it this way. Those island Indians had children who spoke loose and didn't go to Hindu classes on Saturdays. The girls didn't think twice before dating native boys. Pinky called herself black and no one who heard her objected—she never called herself this in front of her parents.

Up until the first two weeks of her senior year Pinky's routine was the same.

"Gita! Get up my love. Gita!" She was the only child and much was made of her. The maid, Mrs. Delroy, would tickle her toes with the straw of the broom until Gita pulled her feet away and bolted upright. She would go to the shower. Which was her shower alone. As she got older her showers became longer and by the second week of being a senior in high school she was taking forty-five minutes—something of a crime on an island where rainwater was stored under the house like treasure. She liked the water hot, despite the heat of the island. She liked it scalding hot. Her mother would come and knock on the door. "Too much heat! You're going to wrinkle young!" Then Gita would blast on the cold water and squeal, turning circles under the shower so that she could erase the wrinkling. For many years she stepped out of the shower and reached for her towel without even glancing at herself in the bathroom mirror that covered an entire wall. But since becoming a senior and since Leslie had lost her virginity last year, Gita has become more interested in her own body, and more bold with it.

Now she would step out of the shower and dry herself off with the delicate pats her mother had taught her would not dry out the skin. When the steam evaporated Gita would hang up the towel and walk slowly to the mirror. She looked at herself as she brushed her teeth and arranged her hair. Sometimes, if she was thinking of Mateo Parone, she would look serious and sexy like she imagined Leslie might when she was doing it with Ben Jamison. Then she would blow a kiss to her reflection but this would be too much and she would collapse into giggles. Her uniform would be laid out on the newly made bed when she emerged.

At the breakfast table her mother and Mrs. Delroy would lay out jelly and tea and tofu eggs. The two women would be quarreling with each other in the way master and servant have quarreled for centuries. Neither one really able to understand the other even after sixteen years making breakfast together in the same kitchen. Mrs. Delroy had a thick Kittitian accent, while Mrs. Manachandi had never lost her northern Indian lilt. This is not to say that the Manachandis treated Mrs. Delroy as though she was less. They called her Mrs. Delroy. They gave her that respect. The other new Indian families called their maids by their first names and talked badly about them at Indian-only functions. When Mrs. Delroy and Mrs. Manachandi stood in the kitchen together they seemed as though they were two halves of the same person.

Mr. Manachandi would also be at the table, reading yesterday's paper. He wished that the island had a paper delivery system so he could read that morning's paper at the breakfast table as businessmen did in England, but it was not so. Mr. Manachandi had never lived in the U.K., coming directly from Bombay, so he would never have the paper delivered to him in time for that morning's breakfast. He always read the news a day late.

Gita and her father ate breakfast together. He quizzed her on yesterday's news, which she had read yesterday before she arrived at her father's store to deliver the paper. He imagined that she would marry the son of one of his fellow jewelry store owners in Tortola or St. Thomas. As each son returned from the U.S. or the U.K. with his business degree Mr. Manachandi would scrutinize him. But either the young man would marry someone already out of secondary school, or there would be a scandal with a native girl and the boy would be sent to St. Vincent to recover. Mr. Manachandi wasn't sure which shop heir Gita would marry but he knew that she would have to be witty and up on local politics to win the best mate. She would also have to know math quite well and the value of different bits of gold. So often at the breakfast table he would test her with problems of centimeters and karats. He might present her with a pair of heart-in-hand gold earrings with diamond studs. "How much do you think I bought this for?" She would smile over her tea. "Seventy dollars a bag." "How much should I sell it for?" She stirred her tea. "Is it Christmas or regular season?" "Christmas." "Is your customer a tourist or a local?" "A local." She tapped her fingers on the tablecloth. They made a thudding but musical sound. "Two hundred dollars at first. Bring it down to one-fifty. If they don't take it wait until they come back the next day. Say something like *Yes, I remember you. And now this is the last pair.* One-twenty is the lowest." "Too high." her father would say. "You'll never sell anything. People will think you're cheating them." But later that day someone would come into his store and he would say, "Look at the diamonds. They're real. These are eighteen-karat gold. Handmade, each one. One-twenty is the lowest I can go. I'll give it to you for one-twenty." Secretly he wished Gita would never have to marry. That she would come to the shop and work with him like a son.

But this had changed in the second week of Gita's senior year. She'd had a quiz in calculus that most everyone was sure to fail, except her. She and Leslie hung about in the school courtyard and talked about college. Leslie would go over to St. Thomas, to UVI. So would Gita. Leslie because it was cheaper and she wasn't incredibly academically inclined. She wanted to play volleyball and the college had a good team that competed on other islands. Gita because, though she was a sure thing for a full Barnard scholarship and even had Wellesley and Spelman as backups, her mother didn't want her to go far away to college. Too many girls came back with American boyfriends or with ideas about never getting married.

"There's Ben," said Pinky, pointing with her chin across the school yard where a pickup basketball game was in progress.

"Screw Ben."

"Why?"

"He horned out on me over the summer."

"How do you know? He was in Atlanta all summer."

"Grapevine, Pinky."

"Why you ain tell me, girl? Dang. We need to get you a next man."

"I ain tell nobody. We need to get *you* a man, period."

"Good luck."

"I telling you. Fine ass Mateo is all over you."

"Mateo's an idiot."

"But he's fine and you're smart enough for the both of you."

"And what I going to do with him? He can't even drive his car without crashing it. Good luck getting a black guy to pass my parents' husband meter."

"He's half black. And Pinky, really. Stop thinking about stupidness. You practice first with boyfriends. Don't even think about husband. Boyfriends are more fun anyway. Husbands are soo boring. You ain noticed?"

Pinky nodded. "Do you think you'd ever do it like on the kitchen table?"

"Do what?"

"You know."

"Oh, you slut." Leslie paused and looked out at the boys across the school yard. "Yeah. I think I would. Would you?"

"I guess if my husband wanted to."

They nodded together. Leslie had only done it three times with

Ben before school let out and he went to Atlanta to spend the summer with his mother. She said that it hurt every time but she expected that if they'd kept doing it all summer by now it would be feeling good. Pinky had shrugged. She didn't like the idea of waiting for it to feel good. Why can't it feel good right away? It feels good to him. She imagined that when she became an obstetrician-gynecologist she would make sure it felt good for all women all the time.

Leslie picked up her schoolbag. "You want a drop?"

"Sure."

"Hey, we gone," called Leslie to the guys still playing basketball.

Mateo dribbled the ball with one hand and put the other one up to signal a time-out. "Hey, I going see you ladies at Vive tonight?" His voice had become deep over the summer and to Pinky it sounded rich and matched the musky way he smelled.

Leslie gave their response. "Maybe."

Mateo was looking at Pinky. "You too, Pinky?"

"You know I'm bagged up."

"Sneak out," said Mateo, dribbling the basketball hard, slamming into the ground, while the other guys waited for him. She laughed at his suggestion. She flipped her hair and then felt stupid for doing so.

In the car Leslie didn't look at her friend as she maneuvered out of the tight space. "Really, Pinky. We've been friends so long and I'm sick of giving you the business secondhand. I mean, I go with you to all the Divali stuff but you never come to the club. 'Bout time. You's seventeen, woman."

"Screw you. Divali is like a religious thing. The club is not."

"It could be."

"Whatever." But she wanted to go. Maybe tonight she would have that fight. She would cry and ask her parents why they'd brought her here to this island only to tell her she couldn't be a part of it. Or maybe she would ask to stay over at Leslie's and even though her mother didn't like Leslie so much she wouldn't have much reason to say no. The last time she'd asked her mother had said she was too old for sleepovers. But that was a year ago. Maybe it's time to ask again.

They kissed on the cheek before Leslie drove off. When Pinky walked into the shop she knew something was wrong. Only the workers were there. Not her uncle Rommy or her father. Just the black women who helped sell the T-shirts. They were behind the counters on both sides of the store. One came out and touched Gita's face with the palm of her hand.

"Gita, girl. You need to call home."

When she did no one answered. Then the phone rang in the shop. The woman nodded into the receiver. When she hung up she motioned for them to start locking up. "Sorry," she said to the customers, with an astuteness Gita had never noticed before. "Family emergency. We must lock up the store now." They closed the store in silence. Gita did not ask the women what was going on. They all went and stood outside in the hot sun. The street was crowded with tourists half-naked in bathing suits speaking French and Spanish, and an English that grated at Pinky's ears. The two women spoke to each other in a patois Gita did not understand. The traffic was heavy with taximen yelling "Back to the ship" as they loaded on any tourists tired of shopping. After half an hour Gita could see her father's sedan inching up the street.

Her uncle was driving. He was sitting straight up in the car and didn't look at Gita as one of the women opened the passenger door for her. "What's going on, Uncle?" But he shook his head quietly and drove. When they turned into the hospital parking lot Gita could feel her bowels growing tight. *Not Dada,* she thought. She held her belly as they walked through the lobby and took an elevator to the second floor. There her father was sitting in a chair in the waiting room. When he saw her he turned away as though she had insulted him. She went to him anyway. "Dada?" She put out her hand. He moved from it. Gita turned and walked past her uncle, who was just standing there dumb, and went to the nurses' station. They called for a doctor. A doctor came. She was young and brown-skinned. Her hair was in a ponytail like a student's.

"Are you Gita?" the doctor asked.

Gita nodded.

"Come, let's sit." Gita followed her to a corner.

"Did you know that your mother was ill?"

"Just tell me."

The young doctor narrowed her young eyes. She seemed to be either scrutinizing Gita or fighting back her own tears.

"Your mother died this afternoon. Your father is very upset and he wanted me to talk to you. I want you to know . . ."

As the doctor talked Gita heard her father let out a loud wail. She turned to look at him. He was looking at her and weeping. At that moment Gita decided that no, she would not become a doctor.

Gita's family was all in India or Britain. Uncle Rommy wasn't even her real uncle. He was someone her father knew from India and had invited to help with the shop. Her mother's family wrote that they would take her in at their house in Mumbai because Gita needed a woman's hand to raise her. Pinky told her father she wanted to stay with him. He nodded absently because he had never intended to send her off. On the phone he fought with his mother-in-law. "She is my daughter. She is my responsibility. What makes you think my Leela would have wanted her to go back to you? So what if I am a man." But really he and his mother-in-law were thinking the same thing. The mother-in-law was saying, "Gita should not be where her mother is not. And I am her grandmother which is a kind of mother." The father was saying "Gita should not be where her mother is not. Her mother is here. Her mother is coming back."

Mr. Manachandi talked to his wife at night. Gita would walk past the door and hear his side of the conversation. At first she thought he was on the phone but then he would say, "Ey, Leela?" and there would be no audible response. He seemed quite normal otherwise. The shop did not falter. He did not crash the car. He did not get mad. He simply talked to his dead wife at night. He simply slept on only one side of his bed.

Mrs. Delroy served them breakfast but for the first week she did it all in tears, then she would go to the kitchen to eat alone and cry. Mr. Manachandi stopped asking his daughter about weights and costs. He started to ask her about her future. "Are you going to college?" he asked her. And she realized that she had only had that conversation with her mother. She was aware of the betrayal when she answered: "I've been thinking of Barnard."

He nodded. "That would be a good school for you." She lowered her head and felt that pain in her bowels again. Her mother was dead and now she would get to go to Barnard.

"What will you do, Dada?"

"I will stay here," he said softly. And if he had been talking more loudly he might have completed his thought out loud as well. "I will stay here because I am waiting for your mother to come back."

Gita's mourning was different. Her mother died and suddenly her own life began. Suddenly she could go Barnard; she even applied as early decision. Suddenly she could spend the night at Leslie's without a fight. Suddenly no one scrutinized her clothes when she went out . . . didn't check the length of her skirts or the transparency of her blouses.

Gita and her father were invited to many Indian houses for dinner. She was the same good Gita with the aunties. They caressed her and gave her their cell phone numbers, saying to call if anything. But those aunties had children around Gita's age and though they were not Gita's close friends they were still like cousins. They knew her business. They saw that she stayed later on campus than usual. They saw that she and Mateo Parone looked at each other with little flirty smiles during class. Her grades slipped just a little in calculus. Soon people were talking: She's changed since her mother died. She's not our same Gita anymore.

But during the Divali celebration she danced onstage with two other girls to a Bollywood song that even the aunties liked. And so no one had the heart to tell the widower to keep his daughter under wraps. But then before school was even out for the fall semester the letter came from Barnard.

When her father dropped the mail on the dinner table it was there among the endless catalogs of her mother's that kept coming. It was a slim envelope, and this made Gita's heart pound. She knew that if the envelope came back thick and heavy it meant an acceptance. A flat letter could go either way. She took it to her room because Mrs. Delroy came in the evenings now and cooked dinner for them and sometimes she even stayed later than that to help clean. Gita stared at the letter and wondered if she should pray over it or just rip it open. It was too late for prayer she decided. She would just rip. But delicately. She found a letter opener and carved at the envelope. "We are thankful but we are sorry . . ." She read it over and over again. She must be reading it wrong. She looked at the back. She looked at the salutation to see if that was her name. Dear Gita Manachandi. They had even spelled it correctly. Rejection. Barnard had said no.

Gita rolled into a ball on the floor and shook. She wanted her mother now. She wanted her mother to come and hold her and say Barnard wasn't worthy of her. Her mother would have said "I told you so." And Gita would have felt better because perhaps her mother was right. She could have told herself that her mother had willed the rejection, that it was her mother's fault even. But now her mother wasn't even there to blame and all she could do was cry and shake and then call for her father who didn't come because he couldn't hear her, and it all seemed anticlimatic when she stood up and went to begin a long shower, taking the rejection letter with her and letting it get wet until it melted down the drain.

How did Gita mourn? She mourned by becoming Pinky only.

She had been walking back and forth in front of the coffin shop for days. Her mother had not been buried in a coffin. She had been cremated. Her ashes were sent to Mumbai to her family as was the custom. Mr. Manachandi didn't mind this. The presence of the urn would only make him think his wife was dead. Gita watched the shop from across the street for weeks. She noticed the small priest go in. She noticed that otherwise mostly women went in. That many of them were older women, perhaps burying parents. She would stand across the street and watch them and her stomach would hurt. Perhaps she was getting an ulcer.

"That place is creepy, Pinky."

"Come on, Les. I just want to see."

"Why?"

"Because."

"I don't think it's a good idea."

"Come on. I'll go with you to Vive. I just want to see inside. Aren't you curious?"

"No, Pinky. Not at all. And you're never coming to Vive. Even with Mateo begging you. I swear if you go he'll ask you out."

"I'll go. Now come on."

"Fine, fine. But I don't think it's a good idea." Leslie brought her friend's face to hers. "You okay?"

"I'm good," Pinky said pushing Leslie's hand from her face. "I'm just curious."

This is how Pinky mourned her mother. She and Leslie went to the coffin shop. They pretended they were there for an assignment. And this one? she'd asked Corban. The treasure chest? And what about this shiny Virgin Mary one? The priest offered a brief history of mourning in the Catholic Church and a conflicting history of mourning in Africa. The dignity of mourning and the shamelessness of it. How in his country, women were hired to cry and men were hired to sing the dead one's praises. How in Catholicism when a husband dies it is custom that the wife is the last one at the grave site on the funeral day. What is mourning like in India? Pinky didn't know. "I'm from Trinidad," she lied. She'd snuck a feel of the Virgin Mary coffin and would have stayed there among the funeral things if Leslie hadn't said, "I'm leaving you here if you don't come now." On the way out Pinky bought some fresh marigolds from the nice old man. In the car Leslie arranged them in her hair. "Tonight, you get Mateo Parone."

Pinky nodded. Yes. She would.

As she was getting dressed and her father was reading his first installment of the *New Yorker* magazine she shouted through the door that she would be staying at Leslie's for the weekend. "Will you be okay, Dada?"

"Yes, my love," he called back.

"I'll call tonight and tomorrow."

"You don't have to," he said and turned a page. Smiled at a cartoon.

"But you'll be alone for a few days."

"No, I won't."

Pinky pursed her lips and walked out into the living room.

But without looking up from his magazine he said something unexpected. "Mrs. Delroy will be here." Mrs. Delroy had just started coming on weekends.

That night Pinky wore a dress to match her name. A magenta dress that wasn't even hers. "The sluttiest thing I own," said Leslie, laughing. But Pinky didn't laugh. She looked at herself in the mirror and thought of her mother in her red wedding sari. In the picture her father wore a European suit and had thick sideburns. Her father looked like a child of an era; her mother looked era-less. She was not sure which was better. Now she looked at herself in the mirror and puckered. Her dress was a spandex that stuck and stretched. It was open at the back and ended above the knee. There was a slit at the left thigh. It was indecent. Pinky thought to herself that she would never look like this again. But in the next instant she said out loud, "This is what I always want to look like."

Vive was not the hot smoky place she had expected. There was a huge balcony for the smokers and no one could smoke inside. "So your hair won't smell bad afterward," shouted Leslie as they walked around the loud dance floor. Leslie had taught her the screw face. The club was about attitude. First they walked. Scoped out the club. They kept their backs straight. They flipped their hair. Keep a screw face. Don't smile unless you see someone you know and then hug and air-kiss, and if it's a guy wait for him to offer a drink. Never say no to a free drink. It was a masquerade. They were pretty. They were desirable. Everyone was supposed to know it. When you dance make sure you're not next to a girl who can dance better than you. Make sure you make eye contact with a good-looking guy, but let him come over to you. Dance even when you're tired. Dance even if you're sweaty and tired. Take off your shoes if you need to; you can keep them behind the d.j. booth. Only stop dancing if a guy offers you a drink. And then ask for something good. What's good? Get like a sex on the beach. Or a fuzzy navel. Or a blow job. No, don't get that. That's taking it too far. Get a painkiller. Never get what he's having. Man drinks taste nasty. Like Long Island iced tea. Disgusting. That's a get-drunk drink. You just want to look good when you're drinking. In fact, stick to sex on the beach. It matches your dress. And me. I'll get blue lagoons all night.

Outside on the deck they drank their colorful drinks and cooled off. Pinky's hair was plastered onto her face. It wasn't hot but they had been dancing and so they had been sweating. The d.j. had played dancehall and hip-hop but not calypso yet. Pinky didn't really know how to move to hip-hop or dancehall. She was waiting for calypso. "They play it last," explained Leslie.

"I can't believe I'm wearing this dress." Pinky felt exposed out on the deck. On the dance floor she had felt hidden by the other bodies. "No Mateo," she said out loud and felt relieved, and then disappointed by her own relief.

"No Mateo yet. You just wait." Leslie lit a tiny black cigar with a plastic tip to protect her lips. She blew out over the balcony.

The bells and knocking of calypso came on. They left their drinks and moved inside. Leslie flicked her cigar over the side of the balcony. Inside the dance floor was wild. Women had their skirts hoisted up and men had their hands in the air. People were dancing on top of the tables and on top of the couches. Women leaned on the back of chairs to steady themselves. Leslie and Pinky didn't look for an empty space. They walked in and danced where they ended up. Pinky felt good now. She didn't need Mateo after all. She swung her hips and her heavy wet hair. And then just like that Mateo came up behind her, as though it was something he did often. He had that rich musky smell and he held her hips in his hands as he pulled her body closer to his. Her first thought was that this was not right. Then her next thought was that this was very right. People in the club were screaming the words to the song. Peolpe were knocking their hips into one another. The bass beat twice and people stomped their feet twice. Pinky put her hands over Mateo's so she could follow his rhythm. She looked around realizing that Leslie was not beside her. But then there she was. A white girl was hard to miss in the dark club. Leslie had her palms flat on the wall, her arms straight and stiff, and her backside rolling on the crotch of a boy who had graduated from school two years ago. Pinky wanted to laugh. It seemed so funny, all of this. All this display. All this. And on Monday they'd all be back in school in their uniforms, and perhaps that was its own kind of pretend. Mateo turned her around and now they faced each other and though this was less vulgar, because less of their bodies touched, it seemed so much more intimate. He leaned his face into her neck and she felt his lips on her wet skin as if he had tapped directly on her spine. She shivered and pulled back. And left the dance floor.

Mateo stood on the dance floor for a moment before following her. "You okay?" he asked once they were outside. "Yeah. Are you okay?" "Yeah." They were quiet for a long time. "I wanted to kiss you in there." "I know." "Can I kiss you now?" "I don't know, actually." "Can I try?" She nodded. He leaned forward and she turned to give him her cheek. "If we get married," he said, smiling, "we'll be doing a lot more than kissing." "What?" And then he kissed her open mouth and she felt his soft lips and his wet tongue and she jumped back. And she smiled and then she backed away some more and then she ran away, back into the cavern of the club, her heels clinking on the deck like knocking bones. She had had her first kiss and it had been with Mateo, and had he asked her to marry him? This was like a Bollywood movie, except with real kissing. She needed to talk to Leslie.

But inside the dance floor was a living mass of its own. It was hot and steamy now. And sticky. And the people were not concerned about the expensiveness of their dresses or the intricacies of their hairdos. And the floor was sticky and difficult to walk on in Leslie's heels. Mateo had kissed her and now Gita did not know what to do. It had felt animal-like. It had felt slutty. She didn't want to see him again. But she wanted to see him every day for the rest of her life. And that was silly. Did she really believe that Mateo Parone was the kind of boy who kissed a girl and then married her? Was he? He would want sex first or at least dating a little. He would want to go to college and all that. Wouldn't he? Would he? Was he playing a game? Why would he say something so serious if he wasn't serious?

She felt sick. Her head felt sick. She thought she might throw up. She wandered to the bathroom. "Are you plastered?" someone asked. She shook her head but felt as though she must get away from the crowd. "Man, Pinky Manachandi is plastered."

She hiked up her pink dress without care for ripping her nylons and sat on the toilet until she felt as though the kiss and the drink were gone from her. When she emerged she felt better and more stupid. Had she even kissed Mateo? And had she run away afterward?

"Where have you been?" Leslie's voice was hoarse from shouting song lyrics.

"In the bathroom."

"Were you puking?"

"I don't think so."

"Mateo just tell me he kissed you and then you ran away."

"He's lying."

"Oh man, Pinky. Now what you going do? Do you like him like that?

"I going marry him. My dad will let me. He's screwing the maid tonight."

"What?"

"Nothing."

"Are you boyfriend and girlfriend now?"

"I don't think so."

"You should find out." Leslie paused. "Do you even have his number?"

"I don't think so."

"Pinky, what the hell? Let's go give him yours."

They walked around the club, which was now playing its jazzy theme song. People were leaving. The lights would go on soon and no one could look good under those lights. Some stood around and waited. Others talked loudly about heading out to Smitie's. No one was dancing anymore. The dance floor looked like a sad dirty place. Mateo wasn't there. Outside they walked over the gravel to Pinky's car. In the floodlights Pinky noticed the ream in her stockings. "Bound to happen," said Leslie. "Take them off. I'll drive."

"That's okay," said Pinky. "I'll take them off right here." She sat in the driver's seat of the sedan that had been her mother's and ripped the stockings until they were little pieces of silk. Afterward she felt cooler and less restrained. She started the car and rolled down their windows with the automatic buttons.

"Hey, Pinky. Stop running away from me."

"Whooo," whispered Leslie from the passenger's seat. "He's good."

Pinky put the car back in park and told her heart to stop. She wanted really to drive away. She wanted really to wave and honk her horn like others were doing and then go to school on Monday and wait to see if Spelman or Wellesley had accepted her in regular admissions. "Can I get your number?" She nodded but just gripped the wheel. Mateo leaned into the car window, nodding at Leslie just briefly. "Gita, girl. I'm not messing with you. I know this has to be on the down low 'cause of your pops. I'm for real. However you want it, girl. Hey, give me your cell." She kept her hands on the wheel. Leslie dug through the little magenta purse and passed him Pinky's cell phone. He typed his number in. "I put in 'Mary.' That can be my code name. That way when I'm calling no one knows it's a guy. Cool?" And then he backed away a little. "Good night, Les. You take care of my girl." Leslie smiled and waved and reached over to honk Pinky's horn. "Now drive away, Pinky," she said under her breath.

Pinky put the car in gear and drove down the hill. "I have a boyfriend," she said as the air whipped around them. They turned onto the waterfront, which was empty except for the few other clubgoers who had driven this way.

"You have a man, Pinky. Now what you going do with him?"

"I have no idea."

Pinky had not thought of her mother all night. Really, she had done all she could to not think of her mother at all. And when the tourists who were coming from a night at one of the touristy clubs turned into her lane, forgetting the left-hand traffic, Pinky still did not think of her mother. She swerved and their sedan went into a tailspin, then hit the sidewalk and flew, upside down, into the water. Pinky was delirious. She thought only *Mama will be so disappointed*.

Leslie was thinking *are we really upside down?* The car slammed into the water like a boulder and sank as rapidly as a stone. It was dark and they were underwater and they were in a car and they were upside down. It was unusually warm but there was no time to notice such a thing. Leslie released her seat belt. She reached out for Pinky who was facing her. They were looking at each other—Leslie could tell that much. She tugged at Pinky's seat belt. Pinky did not tug back. Pinky only looked at Leslie with her eyes wide open as though she were breathing the water and surprised at her new magic. Leslie's body filled with the burn of the saltwater in her chest but she was a child of the islands and she knew how to hold her breath. She tugged at her friend's seat belt. She pulled at Pinky. This seemed like forever but maybe it was only a few seconds. Five seconds maybe. Leslie's chest hurt and her eyes hurt and she was more afraid than she had been at birth. Five eternal seconds and then she turned to open the door but the door would not open and so she flew through the window and she did not look back but went toward what she hoped with all her heart was the surface and not the sand or out into the ocean. She hit the air and heaved and was surprised to see the streets quiet, as if nothing at all had happened. As if the reckless tourists had never been there. As if her friend was not under the water stuck in her seat belt. She swam until she could walk out. Four more minutes maybe. She ran across the street without looking either way, toward a convenience store that was closed. A minute. She ran toward another store that was up an alley. Five minutes. She was wet and dirty and she babbled to the register man who nodded and handed her the phone. She didn't call the police or the fire station. She called her parents. But all she could say was "Mateo kissed Pinky and now she's over the waterfront. She's in the water and it's only me on land. Just me. Help. Come help." And by then the convenience store owner had used his cell phone to call the police. And by the time the police came and Gita's father came with Mrs. Delroy, it had been almost thirty minutes.

"Why don't you go get her?!" the father shouted before the car had even stopped. Mr. Manachandi left his car like a man on fire and rushed past the police who were gathered around Leslie. He jumped into the water. The police did not stop him. "Part of his mourning," one said to another and jotted the occurrence down in his chart. Mr. Manachandi went under and then came back up. "Help me! Please. I see her. Help me." Mrs. Delroy cried and then screamed and then a police officer said, "Get the old man out of the water." And a young cop took off his gun and jumped in and grabbed Mr. Manachandi and hauled him out. The father looked like an animal. He looked like a wild dead animal. The firemen, who were more trained in dealing with human beings, told him that they needed him over here. Over here. Away from where the divers were going down to cut the body out of its seat belt. And by then Gita had been underwater for forty-five minutes.

In the ambulance Leslie howled as though her own mother was dead. She howled, and then for two days she did not speak at all. When she did it was to ask her own mother why they had not tried to resuscitate her friend. "It was too long underwater. Even if they had gotten her back it would not have been enough of her."

Mrs. Delroy walked into the shop and said "Good afternoon" out of custom. Mr. Corban replied out of the same compulsion. She looked around at the coffins. Mr. Corban thought she must be about Usha's age and sat more erectly in his chair. She walked to the mustard-colored coffin with the Virgin emblazoned on it and caressed its satin lining. The Virgin was reminiscent of the girl's mother. Mrs. Delroy thought this would be best, but she wasn't sure she'd have her way. She looked at Mr. Corban behind the glass counter. "Something for a teenage girl," she said. He nodded with the weight of this request and came out from behind the counter.

The jangle of the door was heard again. Mr. Manachandi walked in slowly with his shoulders stooped over and his hands clasped in front of him. "Do you have a chair?" Mrs. Delroy asked. Mr. Corban rushed back and pulled Father Simon's stool toward the man who said thank you in a voice that seemed to have a hard time getting up his throat.

"This one," Corban said and turned back to Mrs. Delroy. He reached his hand toward the Virgin. "Why, I had a young lady in here last week who loved it. Very stylish and holy all at once. Very good for a young person." Mrs. Delroy nodded and turned to Mr. Manachandi.

"No," the man said quietly and breathed out deeply as though settling in.

Corban studied the man for a moment. "Perhaps you need an urn?" He thought on the ornate silver urn he had polished a few nights ago with toothpaste. That one was his own, but there were others that a teenage girl might appreciate.

"No. No. No," Mr. Manachandi began, his voice still small. He shook his head and closed his eyes, as though to muse on his own desires. Mrs. Delroy turned away from the flashy coffin and walked to stand beside her man. Her shoes made an undignified squeaking noise on the polished floor. Mr. Manachandi opened his eyes. "Something pure and natural," he said firmly. "Something like Gita." His face threatened to crumple into tears but instead he only clenched his fists.

Mr. Corban put his hand to his chin and squeezed it. He looked about and saw the simple pine coffin. He did not think this was the right choice. He wished they would go with the golden casket, but he would show the pine to them anyway. They deserved to make their own mistakes. They looked like two people whose lives were about to begin.

KILL THE RABBITS

For Nicholas Friday

1.
Cooper

It is the night of Easter Sunday. I've already been to chapel and received God on my tongue. I sit in my cell with the lights off. Everyone's light is off. I wait for the man with the cross to begin his walk. He's been doing it once a year for the whole twelve years I've been in here. Carnival is coming in a few weeks. The queens have already had their pageants. The steel bands are practicing every night—until late in the morning. But this man. He will come, I believe. He always comes. I wait for him. And I think about why he is doing his penance. And I think about why I am doing mine.

I have a view of the sea. During Carnival I can hear all the music. I can fling a note down onto the parade revelers, hoping it gets to the big-bum woman I like the best. At night I hang my hands out of the bars, palms open, and cup the salt air. They say they will move me to the big jail in St. Croix, but they haven't yet. Maybe they won't ever. From my cell I can look over the parking lot at Fort Christian and think about how maybe in another earlier life I would be locked up in there instead. In a dark cell with thick red stone walls. But even then I'd have a view of the sea. I've only been in the fort once, for a field trip in seventh grade where I feigned disinterest as I closely studied the walls and passageways for how a man in those days could use shadow and color to escape. Now they use it to give classes to the kids who are really good at painting and drawing. Imagine that. An old jail can be used for art classes.

I wasn't so good at art. I wanted to be a magician. My mother bought me videocassettes that came with foam balls and a magic wand. I studied the cassettes. I rewound them until they warped and would stop and skip and pause at the most inconvenient places. They instructed on how to pinch the foam ball between your knuckles and still wave your hands, which words to avoid with a plastic coin wedged under your tongue. But the biggest part of the magic was the trick of convincing your audience that you have indeed yielded everything—look, my hands are empty, nothing behind my ear, my sleeves are loose. The confidence it took to say "look inside the cup, see nothing is there" even though you know that if they decide to touch the cup, if they ask you to pour water in the cup, if they even walk around to your side of the table to see the back bottom ledge of the cup . . . the trick would fail. Confidence is the biggest trick.

When I was about ten years old I learned to lie. This, as with my other vices, came of love. I loved raw brown sugar. I loved that the grains were thick and amber colored. I loved that if you put some in your mouth you had to crunch on them and they wouldn't melt like the dust of the bleached processed kind. I loved the smell of molasses the brown grains gave off. They were real. The white sugar seemed smooth and fake. Like a girl in my fifth-grade class who wore lipstick. White sugar seemed to be trying hard to be something it was not. We didn't get brown sugar in the house often because it was more expensive. But sometimes my mother would need it. And then I'd find ways to devour it.

On the day I learned to lie I poured myself a glass of milk. To sweeten it I poured in brown sugar straight from the bag. I sipped the milk and continued pouring and sipping until I had a cup of drenched sugar with a shallow layer of milk on top. I was impressed with myself for making this new treat and for hiding it—like a magician. I put away the bag of sugar and sat at the table to eat my milk sugar with a spoon. That was when my mother swung in. If you ask me now I think she must have watched me all along. She must have waited for me. She took out the bag of brown sugar and asked me why the bag was so near empty. I shrugged and sipped my milk—careful not to gather up any of the sugar.

"Cooper. How much sugar you put in your milk?"

"None, Mommy."

"So then where all the brown sugar that was in this bag?"

"I don't know, Mommy."

"You better tell me or you going get beat."

What is the need to have the truth all about? If she knew, why didn't she just take the cup from me? Why was it so important that I confess?

"I don't know where the sugar gone."

"Come here."

I got up from the table and walked to her, not once looking back at my cup to incriminate myself. When I was close enough she grabbed me by the arm like I imagine she must grab robbers on the street before lowering them into her squad car. "Why you lying? Just tell me."

"Mommy, I don't know nothing."

She raised her hand and smacked me on the arm. I still didn't know. She unleashed her belt and brought it down on my back. I still didn't know. Again and again, I didn't know. I crouched on the floor crying. She went to the table and snatched up my cup and poured it out into the sink. I stared with horror and disbelief as the sugar came slopping out.

"A whole cup full of my brown sugar. How did it get there, Cooper?"

I didn't know. I had no idea. She beat me again and again until she was tired and my body was welted. I never ever knew how the sugar got into the cup. And finally she let me be. "You scare me," she said as she left me welted on the kitchen floor.

For the life of me I could not figure out how the sugar got in the cup. Somewhere in my body, I knew I had done it. Somewhere in me was the memory of pouring the sugar in, of crunching the sugar in my teeth. But if you had given me a lie detector test I would have passed. The only rule of good lying is the ability to convince yourself.

So of course I became a thief. I couldn't help the cliché. Which didn't go over well with my mother, who is, you must know, a cop.

My guess is that she's the reason they keep me here in the St. Thomas jail. She likes to visit me and make sure the guards are sneaking me in a bit of the skunk ganja from Jamaica. The inmates here know my mother. They remember that she let them off for speeding once or that she only dragged them home when they'd been caught drinking underage at the club. The other officers really respect her, 'cause she doesn't wear lipstick and put her hair up all nice on the job. When she's in uniform she looks like a man—and most folks think she's at least a dyke. They know that if they're in a tough place, she won't worry about her nails or cry—she'll have their back. And because of her I have my own cell almost. My spare bunk is reserved for people passing through.

Most of the time I'm by myself at night. If the moon is big I'll be looking at the tide pulling in hard and slow. Looking at a crazy man jogging and punching the air like a boxer. Looking at a car drive by every now and then. So it made sense that it was me who saw the white man with the cross on his back. No long robe. No crown of thorns. Just a big wooden cross, bigger than his whole body. And when he stumbled and fell almost into the water, there was no Simon to share the burden of that heavy wood. Just me above, waiting and watching.

2.

Xica

When my mother brought me home from the hospital, two days after I was born, she placed me in a suitcase full of her clothes. I slept in that suitcase full of her clothes for the first year of my life. She wanted me to become something transient. Something very much like clothes. Something that should be easily packed and carried with you. Perhaps even checked in at the airport so that during the plane ride the luggage will be in someone else's care.

It turned out that I would not be so easily transported. The clothes took my smell, be it of pissy diaper or freshly powdered behind. They were my playthings. The buttons shone and were pleasant to chew on. The zippers made a jagged sound that was funny to me. The clothes took my weight and my form. A T-shirt that I slept on top of no longer fit my mother when she tried to put it on. It was not surprising then that my mother left me behind with the clothes when she walked out with her big empty suitcase.

I never saw her again. My grandfather let me stay in his house because that is where my mother had left me—among the clothes on the floor in the room that had been hers in his house. But he did not really raise me. He told me stories about my mother. He brought me the letters she wrote—because she wrote every Christmas and for every one of my birthdays. But he was not a Daddy. Many fathers are not Daddys. There are Papas and Fathers and Sirs, even those who go by their first name. Perhaps he was a Papa. Mostly, he was committed to other things. He made costumes for Carnival. That is what he was. A maker of costumes. A maker of pretty things. He made costumes for the parades and for the pageants. Sometimes he made all the costumes for all one hundred members of a troupe. Sometimes he made the one big mass costume. A thing that had to be carried on your back up the parade route. A thing that was taller and wider than the wearer and made the wearer something else.

My grandfather was the best at what he did. And he was busy. Our walls were forever lined with straying sequins. The floors were always slippery with glitter. The dining table constantly being piled with cloth and sewing needles. My bedroom, which was my mother's bedroom before it was mine, was the changing room. Often a stranger who had been trying on a costume would leave her stockings or panties behind. I would wear them—to see what it was like to be someone else. It was a kind of costume.

Many of my uncles and aunts lived in the house for short periods. They were temporary parents. With them I did well, though I came to expect constant newness. I came to expect it and not see it as abandonment but as a new chance to remake myself. I treated all my relationships like this. I was not interested in keeping the same friends year to year. This meant switching schools because on this small island the schools are also small and in two years I would have made friends with everyone who would have me.

I switched schools often and this was facilitated by an uncle or an aunt who wanted me to attend the school she or he had attended. They would hold my hand and march me to their old third-grade teacher. Or their middle school schoolmaster. Or their old high school principal. A uniform would be made quickly and without flare, this was not Carnival, so that my skirts never had the stylish box pleats or paneling of the other girls'. And by the time I graduated from high school I had attended all the public schools and private schools that would have me.

The reputation that followed me was that I had kissed every boy on the island. Or if I had not kissed that boy then I had kissed his friend. I never kept a boyfriend when I moved schools. Even though some of the boys did not want to leave me be. They insisted that love should cross school walls. That we could meet at the movies or the beach and still be boyfriend and girlfriend. That sounded like a trap to me. But I knew that I was not normal and that these sorts of silly attachments were indeed normal, so out of pity I sometimes had sex with a boy. To get him to leave me alone. It was my way of saying Here, you have had me. Now let me be. This left me feeling less guilty when I would not return his calls. The general assumption was that I was a bit of a slut. And this was true. I felt I was a better person for it.

3.
Herman

I figured out what the song meant one day when I was hanging out in Frenchtown. I feel okay around Frenchies. They act like islanders but I blend in with them and they're nice to me. Dutch was drinking his beer and when a car drove by blasting "Legal" he smiled. "You better hide for Carnival."

"What do you mean?"

"I mean the song, partner. You know, *kill the rabbits*."

"What about it?"

"Rabbits are white people," he said.

"Are you serious, Dutch?"

He smiled and nodded. "Don't come to Jou'vert. Don't come to the village or the parade. Dread, you better stay home until Monday."

"And what are you going to do?"

"What you mean?"

"*Kill the rabbits*. Do you think they'll kill us for real?"

"Man, who the hell is *they* and who the frig is *us?*"

I didn't know what I was getting myself into but I could see that Dutch was no longer congenial.

"I don't know," I said.

"The *tourist* color. I ain no tourist. I's a Frenchy—a island man. Rabbits don't mean me."

"But you're white, too, like me."

"Not that. The song means you."

"Not me either then. They mean tourist then. Like those assholes." I pointed to a white couple who were dressed in shorts and walking into a café. I didn't know if those tourists were assholes. I didn't know anything about them.

"You are them," said Dutch.

"No. I live here. They're tourists. I'm local."

"You live here for two years. They live here for two weeks. What's the difference? You're all going back."

"That's bullshit," I said.

He shook his head. "You're a belonger to up there. That's where you'll run if there's a hurricane or a revolution or something."

"So would you. You're a hypocrite."

"I wouldn't belong up there. I'd be running around with a piece of this place on my back; this is my home-home. It might be home to you, partner, but when you think of home-home you don't think here."

"Damn, Dutch. You're a racist—against white people. Against your own kind."

"You ain my kind, Herman. You are not my kind."

Then he walked away and the smell of fish being chopped up yards away was suddenly so high that phlegm came up my throat and I turned and spat.

I'd been on the island for almost a year, since my parents had moved from D.C. I'd been traveling since high school. Trying to find a place I could settle into and feel good about. I wanted somewhere where there was English because I wasn't good with languages. But I wanted somewhere warm. Now I worked in my parents' bar in St. John. Maybe I would live here in the Virgin Islands. Maybe I had found my paradise. I was not planning on going anywhere. I did not want to be a tourist. Not anymore.

4.
Cooper

When I'm not staring out at the sea I lime in the library. I prefer the salt air to the library's a.c. but sometimes I like the quiet. I like the hard wooden chairs with firm backs. It's a small quiet place, like a vault with precious gold bullion. A vault inside the jail. The tile on the floor is scrubbed shiny and clean and my shoes squeak when I walk. They only let three of us in at a time. And we have to sit at different tables. There are only three long tables in the library. There's a computer in the corner that connects to the Internet. I surf, looking up the newest magic tricks. Now I can make plastic forks and spoons disappear. I've been looking up rabbits. How to make one disappear. Turns out those magic rabbits die at a higher rate than pet or even wild rabbits. All that disappearing. I wish this place had classes. Not magic classes necessarily. I wouldn't mind a painting class or even just watercolors. But the one problem with this small local jail is that they don't have things like that. I've sacrificed education for a view of the ocean. I laugh when I think this. I sound like someone who has a choice.

What I find out about "kill the rabbits" or "the rabbit is dead" grinds in my chest and in my head. It's called the Bitterling Test. What a name. German, I think. From before anyone cared about planning a family or about women shoving hangers up their twats. The Bitterling Test was the first pregnancy test—a thing rich women used to check if they were pregnant, so they could decide if they wanted to have the baby or not. If now was a good time. Inject the urine into the rabbit. If the rabbit died then the woman's having a baby. I think of my Xica in the yellow dress. I think of her and how many rabbits she's killed.

I was sixteen when my little brother was born. My mother thought it would be good to have the Christening during Carnival time because of convenience. A lot of family would be down from the States.

There were the days off from work and school that could make the whole affair a family reunion. Plus my mother and her new husband had met during a Carnival and everyone laughed that the baby had been conceived during Carnival—though I didn't want to know about that. I always thought my mother worked during Carnival. They needed more cops because of the crime. But my mother didn't believe in any connection between crime and fêting. She always said that there was more sex during Carnival and more drugs during Carnival but there wasn't really more crime. It made good sense to have the Christening then and it was romantic—even though it was such an island thing for them to do.

It was the Carnival of *Legal,* so the fact that my mother preached her no-crime speech at every opportunity the weekend of the Christening was not to be misunderstood. Everyone expected crime that Carnival. The song was calling for a revolution. A kind of Carnival revolution. The authorities and church people were always demonizing Carnival for its slackness, its degradation. Social workers on the local TV station talked about the great disservice we did our children by showing them how to cock up and wind in the middle of the street. But that Carnival Jam Band had come out with *Legal,* a song that told all the stuck-up people to go to hell. "They tell us: Be on good behavior, for the tourist color. All they want is: stand in a circle spin all around, do-si-do when you come into town. Stop! Who say we wild? It's the Jam Band style. Boom, boom, bam, bam. Hands in the air!" Don't try to impress the white people was the directive. Don't imitate their dancing and their ways just to make them feel comfortable. This is our Carnival. Obey your own culture. Be wild. Let loose. Throw your hands in the air.

For Christ's sake, it was the year I was sixteen. The song was telling us that stuck-up people wanted Carnival to be a legal affair. But legal meant proper. And proper meant fake. And we would not be fake or proper or legal. I understood that they meant a cultural revolution. I allowed myself to misunderstand.

Carnival break started on Wednesday, with a half day of school that nobody attended. Wednesday was food fair and if you waited until even noon, all the best conch in butter sauce would be sold out. But the Sunday before that I had met Xica. She'd been at the Christening. She was related to my brother's daddy somehow. I didn't notice her first. Really. First, she noticed me.

We were at the Cathedral downtown. In days the Cathedral would be locked up as Carnival revelers stamped through the street. Obeying the song that would be the road march. Be wild, it commanded. We own this Carnival, it declared. But now "I am the vine and you are the branches" was being sung by the choir. The priest called for the child to be brought up. The microphone wasn't working and so we couldn't hear the godparents respond to the sacred questions. My mother was wearing a big cream-colored hat and a fluffy dress. I thought she looked silly but hadn't told her so in the morning. Her husband, who had only been her husband since the baby but was now living in our house, told her she looked fabulous and kissed her on the mouth. I didn't like him. His mouth was always greasy and I knew he wouldn't stay.

In the Cathedral I held the Body of Christ on my tongue seeing how long it would take to melt if I didn't chew it. I stared at the Stations of the Cross on the walls, studying the story it was telling. Finally, on the station where Jesus falls for the second time, the wafer slivered into nothing and melted away in my mouth. "Abide in me as I in you." I closed my eyes thinking that in the front pew only God and the priest would see me taking a rest. And I must have dreamed about a girl because when I felt someone slide up against me in the pew I didn't flinch out of my sleep. I just nestled in. A song was playing. My boy cousin was kneeling on one side of me. My mother's husband was on the other side of him. The baby, who hadn't taken the water on his forehead well, started crying and I woke to my mother rustling out of the church with her new son in her arms. The girl next to me was kneeling with her head down like she was praying. She lifted her head to stare at the altar. Then she turned to me. "I stare at the paintings," she said. "I like to look at pretty things."

I nodded. She was older than me, but she didn't look like the religious type. Her yellow dress was grabbed around her waist, and she was wearing big gold hibiscus earrings. But with these girls you never knew. They want diamonds and Jesus at the same time, forgetting that Jesus walked Palestine barefoot with only bread and wine to eat.

"We will be one in love." The song finished. She leaned into the seat but stopped before her back touched the pew. She was perched, ass alone holding her up. She whispered to me. "I like Simon Peter best." Her face was the sweet color of brown sugar.

The recession song came on, "Give me joy in my lamp, keep me burning," and the girl slid out. I followed her. She didn't just dip her finger in the holy water. She cupped it out and splashed on her sign of the cross. Outside the beads of water were still on her forehead and spotted on the chest of her dress. An interesting yellow dress. Tight on top with puffy shoulders and like skin on the bottom. The dress was glittering somehow, like maybe it was done up with gold thread or something. Like something old-timish, like a hand-me-down or costume. People were mingling and taking pictures of my mother and the baby. The baby was wearing a long white dress. The family was supposed to go to brunch at some hotel out East End that was expensive and reserved for such occasions. A car drove by shaking and blasting the song that was the anthem: *Legal.* The hook was playing. "Kill the rabbits! Kill the rabbits! Kill the rabbits . . ." All the adults pursed their faces and flipped their hands as if fanning the car away. The car drove on but the song stayed in the air.

"Paul is the one who carries the pen. He's the scholar. But Peter carries the keys. To the Church. Which do you think is more powerful?" Now she was walking back behind the church. She walked with her back erect. Like a model. I wondered if I knew her. It seemed like I'd seen her around. But St. Thomas is a small island. Everyone looks familiar. I followed her to the side of the church, where the stone wasn't painted over. She nestled behind these big winding stairs that went up to the place where the priests lived. It smelled like pee. I'd never followed a girl to a small smelly corner before. I kept looking back to see if my mother would forget me and go to the Baptism brunch. But this girl said "I'm Xica" and before I could tell her "I'm Cooper, but call me Coop" she had pushed up against me and was kissing me and we were clutching each other and our mouths were wet with their own juices and different parts of my body were going limp or stiff. And then she pulled away, but I pulled her back because I wasn't done with this brown sugar. Our faces were right up against each other. She looked at me hard. She must have been a woman, really. She must have been eighteen.

"That's it," she said. "It was nice." And she pulled away so quickly that her chain busted off in my hand. "Shit," she cursed, then crossed herself. "Keep it." Then she snapped away. I was in love. That was it. I was in love with Xica. And all she had done was kiss me. She didn't come to the brunch. She wasn't close family.

That Carnival I was overtaken by the slapping of steelpan and the clanging of cowbells. The food fair was so rammed that it was easy to stick my hand in a white woman's pockets and take her money as she pressed her puffy twat against my hand thinking I was looking for something else. I stole from tourist women, mostly. It was easier than magic. If you had asked me then why I was stealing I would have said to buy a better necklace for Xica. One that wouldn't break so easily.

I hadn't ever been like this before. Before I just stole to know I could do it. Now I stole and stole and I told myself that this was the Carnival for revolution. Love was a revolution. And stealing was part of the war. I was part of a movement. Anarchy is the word for it. I didn't know that word then. Then I would have said that I was just obeying the song.

At Jou'vert I tramped behind Jam Band, holding on to the truck, swinging to catch the bottles of spring water they threw to the crowd. They played their oldies which made the girls bend down low with their hands on the ground. Whenever they struck up *Legal* the whole crowd, thousands of us there in the street, would go jump and prance and lose our minds. They must have played it five times. A long version that lasted for fifteen minutes. When it was dark everyone sang along loudly and put their hands in one direction and their backsides in the others. "Take off you shirt and wave it!" And in the light of the moon girls took off their shirts to reveal sports bras worn for the occasion. As the sun came up on the Waterfront me and my boys found each other and moved through the crowd like a pack of dogs. Our elbows out and faces hidden by handkerchiefs. We weren't stealing or anything. We were just making room for ourselves. Watch us, we were saying. The sun is up on this street party and you better know that we're here.

Two days later I was a wild clown in the Carnival parade. I tramped with a crew of my friends and I looked for Xica. I saw many women I thought must be her. I touched them. I smelled them. I told myself I would find her after Carnival when we were without masks. I would present her with a new necklace. But that was my last Carnival.

I still have Xica's broken necklace. I had it made into a hand chain and it's the one vanity they allow me—though I only wear it during Mass. It's my talisman. And now I look forward to spying on the thick crowd of revelers of Jou'vert morning as much as I look forward to the one martyr on Easter night.

5.
Xica

I wish to blame my mother. It is the thing we all wish to do and Dr. Freud has given us license so now we are taught that this desire is natural—even though nothing about blame is natural. I have simply made a decision that my pain is inherited. In which case, it is from her. But that still does not make it her fault. Notice that I do not mention my father—since I did not know him at all and so can credit nothing to him. Not even abandonment, because in truth he may not even know that I exist. Fatherhood is a thing that is assigned and accepted.

I will blame my mother. Let me say that living my first year, quite literally, in a suitcase, did me in. In first grade I could not touch my toes. I could do a split and that was thought remarkable by the boys in class. But I could not touch my toes. No one kept track of this inability, except me. In middle school it was the rave to build a body pyramid for pictures. I could never hold anyone on my back. And I was always thought too tall to be the point person. In the pictures of that time I am the pretty thing in the front doing the split. My legs open to the ground.

I always walked very erect. I breathed shallowly. It was thought that walking with my back straight and breathing deliberately was another way I flirted—because once a reputation has been assigned, everything is attributed to it. I could sit only at the very edge of a chair, so that the sharp muscle of my buttocks alone held me up and that was thought to be a way of saying come hither. In truth, if I did not walk straight I could not walk. If I did not breathe shallowly I could not breathe. If I did not sit at the edge of a chair I could not sit. My back was in a constant tremor of pain. Either it felt as though something deep in the muscle was ripping asunder, or it felt as though the spine itself had been lit on fire. When I was feeling the one pain of tearing I longed for the relief of the other pain of burning. But I was never without one. No one knew of this pain. I did not speak of it. It seemed as normal as getting my period every month. Something that happened. Something expected. Something that one did not talk about. The only thing that made the pain stop was something that was not unlike the thing that made bleeding once a month stop. Let us call it slackness. Rudeness. Bad behavior. Call me a slut.

I graduated from high school but I did not walk in a graduation ceremony. It did not seem right to claim one school as my alma mater. Colleges in the States would not have me. My transcripts were too confusing. My grades did not match. I may have been an A student in history one semester at one school, but then there was a D in history at the next. I looked as though I was many people, and I was. I was someone who had traveled. I had traveled my island. I knew it. I knew it like the back of my hand, and when I thought this I did not mean it as a cliché. I meant that my hand was a thing decided by history. That my hand was colored and shaped by something that time had decided. But that my life was about defying that history. And I meant that I knew the land of my island as I could know a book I might read.

One of my many teachers once said that history has no influence on land, that land is outside of history. He lied or he was mistaken.

History has carved down mountains. History has drenched out rivers. History has made the land, and the land has, when under duress, made history. The land had decided that there would not be slave plantations on it and so we in St. Thomas did not have plantation history. No sugarcane for men to slash and suck. That is what women were for. No one and no thing is unmoved by human history and it is a sad, sad truth. But that Carnival the land had decided to defy history. And this, like my body, was a bit of an impossible thing—but an admirable thing as all impossible things are.

But of course I could not be the only one like this. I could not be the only one with this wandering need. This one who longed to be packed in a suitcase and taken. Herman was such a spirit. He was a student. He was living on loans. A year in Texas at a community college. A year in Hawaii at a public university. Before the Virgin Islands he had thought about Alaska. Maybe Eden is a cold place, he said. But then he said that he was home now. That maybe this place was his home. Maybe, he said, he could spend his life traveling this small place and that would be enough. This is what he told me on the ferry ride. That we first spoke on water and not land is a symbol of something. But he was not like me, exactly. He was telling a lie that even he did not believe. He only wanted to be like me. But I did not know this at the time.

He was in the Virgin Islands because his parents had bought a house and a bar. They had arrived on a cruise ship and had decided that there were some niche places here with people like them and that they could live here without having to change themselves too much. They could live what might be called the good life and it did not matter that most of the people they found here, the people who were not like them, but rather were simply characters in this good life, were people who disappeared bit by bit every time people like them arrived. It did not matter to them that their existence meant a space that was absent of our existence.

Herman was white and I was black—we are still so. That he wanted to be like me said something about him. It said that either he did not understand how the world worked, did not know that he was born with the Great Advantage of pale skin (though it is not an advantage, it is only a genetic mutation, but let us put that aside, because it has been put aside long before us), or that he did not want his advantage.

To me he did not have a past. To me he was a transient thing who simply appeared and I expected him to disappear any minute, so I fell in love with him. And I took him to pre-Carnival soca fêtes and on Jam Band boat rides at night. We would be packed in by the heavy crowd and I always won the coveted corner of the rusty barge. It was dark there. As the calypso started up a woman could push her man into the corner and turn her back to him, roll her hips and ripple her waist, hoist up her leg and loose the burning and ripping of her back into the bass of the rhythm box and the lyrics that we called awesome.

He was like watching a pageant with the different segments of sportswear, evening wear, and cultural costume. In one day Herman could be a white newcomer, a Frenchy liming in Frenchtown, a local kid grinding on his woman at a jam session. He knew to stay put. He knew to push his pelvis out and sway it side to side. He knew to follow my lead on the dance floor. This is the way you dance to soca, I told him once and then never again: you always follow the woman. He wore dark colors. He wore a hat low on his head. My aunts and uncles who visited the island in abundance during Carnival called him light-skinned so as not to insult me by calling my boyfriend white. He knew to hold me in the backseat of my car after the party when I curled into a ball and my back burned and tore all at once and I cried and he wiped my tears and said the right thing: Don't ever be ashamed to cry in front of me.

I brought Herman to my house. Carnival does not end at this house. All year long bands and troupes come to my grandfather and he keeps their ideas in drawers alongside his rolled-up socks. His costumes compete against each other to win King of the Band. Every year a Carnival Queen contestant hires him and her sponsors pay him a year's salary to ensure that she wins at least the cultural costume segment.

This is where I would bring Herman. We would make love among the empty costumes that hung in my closet. Those costumes would be living things and it was as if I had many lovers. I felt in control and wild at the same time—in control of my wildness. I felt as though my own clenching and releasing was like an injection, an elixir, a cure.

We visited once with a glittering set of jagged red dragon wings that filled an entire wall of my room. The wings shook as if in flight if we just breathed on them. Herman climbed inside the costume and he became a dragon. Shimmery and scaly and attached to a set of wheels because the wings, though they threatened to launch, were too heavy to be carried on the back all up the parade route. Even for someone with a strong back like Herman's. Herman rolled the dragon cautiously around the cluttered room and I watched him and instantly I wanted to be a maiden in a high tower. And then Herman climbed out and he climbed on top of me and I said: Pull my hair down. Call me Rapunzel. And he said: I feel strong. I feel powerful. And when we left we could not believe that my grandfather had made the dragon with his own hands. And when we left there remained little curls of my hair that were quite unlike Rapunzel's long blond ropes.

That Carnival there was also an entire array of Oompa-Loompa candy cane costumes because one school troupe in the children's parade was doing a vapid Charlie and the Chocolate Factory theme. They hung limp and tiny in my closest. The curling pointed shoes still being worked on up until the day after the food fair because they had to be sized perfectly and children's feet, it seemed, never stopped growing.

My man was brave. Herman said he wanted to be in the Carnival parade. Herman said he wanted to process down the road. Jou'vert wasn't what he wanted. In that you didn't get to put on a costume, really. Your costume was cutoff jeans and sneakers, maybe a fine layer of mud to keep you cool. And perhaps Jou'vert was too dangerous, with those crazy young boys elbowing their way through the crowds. Causing fights. But in the parade the costumes were elaborate. They didn't just make you feel different—they made you a different person, maybe even a different species. You might be a dragon or an Oompa-Loompa for a whole day. I said I would help him. I said that together we could join a troupe. And we did.

I had not been allowed to join the Crushers until I was eighteen. I do not know if this was Carnival rules because the Crushers was a troupe of the adults' parade, or if this was Crusher rules. The year I was eighteen was the year of the lyrics, kill the rabbits, kill the rabbits, kill the rabbits, each sentence a higher octave than the last so that it was more of a taunting than a war cry. Nothing was to be killed with blood. We would kill them with the rhythm. That year was also the year of Herman. That "them" meant my boyfriend was something I understood. But I was not thinking along those lines. I knew he wouldn't last; like all the others he would clutch a suitcase and leave. So I would not wait until next year when perhaps a more benign song was in rotation. I wanted him in Carnival. I wanted him to be one of the pretty things.

We joined the Crushers. We went down to their base and picked out costumes from the sketches tacked to the walls. Their theme that year was professionals. Firefighters and police officers and the military. Did it seem that Herman wanted us to be in the same uniform? I didn't care. This is the Crushers, I told him. We don't have to stay in order. We don't have to stay in our section. We can mingle. We can jump on a steel band truck and pung some tenor. We can sit on the side. We can even jump up with another troupe if we want. I wanted to be a firefighter. That he also wanted to be a fighter I took as a coincidence. We both liked the felt hats and the shiny red jackets. I especially liked the hose that we got to hold. The Christmas tree icicles that came out the front like sparkling water. The song the Crushers chose for the road march, the song our d.j. would play when we entered the field, would be Legal, with its revolutionary lyrics and its can't-be-avoided beat. We did not even need to vote on it. What other song was there that Carnival? In the fêtes when the call came on to kill the rabbits, it did not matter if I was dancing with Herman, I would fashion my arms as if holding a rifle and crouch down low—bouncing, bouncing all the while. It did not matter if I was dancing with Herman; he would crouch down with me.

But then he asked me in my bed one night: Why kill the rabbits.

What do you mean?

Kill the rabbits. What does it mean? Why rabbits?

Just something the singer made up.

Maybe I'm paranoid. Am I?

I moved my body so that I leaned into his chest. I pulled his arms around me so he could feel protective and strong: You're fine. It means nothing. It's a game.

What kind of game, Xica?

I lowered my head so he could kiss my brow. I wanted him to call me his little girl. I thought on childish things: It's from Bugs Bunny. Elmer Fudd hunting Bugs Bunny.

I could feel his arms tighten and then slacken around me. Perhaps he wanted to push me off my bed—to the floor where he'd already pushed the old clothes that I kept on the bed like a teddy bear or security blanket. Perhaps he wanted me gone.

But Xica, in the cartoon Elmer Fudd never gets Bugs.

See, it's a joke. It's a game.

Elmer is a joke, Xica. Elmer can never catch Bugs. It's as bad as Coyote and Road Runner. Elmer gets made a fool of. So killing the rabbits is what foolish people do. The rabbit always wins.

I pulled myself away from him. And looked into his eyes. They were blue and I wished then that they weren't. Any other color but vapid, white-only blue. I asked him: What do you mean?

I mean if the white people are rabbits, then you're Elmer Fudd.

That's not what it means. That's not what it means at all. Stop trying to figure it out. It's code. It's code that you can't figure out.

Perhaps he thought I meant you as in anyone. But I meant you as you and not me. Either way, he reached out for me and turned me back into his chest. I felt my back press onto a set of hard buttons on his shirt. I curved my spine into his belly. I let him protect me because this is what parents do: protect because it makes them feel strong.

6.

Herman

Xica was my girlfriend before I even knew I liked her or that she liked me. I saw her eating in a tapas bar in Cruz Bay. She was listening to some jazz guy from St. Thomas playing an upright bass and saying "Oh, oh, oh" over and over again. She was in a yellow dress that was shiny and out of date—out of place in the tapas bar. Everyone was leaning over a tiny plate of mussels or Brie. She sat at the edge of a bar stool, her back so straight that she reminded me of a librarian. It was painful to watch her. Everyone clapped and someone even hooted when the bass guy took his break. I didn't think of the woman in the yellow dress again. I ate my mussels. I tipped the barman well. I walked out. Outside under a lamppost the bass player had a glass of white wine in one hand and Xica in the other. I stopped. I hadn't seen this kind of thing with the black people here. They were more discreet than this. More stuck-up in a way. Not a bad way or anything. They just didn't kiss in public or even hold hands. The white people did that. Hell, I did it. They were the only black people in the street—this little part of St. John being frequented mainly by white locals and tourists. I couldn't stop watching them. Then the bass player stopped kissing and looked at me. He made a noise that was kinda like his instrument. Then the woman looked at me. I wondered vaguely if she was an African American perhaps. Or a prostitute. Perhaps she was from D.C. She might even have been Ethiopian like so many black girls in the D.C. that had been home to me. She was beautiful in the way they were.

I went back in to wait for the bass player to start up again. I left half an hour later with Xica. Just like that. We took the ferry back to St. Thomas and I knew I'd be stuck there because the ferry wouldn't make a return trip until the next morning. We sat on the top in the open air with the night wind whipping around us. We talked about our pasts and I found myself telling her about the first time I'd had sex. It had been with a Cuban prostitute in Miami where I'd gone to visit a cousin over summer vacation in high school. The cousin was older and cooler than me and I wanted badly to be like him. He screwed the woman first while I waited outside the door in a communal living room that led to other doors. I listened to him grunt. When it was my turn I was scared and the woman didn't comfort me. She didn't even pretend to like me. I was ashamed of the whole thing. I didn't believe in pornography. I didn't believe in using women for sex. Yet, I had done it. And I told Xica this as the ferry pushed through the water. I had never told anyone this before. I'd never even talked to that cousin of mine again. I had made myself believe the thing never even happened. And here I was telling Xica. She cried right there. Her face drying quickly because of the wind. She told me that I was a monster. She told me that God could see me doing that horrible thing and didn't I know that I was participating in a system that made women slaves? Then she nestled into my arms and told me that she had forgiven me. Then she told me she loved me.

Xica took me to her home that night and introduced me to her grandfather as her boyfriend. He shook my hand but stayed at the dining table hunched over his sewing machine. And it felt like I really was her boyfriend after all I'd told her. She took me through this house. Everywhere there were glue guns and monstrous jars of gold dust. And up along the hallway walls were Carnival headpieces and pictures, just the pictures, of plaques that read "Best Costume" or "King of the Band." And there was fluorescent elastic and old sneakers and the sound of the sewing machine going. And I knew that this is what I had come to the islands for. I wanted to be a part of this. I would not be a tourist.

Xica and I joined the Carnival together. Picked out the same costumes for the parade. We did everything together. I was falling in love with my real island girlfriend. Dutch didn't tell me to be careful of rabbit killers anymore. We shared a joint with some other Frenchies.

"Be careful," he said.

"Of what?"

"Is that your bona fide woman, man?"

"Xica. Yeah, that's my woman."

"Then never mind, man. Never mind."

"What do you mean?" I asked.

"She's already your woman. It doesn't matter."

"What do you mean, man?"

"Forget it, Herman. Forget it."

By then I loved her. It didn't matter what anybody said, she was my piece of paradise.

People said she'd screwed around. People said they'd seen her kissing on another guy the same day they'd seen her with me. They said that she'd slept with a ton of guys back in high school and that she would still do it now if you just talked to her the right way. I asked Dutch if he'd been with her, even though if he'd said he had I would have kicked his ass. I wasn't afraid of anyone. I mean, I was afraid. I was really afraid of getting beat down by a gang of Frenchies. But I was going to fight for my woman anyway. Dutch squinted his eyes. "I think I kissed her once in like eighth grade or something. But nothing else, man. That's your woman. Don't worry yourself about history." He passed me the spliff like we were family.

A week or so before the parade the Crusher director called me on my cell phone. He told me he had an emergency at the center. Something about my costume. I didn't have a car. I liked walking. I wanted to be close to the land. Still, I had to hitch a ride to the docks and then take the ferry over to St. Thomas. When I got there it was only me and the director.

"Mr. Man," which was what he called me when he was making fun of me in a way I wasn't quite sure was funny. "Mr. Man, we need someone to be the rabbit."

Immediately, I understood what he meant but I was sure I had misunderstood. "What do you mean?"

"Our troupe. We're doing 'Legal.' That is our theme. Police officers. Firefighters. Crossing guards. Military. Some people have toy guns, others ticketing pads. Have you seen those?" He laughed so that it was clear the ticketing pads were his idea. "They can give them out along the parade route: 'In violation of slackness. In violation of having a big backside.' It's genius." He cleared his throat and then laughed again. He touched the sides of his eyes tenderly. Then he cleared his throat and looked serious. "But we need someone to be the target."

"I'm already a firefighter. I already put the glitter on my felt hat. I just need my hose finished by the tailor, my girlfriend's grandfather, and my costume is done. I'm the only male in the firefighter section. You need me there."

"Yes, yes. And your girlfriend sure will look good in her bikini fire suit. I mean it's made for her."

I stared at him.

"But I mean we don't need men in the firefighter section. The hose is so . . . what's the word? Phallic. It's the kind of thing for a woman to carry around. You don't think? Something for her to wind up on? No, we need you elsewhere. You'll be the rabbit. In the stadium you'll lead everyone in a do-si-do for the judges, but then at the last minute we'll turn the hoses on you and then the military will shoot you down. Then you can go home."

"What?"

"It's a metaphor, Mr. Man. Kill the rabbit. We're just acting out the song."

"I thought the Crushers didn't do routines. I thought you didn't believe in conforming."

"It's not a routine. You watch. Everyone will want to shoot you down without any rehearsal. You do this, you're a hero."

"But I'm not the hero. I'll be the villain."

"Sure. Yes. But by playing the villain you give us a chance to regain our . . . how should I say it? Our cultural dignity. Then you you'll be a hero."

"But you'll kill me."

He put a hand on my shoulder. "Not you, Herman. But what you represent. Come, Mr. Man. Carnival isn't about real. Carnival is about representation. You do this and it shows that you know no people should put on a pappy show for another set of people."

"So you should kill white people?"

"Only metaphorically. Now listen. This will be our secret. You'll go to Mr. John's house to be fitted."

"But that's Xica's grandfather. He's down with this?"

"Yes. He's one of us, you know. A secret Crusher. That's how we win every year. Even Xica won't know about this. And you won't tell her."

I didn't know how to get to Xica's house without her knowing. But it turned out to be the easiest thing. I took a dollar van to meet her for a movie. I got there early. While she was in the shower, Mr. John walked me silently to his own crowded storeroom-bedroom and pulled out a white-haired rabbit suit from a shadowy corner. I had imagined it would be like a Disney suit, where all of me would be covered. Instead it was furry long pants with big rabbit feet that I discovered were just snorkeling flippers covered in carpet swatches. It had a puff tail in the ass of the pants made out of cotton balls. The hood had rabbit ears and wire whiskers and big puffy cheeks that felt like stones at the sides of my face. My face would be painted white and I would be given six gray wires to glue right onto my cheeks as whiskers. But my face would be there. Sticking out for everyone to see that it was me.

Mr. John signaled for me to try it on and quickly he pinned parts and loosened parts while motioning for me to stand straight. At one point he pinched between my legs to make sure my crotch could breathe. Then he made me take it off. He turned while I dressed. I handed him the suit. "Xica is the only constant thing I have," he said clearly. Then he took the suit from me. I had never really heard his voice before. He sounded like a sad old man.

On the day of the parade, I could not do it. We had been dancing and drinking for two hours. Xica let the other firewomen in the troupe grind up on me and I didn't feel too bad when I saw her push up on the other men who were police officers and army guys.

It was a sudden thing. I was there in my fireman suit, carrying the hose at my crotch like I figured was the manly thing to do. I wasn't thinking about rabbits. Our troupe had played the song three times already but every time it played Xica came to me and held on to me tight. But "Legal" wasn't playing when someone I didn't know tugged me into an alley and pulled out the suit from a garbage bag. Perhaps I was drunk. Perhaps I was afraid. I ran up the alley. Away from the strange suit, away from the parade and away from Xica. It had dawned on me that if they were painting my face then why did it have to be a white man? Why did it have to be me? I do not know who played the rabbit. I never knew.

I felt smart and brave when I caught the St. John ferry that was going back and forth often because it was Carnival time. I went to my parents' bar, where I spent most of my time on the island. My father was there and other men were there, drinking and watching the parade on one screen and a basketball game on another. I walked in still in costume and they looked at me as though I was a ghost or at least a dragon with pointy wings come to take something from them, when I was only a firefighter. When my father, behind the bar, let out a big whopping laugh, and all the other men and women allowed themselves a giggle, I knew that I wasn't really a firefighter. I took off my plastic hat. My father poured me a rum and Coke. I turned to the TV screen that was showing the game.

7.
Cooper

"Hey, Coop. Hey, Coopster. Coopadelic!"

That was Sexy. I mean that's his frigging name. No lie. I guess he's sexy, but I wouldn't know about that. He was calling me over to his car. He opened the side door and let me in.

This is how I know Sexy: that Carnival he gave me a gun. That's how everyone knows Sexy. I didn't need the gun. I was making more than enough just picking pockets. Sexy was into other stuff. Sexy was into everything. A real hustler. He had a hustler's job—he worked at the race track organizing the betting. And he had soldiers all over the island. He had found out about me and my quick fingers.

"I ain needing all of that, Sexy."

"So what?"

"And I ain want it."

"You're small time, Coop. You could be making some real money."

"Man, Sexy. I still in high school. Let me graduate, already."

"Take it anyway. It's a gift. A temporary gift. Consider it a loaner but with no interest."

I didn't even know how to use it. He leaned over to me in the passenger seat. "This is the safety. Leave it locked unless you plan on doing something. Too many guys in jail for mistakes. And this is the barrel."

I couldn't tell if it was loaded or not.

"No bullets," he said.

"You know my mother's a cop, man. She going kill me."

"Listen, Coop. Hold it for me. You's a magician. Make it disappear until I need it again."

I took the gun. I hid it in the alley by the church. Behind the stairs. It was so many months later when the cops found it that I'd forgotten about it. As far as I was concerned it really had disappeared. Later, when the cops found it, there were two prints. Mine and someone else's. They never figured out who else. Someone who hadn't been printed before. Someone not in the system. It must have been Xica's, either that or a priest's.

The gun was what cinched me. They said I'd stolen diamonds from this tourist couple out East End. The white people pointed and said that yes it was me. That I'd held them up at gunpoint, taken advantage of the wife, then slammed the husband into sleep with my piece.

I didn't do it. Really. But it didn't matter. Because it was like my mother finding the sugar—when they found the gun behind the stairs I was horrified. There were my prints and not Sexy's. I mean, maybe, just maybe a tourist woman found me roaming the streets that Saturday after the parade, looking for Xica—my clown suit costume zipped down to my waist. And maybe she touched my shoulder and slid her hand under my sweaty undershirt and looked at me like I was licorice. I mean, suppose I went with her back to a time-share and she introduced me to her husband and they both wanted to have sex with me, but I said I would only do the wife because I wasn't about to be a batty boy for their fetish. And maybe I did or maybe I didn't let the woman climb on top of me while her husband watched and chanted "Ride that island monkey, ride it." And maybe I stole the diamond chain around her neck and the diamond tennis bracelet off her wrist and the diamond earrings right out of her goddamn ears, and rolled out with it all when the man tried to make a move.

I'm not a hustler. I'm a magician. But still they got me on rape and assault with a deadly weapon and with illegal use of an unlicensed firearm and with stealing the earrings and the bracelet. But they never found the necklace. I made it disappear.

I pleaded innocent. I'm telling you, I had never even seen that tourist couple before in my life.

8.
Xica

Flesh is also a kind of costume. It is also a thing to hide behind. A thing to move you and to be moved by. It is a thing to encircle a pain. A thing that is a gate to put up between people who are otherwise the same. Skin. The walls of a gated community. Where the man in the gate booth says: Sorry, you do not know the code. And I have to say: I am here to see Herman. Who is Herman? My boyfriend. Girl, don't you know that they don't really love anyone that looks like us? I'll let you in these gates, 'cause it's none of my business. But you should know that they don't normally let black people in here except to clean or fix something and if you were my daughter I wouldn't be letting you in at all. And the gate opened. I'd brought my grandfather's car over on the barge from St. Thomas to St. John and now I drove myself up to Herman's big house a week before Carnival and he was there to greet me at the doors that opened as though to a banquet. And when I walked in the whole place was painted cream and white and I knew that the gate man was right. Perhaps people who were brown in color had built this house. But people who were brown in color would never live in this house. Even though this was my island and I, too, was brown in color.

No costumes to get in the way, said Herman, taking my hand and leading me around the house.

I said: But there are other things to get in the way.

Not here. Not with us.

And now he took both my hands and showed me the study that was bare of everything except of books and a large picture of Saint Paul.

Saint Paul, I said as if Herman was introducing us.

Yeah. How did you know?

He's one of the saints of the church I went to last week.

Oh, yeah. Where you lost the necklace I gave you.

I ignored him: You can tell Saint Paul by the pen and book he always carries. He's a scholar and a writer.

That's what my father says. Said he's the patron saint of modern thought.

I did not think that it was rude of me, I just said what I thought to be true: Your father either makes things up or he lies.

Perhaps both, Herman said. He stopped holding my hands and embraced me from the back. This is why I loved him.

I breathed deeper than I should have. I looked at Paul. I felt Herman's arms. I said: Paul was a martyr and that is the truth. There is nothing modern about that.

Do you like martyrdom?

Who likes martyrdom? Only the martyr. And then he loves it. Jesus, now that is a martyr. He's my favorite saint.

Someone else would have laughed. Someone else would have let me go to slap his knee. Herman only held me tighter.

Saint Jesus, he whispered.

There were many prophets and saints. Jesus is one. Maybe he is the One. I do not know.

I allowed Herman to guide me out and toward the bedroom. I did not want to stay at that house for long. It reminded me of the Cathedral only that these gates were locked and the Cathedral was always open—except during Carnival when it was closed up tight. And only there wasn't anything pretty here. Everything a blanched masquerade.

The morning of the parade we met at the graveyard in town. We all met there. The float was already there and decorated. On the refreshment truck the food was already on the burners and the drinks were already on ice. The graveyard was alive with us. People leaning on headstones as they fixed decorations onto their sequined military boots. Over by the tombs there was a makeup center set up. Someone painted my face yellow. The firefighter jacket was sleeveless. Someone else painted red flames on my arms. I swung my hose around so that the silver shingles shimmered. Herman did not want to paint his face. He only held the hose at his crotch as if it was an extension of himself. The sun dripped down onto my back, rolling down my neck. I blew steamy air from my lips to dry the glitter on my fire hat.

Testing, testing! The speaker coughed and a loud quarrel started from the entire costumed troupe against the music manager. We were unruly. That is how we were supposed to be. Peace is not a part of Carnival. Testing! And then a tune came pounding on. And the speaker hailed us as Crushers. And we screamed back. I stared hard at my headpiece, commanding the glitter to stay in place: Are you read-ay?

Herman and I grinned at each other, eyebrows smashing into our foreheads, and we followed the other hundred people toward the back of the float, a large cup of rum clenched in my hand. It was the Crushers' turn to enter the parade. Our float edged forward. The air was thick and wound like melting glass. The sun dripped down, like it was something shedding itself. The music was churning, turning up, crashing through the sun and air. A huge red and black beetle with the face of a man hustled through our crowd toward another troupe that had started reveling long-time without him. We turned onto Main Street and entered the parade route.

The shops rose on both sides around us, they, too, dressed up with ribbons hanging from wide-opened windows and bows fixed to bolted Danish doors. First, there were just some people walking alongside us heading toward the front of the parade, heading toward the field maybe, where troupes would perform their dance arrangements to be judged for creativity, size, and costume. The Crushers did not have a dance arrangement. We did not believe in routines.

The crowds of paradegoers appeared as we tramped down the route. They had staked out their spots in that grassy section and those shop stoops since seven. They had set up chairs, blankets, and splinted wooden benches. They hid behind dark glasses and generous umbrellas and wide straw hats and building awnings. They brought with them coolers and transistor radios and old Carnival T-shirts and proud Caribbean-country flags and huge smiling mouths and children and cameras and camera film. Then there were faces everywhere and pictures snapping and plain clothes people I did not know throwing arms around and posing beside me. A few tourists dancing stiffly with each other and laughing as if in a glorious hell. Then natives grabbing our hips and waists, dancing close as if we were lovers and not strangers. Hips gyrating, waists oscillating, knees bending, feet stomping, hands stretching to grab the sky. Bodies moved and someone rushed Herman and me and hooked both our necks and spun us around, winded us down until our behinds near scraped the ground, then shook away into the crowd. Herman brought us each a rum and Coke. They make the rum from sugarcane, he said laughing.

My body obeyed the music. No do-si-do. No spinning in a circle. Obey the music. Boom, Boom. Bam, Bam. All inside the Jam Band. The music says to obey nothing but your body. Slave to nothing but the rhythm. Hands in the air if you know you're here. Be here. Be present. Don't let anyone take away your being here. The rabbits are coming! I took Herman and kissed him wetly. We laughed. We screamed. We touched each other as if we were not in public, as if we were not in the middle of the street. Whenever the song came on I found him. I wrapped myself around him so he would know that he was safe.

Rabbit killers are not the same as rabbit traps. Rabbit killers face the prey. They want the victory to be their own and not the heroism of a metal contraption. The wild clowns are the perfect rabbit killers. In the parade they do not even conform to the definition of troupe. They make their own costumes. They do not have a theme. They never have a routine. They may travel in packs. They may travel in pairs. They are the embodiment of the song.

A gang of them came with bells screeching like a hurricane on their sneakers and on their big loose suits. Some with mouths sucking on baby bottles or whistles through a hole in the stocking mask, others with their screen masks down over that first facade—totally anonymous. No velvety suit matched another, no unison in purple and orange and red and green. The suits cut wide so that the bodies appeared slight—perhaps no body within all the clothes. The spirit inside hidden by layers of cloth—no neck, no hair, no fleshy fingers. Gloved hands outstretched, gripping whips of fraying rope and black tape. Whistle in mouth now. The wild clowns made no other noise but their frenzied bells shaking and shrill whistles screaming and their whips smacking the ground as we let them crash through our troupe and join our mad bacchanal.

I must have known some of the masked spirits. I must have gone to school with many of them. I couldn't identify them but they could tell me easily despite my red face paint. This made me feel as if the asphalt under my feet was growing soft. They had whips. Long thick whips tied with heavy black tape that dragged on the ground like fat sleeping anacondas. The whips cracked as if electric when the clowns snapped them on the hot ground or in the hotter air.

The wild clowns moved side to side.

I moved my waist in a circle. I held my hose and acted as if wetting them down. One pretended to be pushed back. I laughed. I was drunk. I was suddenly unsure if I was moving my hips to the right beat. One clown lifted his knees up high, hands out wide; he seemed to be flying like a frantic and colorful bat. And my mind, maybe my body, swirled with sweet rum. I wanted to stop and take a rest. Legal was playing. They say we are too rude. They say we are too rough. They say we cause confusion. And that we never get enough.

The wild clown cracked his whip at my feet and made me skip back. He did not speak. He raised his whip, the snake cracking and cursing at the sky. Now he jumped from one foot to the other, following the music. I could not follow. My head was spinning. My back was beginning to burn. I put the flat of my hand onto the skin of my back. The wild clown reached his gloved hand into my face and moved a piece of stray wet hair that had been blocking my eye.

He stepped back, the bells on his sneakers making a ruckus I could hear even above the song. He raised his whip in the air above me and I felt my shoulders cave in and eyelids snap and I crunched down onto the ground. That this wild clown was a he I did not doubt.

I stayed on the ground, resting in a way that felt comfortable even though I was curled up on the asphalt. But I could not stay there. It was Carnival. I was in the middle of a parade. A costume police officer tapped me with her glittering baton stick and pulled me up. She was wearing dark oversized shades with rhinestones along the rims. I thought then that I should have chosen police officer over firefighter. Get up. Go on the side if you need a break. You going get trampled here.

I got up and I looked for Herman. But I could not find him. For the rest of parade I looked for him. I could not find him. He had left. And this seemed right. But what was wrong was that he did not take me. Perhaps I could have fit in his suitcase if we had tried.

Did I look for him afterward? No. Perhaps I was interested in being found for once. Perhaps he moved to Alaska. He liked being in places where he did not belong. Perhaps I should have gone to Alaska to find him. I never went to his gated house again. I never talked about him to anyone. I thought about him every spare moment I had. I have had many spare moments.

Years after Herman had left, a small package arrived at my grandfather's house, and not in the post-office box as such things should. I came upon it when opening the door for my morning walk. A small square wrapped in brown paper. It had no postage, but there it was on our step as though it might be a pet waiting to be let in. I knew to go to my room. I knew to unwrap it there in the privacy of my bed. It was wrapped in more and more paper like nestled dolls. And then finally the prize tumbled out as though an afterthought. A diamond necklace. I touched its rough edges and smooth surfaces. The silver clasp was smudged and the diamonds dull, as though it had been in that box for a long time. With the collar of my mother's blue polyester blouse, I carefully rubbed it to a shine.

Now I wear the diamonds for the men who are brave enough to let me call them Papa when they join me in the back rooms. I wear the diamonds like a costume. I think of Herman when I wear it.

And now this Carnival, Legal is back. And now I know it is more than just a good song to work up to. I am jumping with the Crushers. Not because I have been faithful all these years. That is not my way. I jump with a different troupe every Carnival. I do not party all year long. I save it up. I help my grandfather with the costumes now. I pick the troupe I want by the costume I like the best. I do not walk around kissing men and collecting boyfriends anymore. So many of the men see me in the street and scream at me and tell me that I broke their hearts or they whisper in my ear at a restaurant where I am by myself listening to music and tell me that they know I am the One for them. I do not think only of Herman. I am still young, not much past thirty. I think of all those boys and men I've kissed, though only Herman has a name in the memories. I cannot remember the other names or faces. I only remember their mouths. I only remember if they held on to me as we kissed or if they let me go easily afterward.

The brace I wear feels like a straitjacket and perhaps it is. I sleep in it even—except when I am sleeping with a man, which is not so often. My grandfather has never liked anyone in the back room where they might see his work and attempt to sabotage any of his costumes. I respect this a little more now. Plus, men do not often want to come to the back room. My mother's clothes lie across the bed like limp bodies and make men feel flaccid. The little children's feathered chicken feet or the Zulu warrior spears make the men uneasy. I sleep with a pillow between my legs when a man is not there.

I take off the brace on Easter Sunday and practice my hip rolling until Jou'vert morning. After food fair when I have eaten all the bull foot stew I can take before noon, I know I am ready for the parade. If the calypso that year is good, the question really is if the parade is ready for me.

This island is like an entire world. But now I have made a circle. I am back with the Crushers. And I am back wanting to hear Legal, because that is the song this year. It too has made a circle. And I am wilding out on the Waterfront. And suddenly there is a piece of paper flying around my head like a mosquito. And it looks like glitter or like a stray piece of costume. But as it falls I stoop to pick it up. I hold my back because I have stopped dancing and I can feel the burn coming on. And it is a note and it says: For you, you all the pretty things.

I felt him. Herman? But he did not answer me. I stood among the other people dancing around me. I stood still as parents tell children to do when they are lost. I let the pain in my back come. I thought of my mother leaving me behind in a pile of clothes. I thought of being abandoned. I opened my mouth and called for Legal. Play Legal! I don't want to be anywhere else but here.

9.
Herman

When I flew back to D.C. my seat was toward the front and the cockpit door was open, revealing all the black dials and red buttons. I heard the pilot order into his microphone. It was not for us, the passengers, to hear. It was for the control deck or someone else on the ground. "Kill the rabbits," he said. I leaned forward to listen for more but nothing else came. I leaned instead on my window and watched the D.C. runway beneath us. A row of bright white lights flickered and then went off. Home, I thought.

Now I dream of kissing Xica. I think of sitting on her bed in her crazy house and our faces touching. Seeing who could hold out. How long we could feel each other's breath—hers coming fast and light, mine coming long and heavy—without reaching for a kiss. She always lost because she always wanted to kiss. Said it made her breathing better. I think now that she was sick really. That she was ill in her body and maybe in her mind, but despite that I still know that not being there for her after the parade was the greatest sin of my life. The greatest cowardice. Cowardice is a sin. I was not there after the parade to hold her when her body shook with pain from being on her feet all day. I did not even watch the parade on the TV, except to laugh or grunt at the women every now and then like the other men in the bar.

I wonder if Xica would have loved me forever if I had played the rabbit. She always said she loved me because I seemed transient. But what if I'd let her kill me in the stadium? "Remember, you said you loved me. You can't love me only because I am transient." That is what I wanted to tell her. What if I don't fit in here? What if I don't feel totally comfortable around black people but I still want to live on the island? Live with you. Is that a crime? What if I love you even though I don't understand you? What if your pussy is made for a black man and I'm too small and that's why you were always with other guys? Is that a racist thing for me to think? Even if it is, does that mean I didn't love her? That I don't still love her?

I live in D.C. again. I'm dating any girl who will have me, which means I seem desperate. So girls call me up in the middle of the night to have sex but none of them want to be seen with me in the morning. I left the island that same month I left Xica. But then not a year after I was gone someone burned down my parents' bar in St. John. My father called me and said, "The niggers finally burned down the bar." Just like that. He'd forgotten I'd dated Xica. Or maybe he'd never known. But my father doesn't usually use that language. He was only mad. He's not really racist.

There was something about his "finally" that made me think that he must have always felt uneasy. Felt he wasn't wanted. The bar was called Crusoe's. Xica once told me that she hated that. But I'd never read *Robinson Crusoe* so I didn't know what she meant. But it dawned on me after my father hung up that maybe she'd burned down the bar. I could see her doing it. I could see her laughing and dancing and pouring kerosene on the bar stools. And I could see her run, her back hurting but running anyway, as the bar went up in flames. And I remembered the song, "kill the rabbits," and I knew that the hunt was on. And I want to tell her, "It's all right. It's all right. I deserve it. I saw you for a flash on the TV curled up on the ground in the middle of the street. The camera flashed away but I knew it was you."

"They want us gone," said my father when I arrived on St. John to help them with the bar. I met with him in the study of my parents' house. "But I'm not going anywhere. I help this damn place. I bring industry. I hire people. What would those people do without me? This is bull. These ungrateful nig . . ."

"Who?" I could not think of any islanders my father had hired except the woman who cleaned his bar and the one who cleaned our house. So I asked him. "Who?"

"Who what?"

"What locals have you hired?"

"Herman. This is not going down easy. It's not right. Just because they're black doesn't mean they can't be wrong. They're like Hitler. They only want their own around them. They're more jingoistic than a damned Texas Republican."

"But we have so much power."

"We're not rich, Herman."

"I mean just by being here. We're just here. We take up space but we don't . . ."

"Are you here to help me or harass me, Herman? You have no idea how the world works." He leaned forward and slipped a book from one of the shelves. He looked at it and then passed it to me. "Read this." It was a book he had written, *Strangers in Their Own Homes: A History of Christian Martyrdom*. He was not a writer but he and my mother had been professors, he in religion and she in literature, before retiring. Part of a professor's job was writing books. I took the book but I did not intend to read it—though I did, eventually. Now I looked up at Saint Paul looking down at us. Religion had never been anything more than academic history to me.

"Saint Paul," my father said as he'd said to me many times before. "He was a scholar and a writer."

"Like you," I said.

"Not exactly. He was a martyr, too. He died for his convictions. Not for himself, really. He died for people who believed what he believed. That's how a martyr is different. A martyr sacrifices for a cause, for many people. And you know it's often public, so that the people can know it's their martyr." He rubbed his chin. Looking suddenly like the professor he had been and not the bar owner he had become. "The Romans were foolish. If they had killed privately it would have been a lot harder to make martyrs out of anybody."

"Will you leave?"

"The island? No. This is my home. Where else would I go?"

"What about the properties in D.C.?"

"No. I'll build another bar. This is home. This is where human beings are meant to live. All human beings need this kind of beauty around them."

I did not know what to say to him. Because he knew and I knew that not all human beings could fit on this tiny island. But I decided to stay and help my parents rebuild the bar. They were my people. Family. Family must be your people.

I stayed for two weeks but I did not hang out with Dutch. I did not look for Xica. And she did not find me.

Then I went back to D.C. I took part-time jobs and temporary internships. I would not commit. I started college again. Spring break and Easter break always coincided. I decided I would visit my parents around that time. Of course, I hoped to see Xica and at the same time I feared seeing her.

I have never seen her.

For the few months after my parents' bar was burned down, I kept up with news on the island by reading various Virgin Islands Web sites. Then one innocent day I read of a new allegation that a black woman had been raped by a white man on St. John. My heart pounded and I wondered if the woman was Xica. They would not disclose her name. I ran to the bathroom and threw up.

Depending on the Web message board the truth was either that the black woman was lying or that she had been raped in retaliation for a white man's bar being burned down, my father's bar. Black women were raped by black men, but interracial rape was something that really was a crime after all. History, Xica would have told me. History makes it worse. The message boards were not shy. The sites talked about another rape, where a young black man had raped a white tourist woman right in front of her husband, then beat the husband nearly to death before running with all their diamonds. Now he was doing time in jail. One posting saw this as an injustice: "They found that black boy so quickly. Why can't they find the white man who raped?" Another posted: "See, they did it to our white women first. It's time we retaliated." I felt sick thinking about who was *they* and who was *we*.

I could not imagine raping any kind of woman. So I could not see how forcing a black woman would make me worse than forcing a white woman but then I thought of the Cuban prostitute in Miami and then I would have to stop thinking.

I decided to make a sacrifice of myself. I started that Easter—a year after I'd left Xica. I have been doing this now for twelve entire years. Each year I visit my parents in their home and each year I make my walk. This year the man who sang "Legal" died. He was a diabetic—too much sweetness in life or not enough. He died but his song has come back to life. And this year I lift up my cross and hope beyond hope that Xica will find me and take me home.

10.
Cooper

I have a view of the sea. I have a view of the fort. I have a view of the bodies dancing wildly in the Carnival parade. I'm in jail. That is my geography. There must be something to this. This must be more than by chance. It is more than chance that this year the calypsonian who wrote *Legal* died. Diabetic coma, for real. Too much sugar or not enough. His songs were still number one on the Jou'vert route. People still lined up to dance up on a boat in the middle of the harbor with his band. But nothing like *Legal* ever again. Nothing that said *I* like *Legal*. Nothing that said *we* like *Legal*.

But this Carnival *Legal* has come back as a veneration because the islands are on fire again. In St. John someone scrawled "nigger" on the side of a car. "White people own this" on the side of building. I read it all in the papers. We're all waiting for someone to burn something down again. Someone to reveal that under our beautiful Virgin Islands there is a whorishness now. That we've been selling ourselves. But not ourselves, really. The land. But the land is us. And even the men who pass through my cell don't want to listen to my preaching. They want concrete proof that our culture is something worth keeping alive. Something worth us. And even then are we talking about culture or are we talking about ourselves? Are we fooling ourselves? The St. Johnians can't even afford to live in St. John. Spray paint on a wall tells them that they don't own a thing.

I watch the people in the troupes. They perform—nowadays they all have routines that they must practice for weeks. They bow or wave at the end and the audience, which used to just be called the crowd, claps properly. But then there are the Crushers. They don't ever do a routine, but they always have the best costumes and they always seem to be having the most fun. Nothing legal about them.

I write "For you, all the pretty things" on a scrap of paper. I've written something to her every year since I've been in here, but this year I believe I see her. The Crushers are masquerading as the weather. She's wearing yellow. She's a sunny day. I swear that's my diamond necklace glittering at her neck. I fold my note tight and pitch it down. I watch this tiny magic wand soar. I can't tell if she's bending to pick it up or if she's bending to push her bum back against the man who is moving up on her. I plunge my hands out of the window because that is the only thing that can get out of the bars. She seems to be looking for me. I cup my hands to share the air with her.

After Carnival is over and the Village is packed up and the rides are dismantled, I think about my martyr. On Easter Sunday, just two weeks before Carnival, I had watched him heave the wood across his shoulders. It could have looked to a car driving by as though the martyr was no martyr but simply a Frenchy kid hauling wood for some secret Carnival thing. But it has always been obvious to me that the wood was not just wood. I can see from up here that the wood is shaped like a cross. And the man is dragging it to no fixed destination. He is simply dragging it up Waterfront. He is not trying to get it anywhere. The dragging is the purpose. I imagine that he must start out at Havensight, where the tourists arrive. Perhaps it is the place where he had first arrived. Where he and his family first disembarked from a cruise ship and into the openness of the Virgin Islands. It seemed a friendly and colorful place, then. Filled with my people who spoke a bizarre English and screwed their mouths in such a way that they seemed drunk or high.

He thinks the sun makes the people drunk, the salt ocean breeze makes the people high. It was a drug place to my martyr when he first arrived. It was a place of hallucination. But what I see every Easter is not hallucination. The man walks with a cross on his back. And the damn cross is heavy and he walks anyway. Past my jail. It is not a walk of full martyrdom, really. No one is meant to see. He is doing a private penance. And why do men walk with crosses on their backs? The answer is the same no matter where they might be or where they might be from. For love, of course. Nothing else is worth it.

ACKNOWLEDGMENTS

Special thanks to the following places where these stories have appeared in some form:

"How to Escape from a Leper Colony"—winner of the *Boston Review* Fiction Prize
"The Saving Work"—winner of the Kore Press Chapbook Prize, and the *Best African American Fiction 2009*
"Street Man"—*The London Magazine*
"The Bridge Stories"—winner of a Pushcart Prize and published in *Sonora Review*
"Canoe Sickness" (under the title: "A Busy London Pavement")—*Global City Review*
"Where Tourists Don't Go"—*Story Quarterly*
"The International Shop of Coffins"—excerpts published in *American Short Fiction*, *Transition Magazine*, and Akashic's *Trinidad Noir* anthology

I could never thank everyone. I hope this will suffice—

Many thanks to the communities of writers where these stories were worked on: the University of Houston Creative Writing Program, Bread Loaf Writers' Conference, the Squaw Valley Community of Writers, Callaloo Workshop, the Rice University Parks Fellow program, Voices of the Nations, Kore Press, Caribbean Cultural Theatre, and the Cropper Foundation Caribbean Writers Workshop.

Thanks to those who read and helped beyond the call of duty or classroom: Jonathan Ali, Bobby Antoni, Cyd Apellido, Diane Bartoli,

Jericho Brown, Vincent Cooper, Justin Cronin, Maryse Condé, Kwame Dawes, Junot Díaz, Andre Dubus III, Percival Everett, Ben Fountain, Patrick Freeman, Elizabeth Gregory, Cristina Henriquez, Arvelyn Hill, Gaelen Johnson, Tayari Jones, Greg Jowdy, Ron and Susan Martin, Nina McConigley, Kevin McIlvoy, Roy and Pouneh McMaster, Keya Mitra, Antonya Nelson, Elizabeth Nunez, Sigrid Nunez, Emily Pérez, Velma Pollard, Emily Raboteau, Danzy Senna, Jonathan Strong, Addie Tsai, Gemini Wahaj, and Lois Zamora; and to my elementary and high school teachers, most especially Dr. Rodio and Mrs. Ignatius. Thanks to Fiona, Polly, Katie, Erin, and the other wolves who made this book possible. Thanks to Elise and Sandy without whom there would be no book.

Thanks to the writer I know as Anexus Corban, who lent his name but bears no other resemblance to my Anexus. Thanks to my aunts, uncles, and cousins who have been champions always.

Every artist needs others who have come before and are willing to selflessly turn back to bring another along. I have been blessed to have Kathy Cambor, Vincent Cooper, Chitra Divakaruni, and Claudia Rankine.

To my loves: Eva Lorraine, Zachary Gundel, and Reggie McGarrah.

Finally and most, to my grandmother, Beulah Smith Harrigan—the one who told me stories.

TIPHANIE YANIQUE is from the Hospital Ground neighborhood of St. Thomas, Virgin Islands. She was the Parks Fellow/Writer-in-Residence at Rice University and Fellow in fiction at Teachers & Writers Collaborative. She has been awarded a Fulbright Scholarship in creative writing and fellowship residencies with Bread Loaf, Callaloo, Squaw Valley, and the Cropper Foundation for Caribbean Writers. She is an assistant professor of creative writing and Caribbean literature at Drew University and an associate editor with *Post-No-Ills*. She lives between Brooklyn, New York, and St. Thomas.

This book is made possible through a partnership with the College of Saint Benedict, and honors the legacy of S. Mariella Gable, a distinguished teacher at the College.

Previous titles in this series include:

Loverboy by Victoria Redel

The House on Eccles Road by Judith Kitchen

One Vacant Chair by Joe Coomer

The Weatherman by Clint McCown

Collected Poems by Jane Kenyon

Variations on the Theme of an African Dictatorship
by Nuruddin Farah:
Sweet and Sour Milk
Sardines
Close Sesame

Duende by Tracy K. Smith

All of It Singing: New and Selected Poems by Linda Gregg

The Art of Syntax: Rhythm of Thought, Rhythm of Song
by Ellen Bryant Voigt

Support for this series has been provided by the Lee and Rose Warner Foundation as part of the Warner Reading Program.

Book design by Connie Kuhnz. Composition by BookMobile Design and Publishing Services, Minneapolis, Minnesota. Manufactured by Versa Press on acid-free paper.